Approaching his sister's dance studio to the right, he heard a pounding beat, not at all similar to the classical music that fueled Carrie's usual dance practices. He stopped to watch through a small square window off to the side. Ava, dressed in a black leotard and tights, leaped and twirled through the air like a spinning top, set on its course around the circumference of the room while Carrie spun in a more confined area in the center of the room.

Brian's eyes sought Ava as her tight body coiled and released, coiled and released. Her arms were at once fragile and muscled, highlighting biceps and long, graceful fingers, sweeping through the air to mirror her legs. Her leaps were huge, with powerful extension and maximum air between her and the floor. No sooner would she land than she'd pull her limbs into herself and pirouette on her toes, spinning fast enough to make him question the physics of it all. This was no prissy ballet. This was fast and furious modern dance where you could feel the beat in your throat. Okay, maybe he'd experienced a little too much dance in his life, but this was definitely as good as anything he'd seen on the New York stage. Ava was even better than his sister.

What happened to the shy, vulnerable girl he'd just met? On the dance floor she was a powerhouse. Full of confidence, energy, and magnetism.

When the music ended, he stood rooted to the floor, and his hands came up in a spontaneous clap.

Praise for Maria Imbalzano

Ms. Imbalzano's book *UNCHAINED MEMORIES* won the Wisconsin RWA Write Touch Readers' Award 2014 and finaled in the 2014 NJRW Golden Leaf and the 2015 NECRWA (New England Chapter of RWA) Readers' Choice Award.

Dancing
in the Sand

by

Maria Imbalzano

Bernie,

All the best!

Maria Imbalzano

Dancing in the Sand

COPYRIGHT © 2015 by Maria Imbalzano

Cover Art by *Kim Mendoza*

The Wild Rose Press, Inc.
PO Box 708
Adams Basin, NY 14410-0708
Visit us at www.thewildrosepress.com

Publishing History
First Champagne Rose Edition, 2015
Print ISBN 978-1-5092-0304-8
Digital ISBN 978-1-5092-0305-5

Published in the United States of America

Dedication

To my husband, Chris,
and our daughters, Alex and Mackenzie,
who will always dance with me.

Chapter One

Ava's eyes flew open at the blaring siren. She sprang up, confusion marring her sleep-addled brain. The unfamiliar room didn't click into her consciousness. Then she remembered.

Brian.

The other side of the bed was empty. The neon numbers on the nightstand clock beamed 6:15. Had he left the guesthouse?

Anxiety heightened with the pitch of the piercing sound.

"Brian?" she called, her voice hoarse with sleep and mild panic.

No answer.

She jumped out of bed and pulled on the jeans and tee Brian had removed from her last night, then shoved her feet into a pair of flip-flops. Her heart hammered against her ribs as the flashing lights of an ambulance intermittently lit up the room. What had happened?

She yanked open the door. The sun hadn't appeared yet, although it must have broken the horizon since she could see as far as the horse barn. An ambulance was just leaving the long driveway of the Stanhope estate, obviously carrying its patient to the hospital.

Ava ran, kicking off her flip-flops, determined to cover the distance more quickly. Did Mr. Stanhope have a heart attack? Did Mrs. Stanhope have a riding accident? Breathless, Ava approached her destination. Mr. Stanhope and his daughter Carrie, Ava's best friend, were outside the barn talking in hushed tones with one of the grooms who pointed toward the tree line. Then Carrie took off in the direction of the garage.

Ava picked up her sprint. "Carrie. Wait." Carrie threw a glance over her shoulder, but didn't stop. Ava ran faster to catch up. "What happened?"

Tears stained Carrie's cheeks and fell unchecked. "Brian must have fallen from his horse. Michael, our stable hand found him on the ground, unconscious, after his horse wandered back to the barn."

Ava's breath caught in her throat and threatened to cut off well-needed oxygen. When had Brian left her bed? How long had he lain on the ground? But any question might give away their secret.

"Where are you going?" was all Ava managed.

"To the hospital. My mother went with Brian in the ambulance."

"I'll come with you. Maybe I should drive." Although she really was in no better shape after hearing the news.

"I'm going with my father. You stay here. Tell the others what happened. I'll call you with any word."

Carrie jumped into the Mercedes SUV and gunned it up the driveway, stopping to pick up her dad at the barn. Ava stood in the dust the wheels had kicked up, feeling nauseous and faint and scared. With legs buckling, she sat on the crushed stones covering the ground, putting her head in her hands, before she started to sob.

Last night was magic. They had made love for

hours before Brian took her on a romantic horseback ride under the stars. How could this morning be so horrific? She needed to think positive thoughts. Send her energy to Brian so he would be fine. It was probably just a bump on the head. A concussion that would be monitored at the hospital for a day or so, and then he'd be released.

At least that's what she hoped.

Ava pushed herself off the ground and headed toward the main house. On the way, she ran into Zack, Brian's best friend from Harvard.

"What's going on?" he asked.

Ava told him what she knew, trying to keep the catch in her voice from turning into full-blown hysterics. "Carrie said she'd call with news."

Zach nodded, but a frown furrowed his brow. "Brian's a good sportsman. He's ridden horses since he was five. But I guess if he was riding at dawn, or the horse got spooked…" He shrugged. "Things happen." He turned to Ava. "I wonder why he was riding so early?"

Ava ignored his question. He clearly wanted to leave the guesthouse this morning before any of his friends, or maybe Carrie, saw him there. He didn't want Ava to be the subject of gossip or speculation. She'd been the stranger of the group this weekend, having joined Carrie, her roommate at NYU, for her brother's celebratory bash at their Newport estate.

Ava and Zach entered the huge colonial manor through the kitchen and sat at the table, reiterating the story as each of Brian's weekend guests surfaced to find out about the commotion. It was a somber group— much different from the prior evening's partiers. They had come to celebrate Brian's graduation from Harvard, as well as their own, and now a black shadow fell over the once happy group.

The fact that Ava had been the last one to see Brian before the accident weighed heavily on her. When questions arose as to where Brian had disappeared to the night before, Ava kept to herself. She wanted their time together private. Sacred.

Guilt niggled at her throughout the morning. In her head, she knew there was nothing she could have done to prevent the accident, but in her heart, she still questioned that fact. Unfortunately, there was no one with whom to confide. No one to lessen the angst or the guilt. She needed to talk to—or at least see—Brian.

As the day wore on with no word from Carrie, Ava became more and more agitated. She covered every inch of the Newport house, roaming from room to room, straightening up when a room needed straightening, and avoiding Brian's friends so she could be alone with her thoughts. She punched in Carrie's cell phone number at least a dozen times, but it continually went to voicemail. Should she call the hospital, pretend to be a family member, and ask about his condition? Or maybe hire a cab—if they had any in Newport—and go to the hospital herself.

Carrie was her best friend; Ava should be there with her, she rationalized. They had met three years earlier on the first day of class—both dance majors—both chasing their dream to become a member of a national dance company. They practiced endlessly, worked tirelessly on choreography, and attended as many professional dance performances as they could squeeze into their schedules. Even now, although the spring semester was over, they had both enrolled for summer classes and were choreographing a piece for the dance showcase at the end of the summer. They'd been inseparable.

One by one, Brian's friends left for home, exchanging their numbers so someone could get in touch with them once the news was delivered. With only a few of them left, Ava could stand it no longer. She googled taxi services and found a cab, allowing the others to believe she was heading for the train to New York City, since she didn't want company.

The twenty minute cab ride to the hospital turned her stomach into a bunched-up tangle—not because of the erratic driving, which she had become used to in the City, but because of what she would learn. Perhaps Carrie's incommunicativeness was due to a much more serious injury. How would the Stanhopes react to her showing up to intrude on their family gathering? Would they think it inappropriate and refuse to discuss Brian's state of health with her?

The waiting room outside the ER was packed. A quick scan produced no familiar faces, so Ava walked up to the reception desk and told the woman her mission. "Could you please tell me Brian Stanhope's condition? Do you know where his family is?"

"What is your relationship to the patient?"

Ava lied, keeping her voice to a whisper. "I'm his girlfriend, but his parents don't know we're involved. Please don't mention it to them." She should be struck by lightning for turning her incredible night with Brian into a relationship.

Thankfully, the woman gave her a sympathetic look. "I can't release Mr. Stanhope's medical condition, but the family is in a private room on the surgical floor. I'll call and see if I can get one of them to come down to see you."

Her intestines cramped a little more. Brian was having surgery. That couldn't be good. "Could you ask for Carrie, please? She's Brian's sister and a good friend. I don't want to bother his parents."

The receptionist punched in a few numbers. After a second, she looked up and smiled. "Your friend will be right down."

Ava exhaled, then thanked her before joining the masses in the waiting room. She rolled her shoulders to relieve the tension that had been building all day, but she felt as tight as a coiled spring. She focused on the wall clock, watching the minutes tick by ever so slowly.

"Ava. What are you doing here?" Carrie's voice was hoarse, tired.

Ava threw her arms around her friend. "I couldn't stand not knowing, not hearing from you. You said you'd call. It's been over eight hours." She looked at Carrie's face, drawn and pale. "Please tell me he's okay."

"He's in intensive care. He has a head injury that caused his brain to swell. They had to operate to relieve the pressure. They put him into a medically induced coma until the swelling goes down."

"Oh, my God." Ava felt the pent-up tears escape. "I was praying it wasn't serious. But I knew it must be bad when you didn't call." She dug in her purse for a tissue. "Have you seen him?"

"No. Not yet." Carrie looked over her shoulder, as if searching for someone. "I have to get back upstairs."

Ava clung to Carrie's arm. "Can I come with you?"

Ava was desperate to be near Brian. To learn at the same time his family did, that he would be fine. He had to be. He couldn't have brain damage. He couldn't...die.

"That's not a good idea. My parents don't want anyone but family here."

A slap to the face, but not surprising. Would they feel any differently if they knew their son cared in some way for Ava? Probably not. Brian had dozens of girlfriends over the years. One was interchangeable with the next. Carrie had told her as much when she'd warned her to stay away from him—for Ava's own protection.

"Maybe I could wait down here and you can come and tell me when you hear more news." She held onto the thinnest of threads connecting her to Brian, hoping Carrie wouldn't cut her off. She had to know.

"No. Go back to New York. You have classes tomorrow. I'll call you."

Sure. Like she did today. But, of course, Carrie didn't know how important her brother was to her. Despite Carrie's well-intentioned advice.

Slipping her arm from Ava's grip, Carrie pursed her lips, unable to give even a half smile, then turned and headed through the doors leading to a long corridor.

Ava was left to return to New York City alone, after the best and worst weekend of her life.

Chapter Two

Zombie-like didn't come close to describing Ava's demeanor. She attended summer classes, but her mind refused to accept one morsel of knowledge unrelated to the tragedy she'd left in Newport. Not only did she fret over Brian, but she didn't even have her best friend and roommate with whom to commiserate.

Maybe Ava's sister Kim, an ER nurse, could shed some light on what to expect. Remorse plagued her as she located her sister's number on her cell. She'd been neglectful in responding to Kim's messages, her sole focus on Brian. But now she had a reason to phone. Surprised at reaching Kim on the first attempt, Ava jumped right into the reason for her call.

"I need to ask you about a medical condition. I know it might not be your area of expertise, but I didn't know who else to ask."

"What is it, Ava? Are you okay?" Her sister's concern wrapped her in a warmth she craved, and Ava was glad she made contact.

"Yes. I'm fine. Although a good friend of mine isn't." Is that what she should call Brian, or should she share with her sister her real feelings toward the man with whom she was falling in love? After explaining what had happened, she asked Kim the scary question. "What can we expect when he comes out of the coma?"

"Oh, honey, that's a hard question to answer.

Without knowing the specifics of his injury, it would be impossible to speculate." And she clearly didn't want to, but Ava needed to know.

She bit her lip, then forced the question. "What's the worst-case scenario?"

"Well, he didn't die from a bleed into his brain within hours of the accident. So, that's a positive. He's being monitored in intensive care and you said he's in a medically induced coma?"

"Yes." Her response was barely above a whisper, and she clutched the phone so tight, her fingers hurt.

"The extent of secondary damage due to swelling of the brain will determine the permanence of the initial damage. Because the brain is confined to a tight space, inflammation or internal bleeding can cause pressure on the nerves. If the pressure doesn't subside, the nerves will start to die. If that happens, he can lose his ability to move, think, see…" Her words trailed off. "But I'm sure that won't happen. What hospital is he in?"

"Newport Hospital. In Rhode Island. My roommate and her family have a house there. It's her brother, Brian who was injured."

"Oh."

"What do you mean, oh?"

"Nothing. Just that it's a small hospital. But I'm sure his parents have brought in the right specialists and decided on the best treatment for him. You said they're wealthy, right?"

"Yes."

"Ava, are you sure you're okay? Is Brian more than a friend?"

Just hearing the question, opened the well. Tears poured down her face and her throat constricted. "No," was her only response; a truthful answer to the first question, a lie to the second.

There was silence on the other end, then "I'm sorry, Ava. Please don't tell Carrie the worst-case scenario." Her voice was soothing, calm. "Think positive. Pray. Send all your optimistic thoughts his way. I'm sure he'll pull out of it. He's young. The best-case scenario is that he'll wake up and be fine. You have to believe that will happen."

Ava shook her head, unable to speak.

"I wish I was there with you, honey. Do you want to leave school for a few days and come to our house?"

"No." Her voice sounded like a child's, high-pitched and thin.

"Are you sure? You sound like you could use a big sister to lean on."

Kim's invitation was tempting. She'd like nothing more than to be comforted and cared for in the loving embrace of her sister—in her mind her only family. But a stronger pull in the other direction was the need to be closer to Brian. And to be available for Carrie. A week had passed since the accident, and she longed for Carrie to show up, bringing good news and a return to normalcy. Ava couldn't leave with that possibility hovering over her.

"Thanks, Kim. But I can't miss classes. Besides, I want to be here if Carrie comes back."

"Of course. I understand. But if you change your mind, the invitation's open, as always."

Ava smiled. She and her sister had been close since the day Ava was born; their bond even stronger after their mother deserted them. Ava vowed to make more of an effort to visit, at least on the holidays. She couldn't allow the crack in her relationship with her father to affect her relationship with Kim and her husband Dan.

"Maybe you'll come for the July 4th weekend." There was hope in Kim's voice and Ava didn't have the heart to deny her. "Dad, and Dan, of course, will be here. We haven't all been together since Christmas. Try. Okay?"

"I'll let you know." She couldn't promise anything right now. "Thanks for…" For what? For telling her Brian could have died, but he didn't? That he could lose his ability to talk, walk, see? "For being there," she finally said.

Then she hung up.

That call had been a bad idea.

****

It was eight weeks until the showcase and Ava faced the possibility of being without her partner.

During dance classes, her steps were flat-footed and uninspired. She even skipped her studio time, the one thing she had never done in her life, either in sickness, bad weather, or an invitation to die for. Conversations with friends bordered on monosyllabic and all joy had whooshed from her system. Replacing it was a mean depression that encouraged her to stay in bed and sleep away the hours so she wouldn't have to think about Brian lying comatose in a hospital bed.

Ava relived their weekend together as if Cupid had programmed her brain with only two buttons: Play and Repeat. From the first time she had met him standing outside Carrie's dance studio in their Newport home to the incredible night she had shared with him in bed—and every moment in between, no matter how insignificant or brief—it was all there, stored in her right frontal lobe for easy access.

Another week passed, although it felt like a month. Ava called Carrie daily. Sometimes she felt as if she were a nuisance, sometimes a consoling friend, depending upon Carrie's mood. But while her friend's attitude changed from day to day, nothing changed with Brian. He was still in a coma. And there was still no word on how he would come out of it. Only time would tell.

"Any news?" Ava's voice sounded dull, even to her, and she castigated herself for not trying to inject some positivity, at least for Carrie's sake.

"Yes." Carrie sounded stronger than usual, and Ava didn't hear the strangled tightness that signified tears. "Brian's conscious."

Her heart jumped with hope and every nerve in her body came to life, as she paced back and forth in her bedroom. "What does that mean?" Ava held her breath, waiting for the good news to wash over her.

"He's stable but having trouble with words, and he doesn't remember anything that happened since he first came to Newport. The doctor says we need to be patient. Once they see how much normal activity he recovers during this next month, they'll be able to determine whether he'll have any permanent damage or disability."

Oh my god. Permanent disability was a possibility.

"Ava? Are you there?"

"Yes. Yes." She struggled for something to say. "How are you holding up? Are you okay? Are you coming back to school?"

"Not yet. I withdrew for the summer term. I want

to stay here with my family."

"Of course." While Ava understood perfectly, she missed Carrie. And she selfishly wanted Carrie with her during this awful time. They could rely on each other for strength, help each other through this tragedy.

But Carrie had no idea how Ava felt about her brother—had no clue she was also devastated by this incident.

"If you need to get away for a few days, come down to the City. We can work on our choreography. Go see a ballet performance." Ava hoped the lure of dance would entice her friend to at least come and visit once in a while. "Or I could come there." Ava tamped down her desperation. "We can visit Brian together and when we're not at the hospital, we can work in your studio." Was she really offering to skip classes and possibly fail out for the chance to spend time with Brian?

"No, you shouldn't come here. Brian won't know who you are. And my parents don't want him to feel any more confused than he already is. I'll have to see how things go. If he starts doing better, maybe I'll come down for a break. I'll let you know."

Brian wouldn't know who she was. The squeeze on her heart was palpable. They'd spent hours together over that weekend talking, getting to know each other. He'd kissed her like there was no one else in the world. They'd made love, studied the stars by horseback, and planned to see each other again. But she couldn't say any of that to her friend.

Carrie's lukewarm consideration of Ava's suggestion was obviously as good as it was going to get. At least for now. All Ava could do was cling to the hope that Brian would recover rapidly and fully, and he'd move to New York as planned with his memory intact.

****

"Higher, Ava. Put some power into your leaps."

The oft-repeated refrain from her ballet teacher did nothing to elevate Ava's legs. Although she had slept for ten hours straight the night before, her body felt heavy and sluggish, and her usual zest for dance was missing.

Which shouldn't have been the case. After she hung up with Carrie yesterday, she called Kim, and Ava's spirits were buoyed by the conversation. This time Kim stayed away from the gloom and doom possibilities and focused on the positive, sending Ava into a euphoric state compared to what she'd been experiencing. Not only did Ava's appetite kick in, but for the first time in three weeks she slept without the nightmare of Brian's disastrous fall piercing her fitful sleep.

So why was she moving as if dancing in the sand?

Ignoring the queasiness in her stomach, she took her place behind the other ballerinas and started her pirouettes across the floor, spinning like a top as she focused on Baryshnikov's photograph at the other end of the room. All of a sudden, dizziness washed over her, and she stumbled to a halt attempting to remain upright.

"Ava, what's wrong?' Ms. Drimmer's words hovered around her head, echoing in her ears, while the dancer behind her smacked into her with amazing force. As if in slow motion, Ava met the floor, barely feeling its hardness. Although voices surrounded her, all she

14

could see was black. A sizzling heat burned through her body and broke through her pores in an all-encompassing sweat as the noise died down and quiet insinuated itself.

The next thing she felt was a cold cloth on her forehead with stray drops of water running down her face and tickling her neck. Eight pairs of eyes belonging to her teacher and classmates stared at her from above. "Ava, can you hear me?" Her teacher knelt beside her as she applied the cold compress.

"Yes." Ava struggled to sit up, feeling foolish and embarrassed for having fallen during their routine floor work. "I'm sorry. I must have tripped on something."

"You didn't trip. You fainted." Her teacher's words held concern. "Did you eat anything today?"

She tried to remember whether she'd bothered to open a container of yogurt, her usual breakfast before an intense ballet class. "I don't think so." Now she remembered. She'd been starving, but there was nothing in the refrigerator and she was running late. So, she skipped it.

"Girls, this is an excellent example of what will happen if you don't eat properly." Their ballet mistress had stressed over and over the importance of proper nutrition to feed their bones and muscles. And now here was Ava—the poster girl—for atrocious eating habits. "Lisa, when Ava is feeling a little better, I want you to take her to Medical Services."

"Yes, ma'am."

Ava stood, with the help of her teacher, who walked her to the bench across the studio. A blush rose to her face at the humiliation of it all. Why hadn't she just grabbed a smoothie at the café next door? She knew how exerting these classes were. She also knew the scrutiny dancers were under at the school to assure they didn't develop eating disorders. Now she would be subjected to her teacher's constant monitoring over her health when all she wanted was to be studied for her technique.

Could this month get any worse?

Chapter Three

Yes. It could.

The efficient woman doctor at the University's Medical Services Clinic diagnosed Ava with speed and efficiency. "You're pregnant." A smile accompanied her words.

Ava stared at her, as if she were an alien speaking in Martian tongue. "That's impossible," she rasped. "We used protection."

The doctor shook her head as if she'd given this lecture one too many times. "Condoms are not one hundred percent effective."

"Yes, I realize that but..." But what? Ava was an idiot who relied on a piece of latex in the intensity of the moment. Hot tears leaked onto her cheeks. "I can't have a baby. I'm twenty. I'm a dancer." At least her irrational words didn't annoy the doctor.

"There are options, of course, if you decide against keeping the baby. Abortion. Adoption. But you shouldn't make any rash decisions. Think about it. Talk it over with the baby's father. See what you decide together."

Was now a good time to tell the doctor the father didn't even remember her? That he had a traumatic brain injury and was lying in a hospital in Newport as they spoke? What was the point?

Instead she bucked up and gave the bearer of this

horrendous news a wobbly smile. "Thanks. I'll do that."

The doctor then gave her a prescription for pre-natal vitamins and instructed her to eat a balanced diet. Ava tossed the prescription in her backpack and zoned out of the one-sided conversation on nutrition, promising to do what she was told, just so she could get out of there faster. Once out, she meandered aimlessly, hoping to wear off the shock and clear her mind.

Ava walked for hours, covering Washington Square Park as well as the zigzagging streets of the West Village. She analyzed her options, which weren't many. Keeping the baby was out of the question. She was too young. She had her life ahead of her. And that life did not include a child. Even more so since the father had no idea who she was.

She could never get an abortion. She was Catholic. And although she hadn't attended church since her mother left when she was fourteen, she couldn't fathom killing the tiny human life growing inside. At the thought, a wave of nausea swept through her system and she crouched on the ground, hand to stomach. But there was little to throw up.

Inhaling deeply, she stood, holding onto the filthy trashcan beside her.

Food. She needed to eat, so she stopped in a health food grocery and purchased a nutrition bar, then pushed a cart up and down the aisles, tossing in provisions. But her mind was barely on the task at hand.

Option number three had to be considered. Adoption. That might be the best alternative. She would carry the baby while she settled on an agency that would find the perfect parents for her son or daughter. She would turn the child over and never look back. Ava would regain her life, go back to dancing, and pretend these nine months never happened.

That seemed reasonable. Yet, the words cold, cruel, and despicable collided in her mind and assaulted her conscience. This baby was her son or daughter and not a soulless, formless blob she would be happy to present to the most competent bidder. Ava held her hand to her abdomen and rubbed it slowly as she stood in front of the whole grain cereals. How could she spend nine months feeding, caring for, and worrying about delivering a healthy child only to turn that baby over to a stranger?

That was just emotion taking over. Perhaps she should put this decision on hold for a few days, maybe even a month or two. Nothing needed to be decided immediately. The shock of her predicament was clouding her thinking. Given time to adapt to this new development, she would surely reach a point where she could look at the situation in a more analytical light. Decide what was best for the baby—and her.

In a month or so, maybe Brian would be better. She could see him, talk to him. He'd remember her and they could decide the outcome together. At the thought of bringing Brian into the loop, Ava's stomach plummeted and her heartbeat quickened. Though they'd shared a fairy-tale weekend together, they barely knew each other. Telling him he was about to be a father would send him running for the hills.

That's if he recognized her. If he didn't… She didn't want to think about that.

For the next few weeks, Ava managed to keep up with her academic classes, but she couldn't bring herself to attend dance classes. What was the use? In a few months her belly would be protruding and she'd look more like an elephant than a swan—just in time for the students' showcase where she and Carrie were supposed to present their self-choreographed masterpiece. It would have been their chance to put their talent in front of directors from many of the major dance companies in the City. But now, Ava would have to drop out. All because of one fateful weekend that had brought her and Brian together, leaving him with a serious head injury and her with an unwanted baby.

Their intersecting paths had changed both of their lives forever.

****

"I'm coming to see you; I don't care what you say." Ava held her breath as she waited for Carrie's response, hoping her forceful statement would banish any willful denial Carrie may have been about to utter.

"I'd like that."

"You would?"

"I could use the distraction. I'm here at the rehab center every day with my parents, staring at my brother as if we can make him better by our mere presence. It's exhausting."

"How is he?"

Ava had been so relieved when he'd been discharged from the hospital and sent to the Newport Rehabilitation Center last week. But she hadn't kept up with her daily calls after she learned of her pregnancy, afraid her shell-shocked attitude would wend its way through the atmosphere via cell towers.

Carrie sighed. "His words are a bit mixed up and sometimes we don't understand what he's saying. And he's dragging his right foot. But he goes to speech and physical therapy every day. The doctor and his therapists say he's recovering nicely; it's just going to be a long process. I feel bad for him. He gets so frustrated when he's talking to me, especially when I give him a blank stare. It's like he has to learn the English language all over again."

While not great news, it was ten times better than when he was in a coma. At least now, he was conscious and moving around. Ava bit her lip, hoping her next question wouldn't give away any secrets. "Has Brian's memory come back?"

"No. The last thing he remembers is driving to Newport with his packed Jeep. We've talked about the weekend, the tennis tournament, the parties... He doesn't recall any of it."

Great. But maybe if he saw her it would stimulate his brain cells. She had to try. At least the first step was coming to fruition. "I'll take the train up Friday afternoon after my two o'clock class. Do you want me to come straight to the rehab facility?" Ava was pushing it, but she had to do this.

"I'll pick you up and we'll just head back to the house. It will be nice to dance with someone in the studio. You can show me what you've been working on in class."

Thankfully Ava wasn't showing yet. She could put on a leotard and share what she'd been learning up until a few weeks ago. No way was she telling Carrie she hadn't been to class since then.

Now, she just had to work out a plan to come into contact with Brian. Depending upon his reaction to her, she would follow a predetermined path. All she could do was take one step at a time.

****

Beads of sweat dripped down Ava's back, and she fanned herself with a dance magazine as the taxi sat in Newport's Friday traffic. She had to see Brian. Changing Carrie's plan to pick Ava up at the train station, Ava didn't telephone her. Carrie might try to keep her from the rehab center the entire weekend.

Surely Brian would recognize her the second she appeared. Maybe her presence would even help him recover his memory. Ava just couldn't take the chance of Carrie denying this visit.

Yet, fear of angering the Stanhopes, Carrie included, had her stomach even more queasy than usual. She nibbled on another cracker, all the while rallying her courage.

Ava glanced at her watch: 7:10. Maybe Carrie and her parents had gone home for the evening. Or left the facility to grab something to eat. She leaned back against the vinyl upholstery of the odorous cab and allowed that possibility to take hold. *Please, please, please*, she chanted. But her lie to Carrie would surely tempt fate. She told Carrie the train would be at least an hour late, maybe longer, giving Ava the time needed to get to the center. What she would tell the Stanhopes about her presence, she hadn't yet formulated.

Finally arriving, Ava paid the driver, grabbed her duffel bag, then strode through the revolving doorway, unwilling to be waylaid by fear or indecisiveness. It had taken over four hours to get here and she felt disheveled and wilted, not the look she wanted to present to Brian after over a month of not seeing him. Dashing into the ladies room in the reception area, Ava splashed cold water on her face, passed a brush through her long, dark hair, and dabbed on some lip-gloss. That would have to do; she couldn't spend another minute delaying her goal.

After learning Brian's room number from the receptionist, Ava took the elevator to the fifth floor. Her senses on high alert, Ava jumped at the ding signifying her destination. Anxiety slowed her steps, but she forged on, following the room numbers in a semicircle until she came to his. She knocked on the half-closed door, barely hearing her knuckles rap as blood whooshed through her veins.

Carrie opened the door, surprise or maybe shock etched on her face. "Ava. I thought you'd call when your train got in."

"I didn't want you to bother dealing with the traffic."

Carrie hugged Ava, and Ava finally took the deep breath she craved to settle her nerves.

"My parents ran out to get something to eat." Carrie pulled Ava into the room, swathed in a dim light.

Brian sat up in bed changing the channel on the television with the remote control. Her heart leaped at the sight of him. He looked normal, except for his thinness and pale skin. Not quite the vibrant man who had galloped across the field on his horse, or skirmished during their water polo match, or made passionate love to her—but gorgeous nonetheless. She tried to look away, but her gaze refused to cooperate. The more she drank in, the more it hurt. Finally, he glanced over, a quick dart of his eyes before he refocused on the TV screen. Her heart squeezed. He had to know who she was. Everything they had together couldn't be gone.

"Hi, Brian." Ava moved closer, the long absent

smile finding its way to her lips. "How are you feeling?'

He looked at her again. "Are y…you a…an…other thera- thera- doctor?" His words were halting, as if he had to think about each one before he said it. "I th…thought I m…met…every…one b…by now."

Ava stood her ground, knowing it might take some time to nudge his memory. "No. I'm Ava. Carrie's friend from school. We met the weekend of your graduation party." Ava heard the tightness in her voice and attempted to smooth it out. "We had a conversation in the gazebo the first day I arrived."

The memory was crystal clear to Ava. He had to remember.

Ava stood in the gazebo overlooking a pond with lily pads.

"Do you mind if I join you?" A man's voice broke into her mental dance and she spun around.

Her heart quickened at the sight of Brian, incredibly gorgeous with blond hair, aqua eyes, and a perfect white smile. He looked like a model for Abercrombie & Fitch.

"No. It's your gazebo. I'm just visiting."

"So you are. My sister never told me she had a beautiful roommate."

Ava laughed, now feeling self-conscious. "That's because I'm not beautiful. I'm sort of plain. And pale." In her mind, no one compared to Carrie's beauty, with long, wavy blonde hair, sun-kissed skin, and huge hazel eyes. The guys at NYU followed her around like stray puppy dogs.

"I like your kind of plain. And if you're concerned about pale, a little fresh air and sunshine will give you

some color. You should come sailing with me tomorrow. We could ditch the crowds and take off on my boat before anyone wakes up."

"Thank you. But I'm here as Carrie's guest. I don't know what she has planned for us tomorrow."

"Kind. Considerate. I like that, too."

Brian held her hands, sending warmth, then fire up her arms and through her body. His eyes sought hers and held them. She felt dizzy, lightheaded, as she gazed back at him, unable to break the connection. Just inches kept them apart, their lips at opposite ends of an imaginary hypotenuse, one with magnetic poles. It would take no effort at all to close the gap. To kiss the golden boy.

Carrie placed her hand on Ava's arm. "He doesn't remember that weekend," she said matter-of-factly. Then turning to Brian, she explained, "Ava came to visit me this weekend. Remember, I told you she and I are roommates at NYU. We dance together."

"Oh. R…right." He kept his eyes on the television, although the sound was off.

Ava tried again. "You watched us practice in the studio that weekend. You really liked the dance we were choreographing." Ava moved closer, mentally begging him to reconnect with her. Then a brilliant smile broke over Brian's face and he nodded. Joy bubbled up in Ava. "Do you remember me now?"

"I al…always w…went to Carrie's, to Carrie's recitals. She's g…great." His statement burst Ava's optimism, but she waited patiently while he continued. "I don't re…remember m…my par…party." He shrugged, as if it was too bad, but what difference did it make? Or maybe he didn't want to admit how much it bothered him, so he downplayed its importance.

Either way, the result was the same. He didn't know her. And Ava's prayer went unanswered. She decided on another tactic. Unable to share with him their intimate time in the guesthouse, she ventured toward an activity.

"That weekend was the first time I ever played water polo. You put me on your team and taught me the rules. When Carrie and Zack wanted to join our team, you separated them to keep Zack at a reasonable distance from your sister. Carrie was so annoyed with you."

Ava's laugh seemed brittle to her own ears, yet a thrill tickled her nerves as she relived his fleeting touches, whispered secrets, and furtive glances, all while moving around the pool with ease. He made her feel like she was the only one he saw. She shivered at the thought of his breath whispering against her ear as he coached her on where to throw the ball.

Ava ached to go on, to dangle other memories before him, but tears clogged her throat at the impassive expression on his face. Nothing. She bit her lip, trying to keep from crying. He wouldn't understand her emotion. Neither would Carrie.

Brian filled the quiet void. "C…Carrie's been…visiting me every day." He tapped his fingers on the bed as if the mattress would release the words he needed. "She hasn't s…seen Zack." His words were slow in coming and his sentences simple, but a marked improvement from what Carrie had described a few weeks ago. "Go. Have…fun." He gave his sister a lopsided grin showing his gratitude, while at the same time pushing her to get out of there. "I'll…watch the…Yank…ees." He turned his attention back to the TV, increasing the volume by remote, effectively dismissing them.

"Come on, Ava, let's go. See you later, bro."

Brian gave a half-hearted wave and laid back against the pillows, focusing on the game.

Ava felt hollow as Carrie escorted her out of the facility. The only words that circled her brain were: He doesn't know me.

She finally squeaked out, "He looks good."

Carrie nodded. "Yes. To look at him you wouldn't know he's been in an accident. But the injury is affecting his gait; he walks like a drunken sailor." She laughed. "The doctor says that will improve with therapy and time. His speech is still slow, but it's so much better than it was."

"Will that also get better with time?"

Carrie nodded. "So they say. I think he's embarrassed when he can't remember a word, so he sticks to the basics. I'm sure that's why he wanted us to leave so quickly. He's okay with me around, but he doesn't want to mess up in front of a beautiful woman."

If Ava had been capable of conversation, she would have denied her friend's compliment. But while her plan to see Brian had worked flawlessly, the result was devastating. There was no glimmer of recognition she could work with, no thread she could tug on to bind them together.

The baby growing in her belly would be hers alone.

She, the sole decision-maker.

Chapter Four

"That's fabulous. I love it." Carrie clapped as Ava pirouetted, leaped, and glided around Carrie's studio, showing her the ballet they'd been learning in class.

Despite Ava's predicament, she made a focused effort to rid herself of despair and embraced the pure joy that came with marrying motion to rhythm. Besides, it might be the last carefree weekend for a long while. Catching her breath, she beckoned Carrie to the center of the floor and went through the progression more slowly, so Carrie could join in.

"I've been practicing our showcase dance on my own." Carrie did jetés in place just behind Ava.

Ava's feet came to a stop, dread simmering through her body. She turned to face Carrie, but kept her eyes trained on the floor. "About that. I'm not performing in it."

"What? You're kidding, right?" The disbelief in Carrie's voice would have been comical if the situation hadn't been so serious.

"No. I've decided to drop out of the dance program and focus on pre-law." She rushed into her explanation so Carrie wouldn't have the chance to argue. "It was always my intent to go to law school if the dance thing didn't work out. I'm just being realistic. I'll never get picked up by a professional dance company. It was a silly dream." She shook her head. "A dream that started with my mother's enthusiasm. I should have never let it get this far."

Carrie grabbed Ava's hands and shook them, as if to get her attention. "You are unbelievably good, Ava. All our dance teachers have told you so. How can you drop out without even trying? The showcase is a no-brainer. We're ready. We're signed up. All we have to do is perform the best we can on that one night. Everyone will be there. The people from Alvin Ailey, the Manhattan Ballet Company, New York City Ballet, American Ballet, Paul Taylor. Need I go on?"

Ava shook her head as tears burned her eyes and threatened to spill down her cheeks. "I know who will be there." Maybe she could blame her choice on Carrie? Maybe Carrie would forgo her argument if she felt somehow responsible. "I figured you had already decided against it. You've been here in Newport for almost a month. You dropped out of your summer classes and we haven't practiced together in weeks. I assumed you made the same decision. How can we possibly compete against everyone who's been practicing morning, noon, and night? We'll just make fools of ourselves."

Carrie held her hand to her heart as her face contorted. Sobs escaped her mouth and Ava kicked herself for taking that ploy. She put her arms around Carrie and hugged her. "Please don't cry. Everything will turn out okay."

In hiccupping breaths, Carrie apologized, making Ava feel even worse. "I'm so sorry, Ava. I didn't think about how my absence would ruin your chances. I'm a terrible friend."

No. Ava was the terrible friend making it sound

like this was all Carrie's fault. "No one's to blame. Your brother needed you. I'm sure your presence helped him get as far as he has." Ava rubbed Carrie's back as she waited for her words to sink in—to let Carrie off the hook she'd speared her with.

"Maybe," Carrie allowed, pulling away to grab some tissues. "This has been such an awful time." She blew her nose and dabbed at her face. "But no matter how bad it's been for me and my family, it shouldn't affect you. You can't quit dancing. Maybe we have to postpone our appearance in the showcase. There'll be another one next year. I promise to work every damn day with you once I get back to school in September to make it up to you. We'll be that much better, that much stronger for practicing another year. We'll get offers. I know we will. I know you will. You're the best dancer at school, Ava."

Carrie's positive attitude and conviction almost made Ava pump her fist in the air and sign on. *But I'm pregnant.* Those three words skidded any misplaced optimism to a halt. Besides, she couldn't lead Carrie on. That would be worse than what she'd already done. "You're sweet to say that and I love you for believing in me. But I have to look at my future. I need a job, a career that will support me. Even if I did get picked up by a dance company, I wouldn't earn much." *Not enough to support a child.* She still hadn't decided what to do about the baby once she gave birth.

Carrie placed her hands on her hips and accusing disbelief punctuated her words. "You've known that all along. You can't tell me now you're throwing away what you've worked at for the past fifteen years because of money. Artists don't care about money.

They care about their passion. And your passion is dance."

It was. But passion wouldn't pay for her baby's food or clothes or a place to live. "Things change. I guess I'm growing up." Not that she wanted to. She'd like nothing better than to inhabit the body she'd had six weeks ago and embrace the motivation she'd had then as well. She wanted to go back to being selfish, forging the career she coveted, without worrying about another human being.

A small seed of envy began to grow in her heart, which segued into anger. Carrie would live the life Ava had anticipated, twirling and soaring over a stage as the crowd roared with appreciation. And Brian would skate through his life, unaware of the destruction he'd caused by flirting with a naïve dancer who'd unwittingly fallen in love with him.

Life was just not fair.

****

Brian watched Carrie pace his small room as if she were a caged lion. She'd been acting strange ever since her friend came to visit two weeks earlier. "What's b...bothering you?" he finally asked, unable to concentrate on the article he tried to read as she unsettled the air around him.

"I'm restless."

"No k...kidding. Go b...back to New...York. Stop hang...ing around this...here." When he couldn't find the right word, which was often, he substituted a simpler word. So frustrating. But this whole scene had to be frustrating to Carrie as well. Most people at the rehab center were approaching their eighth decade. He didn't want to be here. Why would she?

31

"I'd feel guilty not being here for you."

So the truth finally came out. "Why? You've been g...great. I really a...ppreciate your...showing up...every day. I'm doing better. Don't...you th-think?"

She nodded and gave him a smile. "Yes. I just don't want to desert you. If I were in your place, I know you'd be here for me."

He put his magazine on the bedside table and patted the bed next to him. "Come...here."

She sat where he indicated and he held her hand. "Th-thank you for help...ing me get...through this. Having you...here...kept my...spirits up. Y-you've been a...rock. But it's time...for...you to get back...to your life. Mom...said you and your f...friend dropped out of the show...case. She was up...set."

Carrie rolled her eyes. "You know Mom. She expects me to be all things to all people. If I had gone back to the City after the accident, she would have had a fit. Although I would never have left you to do that," she added. "But now that I'm missing my opportunity to dance in front of the professional companies, she's making it sound like I should have been able to keep up with my practicing." Carrie sighed. "I'm letting everyone down."

The sadness in Carrie's eyes confused him. "What do you...mean?"

"Not only is Mom disappointed in me, but my friend Ava is quitting dance."

He recalled the pretty, young woman with long, dark hair and royal blue eyes who seemed intent on prodding his memory about the time they'd supposedly spent together. It hadn't worked. "Why is she qu...quitting? I...thought she was an...incre—a good dancer."

"She is. She's the best. You even thought so when you saw us dancing together in the studio."

"I don't re...member." But if she was anywhere near as good as his sister, then she had to be fabulous.

"Was...there some...thing between us? Ava...and I? She seemed in...tent on jog-jogging my...memory."

Carrie averted her eyes, then smoothed a wrinkle in the sheet. "I haven't said anything to you before this, but now that you ask, I guess I would say you were enamored with her that weekend."

"Why...do you s...say that? What did...I do?"

"For starters, when you were supposed to be playing tennis, you came by the studio and watched us through the window. You were really blown away with her talent. Then you spent a lot of time with her at the barbecue that night. And when you weren't with her, you were watching her." A smug smile twitched over Carrie's lips. "The next day you came to find us horseback riding. I went to meet Zack, and you stayed with Ava. That night, after the big formal dinner party, the two of you disappeared. No one saw you leave together, but..."

"That...doesn't mean...anything." He could have been with any of a number of beautiful young ladies that weekend. Brian searched his mind for any snippet he could locate concerning that weekend, but they must have been buried deep. Or knocked right out of him when he fell, never to be found again. Had he been with Ava?

Carrie's sadness returned. "I just can't believe she's quitting dance."

"Why…is she?"

"It's my fault. We were supposed to do the showcase together. We'd been working on our choreography for months. It was really good." Carrie looked toward the wall, her shoulders slumping. "Since I wasn't around to work on it, she dropped out. She must have looked at that showcase as her only opportunity to get picked up by a major dance company. She doesn't want to wait another year. So she's withdrawing as a dance major. I just learned she's transferring to Columbia for pre-law." A tear slid down Carrie's face.

"I'm…sorry." He wiped the tear away with his fingers. "C-couldn't she have…performed on her own?"

Carrie shook her head. "The piece we created was for two people. We played off each other when we were dancing individually, but there were a lot of jumps and spins that required a partner."

He didn't pretend to know the intricacies of collaborative dancing, but he did know how important this all was to his sister. He guessed it was like Ginger Rogers losing Fred Astaire. Or the more modern version of them.

"What…about you?"

"I'll perform next year, of course. Nothing would make me drop dance. I didn't think Ava would either. But all of a sudden she says she needs to concentrate on a career where she'll earn money. I know she has some student loans to cover living expenses, but her father's paying her tuition. Even so, if you were to ask me a few months ago if I thought she'd throw her passion to the wind, I'd say no way."

"Maybe you...could ch-change her mind. Con...vince her to d-dance in the show...case alone doing a diff...erent dance."

Before Carrie could answer, their parents entered.

"It looks like you two are having a heavy conversation." His father pulled a chair toward the bed for his mother.

Carrie shook her head slightly, advising Brian to keep from sharing. So he came up with a topic his father would bite right into.

"Dr. Hast...ings said I'm...coming along...much faster than he...expected. That I m-might be re...leased in a week. I could g-go to out...patient th-therapy in the...City." He looked at his father. "I c...can start work."

His father's chest puffed out a bit, as if so proud of his son for suggesting it. "The job is there for you as soon as you're ready. But you don't have to rush it. Just get better. Focus on your therapies. And what about your trip to Europe? Aren't you going?"

"Not...any more. I t...told Zack and...Rob to go with...out me. They don't n-need a cripple tag...ging along."

His mother chimed in at his crass description of himself. "You are not a cripple. Your leg drags a little, but Dr. Hastings says it will improve with physical therapy. In no time, you won't even be able to tell you had an accident."

That remained to be seen, but he had no intention of holding up his friends' vacation while he slugged through each day training his muscles and brain to cooperate. Work would be good for him. His speech was still slow, but he was going crazy doing nothing intellectually.

He turned to Carrie. "You could…help me…set up my a…partment."

She smiled, seemingly grateful he didn't raise the issue of the showcase in front of their mother. "I'd be happy to. I could get Ava to help too."

His mother pursed her lips. "I thought you said Ava was transferring to Columbia?" As if going to that Ivy League school was distasteful.

Carrie groaned. "Just because Ava isn't dancing any more doesn't mean I can't still be friends with her." Carrie's voice held more than a touch of exasperation.

But their mother didn't seem to care. "You should stick with the other dancers. You all have so much in common. You'll push each other to do better. Obviously Ava didn't have the hunger to stick with it. You don't want her ambivalence to rub off on you now, do you?"

Carrie's face flushed and her fists balled. "Mother, you know nothing about Ava. She's the best dancer at school. It's my fault she's quitting." Her voice broke, and Brian thought she was about to cry. Instead, she got up and walked toward the door, tossing angry words over her shoulder. "I'm going back to New York. I need to fix this."

With that, she was gone, leaving their meddling mother for once, without words.

Chapter Five

"Ava! What are you doing here?" Kim's eyes nearly popped out of her head as she stood in her doorway gawking at her sister. Then concern took over. "Is everything okay?"

Ava dug deep for a smile to assure her sister there was nothing life-threatening spurring her Saturday visit. "Fine. I'm sorry I didn't call first. But I needed a break from school this weekend and thought I'd come see you." A little lie to help her sister get over the shock.

"You're always welcome. You know that." Kim hugged her, bringing tears to Ava's eyes, courtesy of the hormones raging in her body. "How'd you get here?"

"The train to Princeton Junction, then a cab." Ava lowered her lids and moved into the house with her backpack, taking in the newly furnished living room. "You've redecorated."

"It was time to make this house appear like two grown-ups live here. I was tired of looking at Dan's grandmother's couch and my compressed wood end-tables." Kim surveyed the room with a smile, as if seeing it for the first time. "Of course now our credit is maxed out, but we're no longer embarrassed when we entertain."

Ava dropped her bag next to the sofa. "Where's Dan?"

"He's working overtime on a new project. It came just in time since we could use the money. The costs of my fertility treatments are over the top."

"I wanted to talk to you alone anyway." Ava couldn't keep the melancholy from her voice.

Kim eyed her with suspicion. "There is something wrong. Come to the kitchen and sit. I'll make coffee."

"Do you have decaf?"

Kim led the way into a bright sunny room with sliding glass doors leading to a nice-sized backyard, complete with picnic table and grill. So suburban. Ava stood at the door viewing the neighbors' yards. A rocking horse caught her eye, and her mind spun back to a few months ago at the Stanhope estate.

The clip-clopping of another horse had Ava turning in her saddle. Her pulse picked up the beat, then pounded erratically. Brian headed toward her and Carrie, looking like a sexy cowboy. His blonde hair, a little darker than his sister's, but streaked by the sun, blew away from his face—allowing the chiseled angles to become more prominent.

"Hey, I've been looking for you." His blue eyes locked on Ava, as if he were speaking only to her.

"Are you sure you've been looking for us*?" Carrie's emphasis made it clear she noticed his myopic focus.*

His grin widened at her sarcasm. "Yes. I'm supposed to deliver a message to you from Zack." He waited a beat to take in Carrie's quick blush—or was he waiting for an apology?

"What is it?" Carrie's impatience cut through the momentary pause.

"He said to meet him at the gazebo. He apparently

is smitten with my little sister. For the life of me I don't know why."

Brian's teasing chuckle had no effect on Carrie. "What time?"

"Three. "

Carrie looked at her watch. "It's three ten. I better get going."

She took off without a backward glance, leaving Ava alone with Brian.

"Why do you tease her like that?" Ava chastised, but couldn't hold back her grin.

Brian's lazy smile returned. "Because that's what big brothers do to little sisters. Don't you ever spar with a sibling?"

Not wanting to get into a conversation about her family, she shrugged instead of answering. Then she pulled on the reins to stop her horse from eating. "I guess I should get her back to the stable. But I don't know what to do with her once I get there."

"I'd be happy to show you." His tone sent chills up her arms, hinting at more than just returning their mounts.

Arriving at the barn, Brian easily dismounted his horse, then placed the reins over a post. Ava swung her left leg over her mare and would have jumped to the ground, but before she could push off her saddle, Brian placed his hands around her waist and eased her down the length of his long, hard body. She kept her lids lowered, as heat rushed to her cheeks at the intimate contact. Once her feet firmly hit the ground, he backed up a few inches, but still managed to be in her space, making breathing difficult.

But a little less oxygen was so worth it if she could

be in his orbit a little while longer.

"Who drinks decaf in the morning?" Kim asked as she searched her cabinet for the requested coffee.

Ava turned back toward her sister. "I try to be careful with caffeine. According to my ballet mistress, everything we eat or drink affects our body." While true, the real reason was the baby. The doctor had stressed caffeine wasn't good for the fetus, so Ava cut out coffee and soda, although she couldn't bring herself to stay away from chocolate. At least not completely.

Kim riffled through the cabinets and finally came up with an old jar of instant coffee. As soon as the water boiled, she brought it to Ava, joining her with a cup of the real stuff. "I'm so happy to see you. I'm really glad you came to visit." She took Ava's hand in hers and studied her face. "You look tired. Tell me about school. About dance. Or anything else you'd like to talk about."

Where to begin? Ava poured milk into her mug. Brian's graduation party weekend in Newport? The accident? Carrie's focus on her brother instead of their showcase dance? Her fainting in class? She shook her head, discarding thought after thought. This wasn't a story to tell. This was real life—interrupted. "I'm pregnant." The words came out uncensored, without preamble.

Her sister's reaction was slow in coming, almost as if her brain had to catch up with her ears. But then Kim's eyes dimmed, her smile fell, and her mouth hung open. Message received.

"Oh," she finally responded. Kim stared at Ava, as if she could glean more information from her face without asking a direct question.

"I'm sorry to blurt it out like that. I just didn't want to bore you with a whole story before delivering the news. I had to get it out before I burst. Now that it's out there, we can go backwards, if you want." Ava rolled her shoulders, feeling the emotional weight slide off. As she suspected, telling her sister, whom she trusted with her life, helped tremendously.

"From your demeanor, I take it this is not happy news?"

"No." The sigh that had been building up, escaped. "It's disastrous."

Kim bit her lip as if contemplating her next question. "Do you know who the father is?"

Ava felt the proverbial punch to her gut. That question, she wasn't expecting. "Of course I know who the father is. I don't sleep around."

"I'm sorry. It's just that you never mentioned you were in a serious relationship in any of our conversations, so I didn't think you were seeing anyone special." Her sister's apologetic words made Ava feel even worse.

"I'm not seeing him any more," Ava mumbled, swallowing the bile that rose in her throat every time she thought about Brian and his memory loss.

"Is it because of the baby?" Kim's mouth turned down, as if she knew that was the answer.

"No. He doesn't know about the baby." Ava's eyes stung with tears. Again. "He's the guy I told you about two months ago. He has a brain injury and doesn't remember me." The tears flowed as if a dam had been broken.

"Oh, honey, that's awful." Kim came to Ava and hugged her, rubbing her back like her mother used to when she was upset. "Don't cry. We'll figure this out."

When Ava finally pulled herself together, the sisters talked about Brian's condition, then Ava's choices.

"I can't believe I'm going to have a child," Ava said miserably. "You're the one who should be delivering this news. You're the one who's been trying so hard to get pregnant."

As Ava pondered the injustice of her predicament, a germ of an idea took hold and sprouted like a beanstalk.

"You and Dan should take this baby. Adopt it." Ava's words came out so fast, they blurred together.

"What?" Shock punctuated Kim's question. "You're not serious."

Even though the thought had just occurred to Ava a mere five seconds before, it grew roots. "I'm very serious. I don't want a baby. I'm in college. I'm twenty, and I haven't figured out my life yet. I'm not equipped to take care of a baby. Especially without the father." Now the words tumbled out as fast as she could say them. "This is perfect. You've been trying to get pregnant. You just said yourself the cost of fertility treatments is outrageous."

Kim's eyes clouded. "True, but…"

Ava jumped in, not allowing Kim to manufacture an excuse. "If you adopt my baby, I'll know he or she will be loved and cared for by two of the best people in the world. And you wouldn't have to keep going through IVF. What's not perfect about this scenario?"

Kim held up her hand as if to stop Ava's out-of-control excitement. "Hold on. You can't just come in here and offer us your child. There's something wrong about that."

"Why? You're dying to have a baby. You're going through hell with IVF and there's no guarantee it'll work. It's cost prohibitive. And wouldn't it be better for my baby to be raised by my sister than some stranger?"

Kim stood and started pacing, clearly agitated by Ava's simple and reasonable suggestion. "So you've decided to put the baby up for adoption?"

"That's where I'm leaning. So what do you say?"

"This is a huge issue—one that can't be dropped on me like this. And no using guilt." She turned to Ava and pointed her finger, driving her statement home. Then she continued her trek around the kitchen. "I've been taken totally off-guard here. You come by, unexpected—which is great, don't get me wrong—and before you've been here five minutes you drop a bomb. Fine. We can discuss your options. Figure out what's best for you and the baby. But you can't ask me, without thought, to adopt your child. It's crazy."

Kim dragged her hands through her dark brown hair, practically pulling the strands out of her scalp.

"I'm sorry," murmured Ava. "I didn't mean to get you so upset. I know this solution came out of left field. It fell out of my mouth." She rose and went to Kim. "Sit down. Relax." She took her arm and led her back to her chair. "Have some coffee."

"That will not relax me." Kim pushed the cup away, liquid sloshing onto the table. "Let's start over." She inhaled, then let her breath out in a whoosh. "Any decision you make shouldn't be made impulsively."

Although Ava felt like a reprimanded child, it didn't douse her resolve to explore this option more fully. "Listen, Kim, I know this just came out of the blue. But there aren't many options to explore. I won't have an abortion, and I can't keep the baby. Adoption is the only solution." Ava tamped down her excitement over the possibility Kim would step in. "I didn't come here to ask you to take my baby. I came here to get support from my sister. I already obtained names of adoption agencies in New York." She planned to set up appointments with a few of them in the coming weeks. "But it's so perfect. You want a child. I don't. My baby would remain in our family. Only you'll be the mother and I'll be the aunt, instead of vice versa." The more she talked, the more she knew this was the right thing to do.

Kim stopped pacing. "I need some air." She barreled through the back door and stayed out there for the next fifteen minutes, crisscrossing the yard talking to herself.

Ava gave her the time, hoping she'd come to the right conclusion.

When she finally returned, she came in sputtering. "What if you change your mind, either when the baby's born or later? You'd think that would be okay because I'm your sister. But it wouldn't. If you want me to seriously consider this option, I need to know you're going to let Dan and I adopt your child at birth. That you're not going to see the little baby and fall in love with him or her and decide you can't go through with it." Kim's stern look focused on Ava. Then she softened. "I'm afraid. What if you change your mind after the fact? What if you decide years from now, and because I'm your sister..." Tears flooded Kim's eyes and she couldn't go on.

Ava's eyes watered in response. "I hear you. I

understand what you're saying. Why don't you talk it over with Dan. We'll all think this through for a week or two, then we'll get back together. If we think it's the best alternative at that time, you can hire a lawyer and I'll sign whatever you want me to sign to assure you I won't take the baby from you."

Kim shook her head. "I'm not going to make you sign something. If we go ahead with this, we will trust each other to do the right thing."

"If you're adopting this child, we have to do it formally. What time is Dan coming home?" Ava's angst had her zooming to her next target.

"Not until five. Which is good since it will give us the afternoon to discuss this crazy plan in more detail."

"I do have one condition though." It had just occurred to Ava.

"What is it?" Kim's radar was already on wary and now she looked downright skeptical.

"I don't want Dad to know."

"How do you intend to keep your pregnancy from him?" Kim's incredulity irked Ava. It wasn't like she and her father were best buddies. If they saw each other once every couple of months, that was a lot.

"For the next few months, I don't think I'll show, and if I do, I can cover it up with an oversized top. I plan to tell Dad I'm going to study in Paris for six months, starting at the end of September. I've talked about it before, so he won't think it's odd. That way I won't have to come up with an excuse for Thanksgiving and Christmas. I'll just stay in New York. I'm transferring to Columbia, and I'll be bombarded with schoolwork anyway. Changing my major to pre-law at this late stage will have me doing double-duty to catch up."

"If you give up the baby for adoption, whether to us, or someone else, why are you transferring from NYU? Why are you switching majors? What about dance?"

"I know I'm saying I don't want to raise this child, but I don't want to desert it either." The painful thought of her mother's choice pierced her heart. "I plan to save money to help you, if you agree, or whoever adopts it. I also want to start a fund for his or her college education. In order to help out, I'll need a good job, a stable career. I won't have that with dancing."

"You shouldn't give up your ambition. At least not right now. If, in a few years, you decide to change careers, you can do it then."

"I've made up my mind." Ava walked over to the window and looked out at the yard rimmed with colorful flowers. She couldn't let Kim see the agony ravishing her soul over this decision.

Ava's entire life had centered around dance, from the time she was five years old until two months ago. Becoming pregnant had ruined her goal. It was her fault. She'd relied on a condom, but worse, she'd stupidly fallen for Brian. The guy who played around—the guy whose sister warned her to stay away from him because of his penchant for breaking hearts. Yet, she still fantasized about building her world with him. Her prior world—where he would come to her performances, smiling with pride at her accomplishments. And she would attend his business dinners, basking in the glow of his success. They'd be the perfect New York couple, hardworking, successful, and most of all, happy.

Then reality would strike and kick that dream to the curb.

How could one weekend produce such devastating consequences?

She of all people should have known better. She learned early on she couldn't rely on anyone else. Not on her mother. Not on her father. And now, not on Brian.

At that moment, in Kim's kitchen, she vowed to trust no one but herself.

Chapter Six

Seven Years Later

There are other Stanhopes in the world, Ava murmured to herself as she left Peter Dunhill's office to begin the initial consultation with Peter's client. But no amount of rationalization would stop the stampede in her gut.

All Peter said was, "Cover for me for a few minutes while I take this call. A Mr. Stanhope is my next client. You know the drill. I'll meet you in the conference room." Then he picked up the phone and began talking, giving her no chance to find out more information. Not that she'd be able to decline. As a second-year associate, she did what was requested.

Ava stopped before she reached the lobby of Calloway and Burnett, the Park Avenue law office where she'd been working for the last year and a half as the newest associate in their environmental litigation department. Holding a hand over her abdomen, she pressed hard as if that would settle the kicking hooves. Inhaling for strength and praying for a stranger, Ava walked confidently into the reception area to collect Peter's client.

"Mr. Stanhope." She waited for the man standing near the window to turn.

Her vision blurred, but she powered through as she

held out her hand. "I'm Ava Harrington. Peter Dunhill's associate."

"Brian Stanhope." Hopefully, he didn't notice the tremor in her fingers when he shook her hand.

His familiar blue eyes shone with warmth and a smile touched his lips, but there was no recognition on his face or in his manner. Not only did he lose his memory of her from that fateful weekend, but apparently she'd made no impression when she visited him as Carrie's roommate at the rehab center either.

"Why don't you come this way?" She turned and led him down a short hallway into a conference room with floor to ceiling windows on two walls, a large Mondrian print on another and a black rectangular table with hard edges anchoring the room. "Have a seat."

Ava bit her lip as she grabbed a yellow legal pad and pen from the built in credenza across the room. Sitting at the head of the table, she glanced at him.

"Peter's on a conference call and asked that I meet with you to get some basic information. He shouldn't be much longer." He better not be because she wasn't sure how long she'd be able to hold herself together.

"Fine."

After answering Ava's preliminary questions, Brian opened his briefcase and extracted a thick packet of paper. "Our company, Stanhope Natural Gas, is negotiating with several landowners in Pennsylvania to drill on their land for natural gas. The contract we've been using isn't up to par and doesn't cover all the contingencies that might arise. This is the current contract." He pushed the document across the table toward her. "I understand you and your firm have experience in this type of work."

Ava frowned, leaving the contract in the middle of the table. "We usually represent community associations and nonprofit groups against those drilling for natural gas."

"I know. But business is business, right? I figure, since you know what we're up against with the nonprofits, you'd be better able to advise our company of the potential problems, which we can then cover in the contract with the landowner." His tone was no-nonsense, his demeanor, straight to the point.

Brian had obviously done his homework. He knew the type of clients the firm represented and wanted to use their expertise to his advantage.

"I'm low man on the totem pole, so I can't comment on your request for representation." Although, if she were in charge, she'd send him packing. His company, and those like his, were ruining the environment by pumping water, sand, and chemicals into the ground with the hope of untrapping natural gas. Fracking. Is that what they'd been doing seven years ago? She had no idea what Brian's family business involved. It was never the topic of conversation between she and Carrie. They only talked dance.

She studied his face.

"Is everything okay?" he asked.

Her cheeks flushed, and she quickly made some notes on her pad. "Fine. I appreciate you interviewing our firm to represent you. I'll go see if Peter is ready." She pushed back her chair.

"Wait." He gave her an awkward smile. "I feel like we've met before."

Ava's heartbeat tripled, and she looked down at the table. "I was friends, actually roommates, with your sister in college. I met you at your Newport house one weekend."

"Ava Harrington, Ava Harrington." He uttered her name as if saying it would bring back his memory. "I'm sure I'd remember meeting a friend of Carrie's, but I can't place you. I apologize. When were you there?"

"The weekend of your graduation party."

"Oh." A shadow crossed his eyes, and all traces of his smile disappeared. "Carrie might have told you I have no memory of the weekend leading up to my fall, and honestly that whole two-month period in the hospital and rehab, I've tried to push out of my mind." He chuckled without mirth as if to make light of the situation.

Ava couldn't find a single word, much less a sentence in response.

Filling the silence, Brian took up the conversation. "How did you end up a lawyer? If you were Carrie's roommate, I'm assuming you were a dance major."

Ava's heart thudded, and she clasped her hands in her lap to keep them still as she once again told the lie she'd perfected. "With all the qualified dancers vying for positions with the New York dance companies, I knew I was headed for disappointment. So I decided to be realistic and switch majors." Ava avoided his eyes while spinning her tale, even though now, she segued into the truth. "I chose law because there was more stability in this field." She babbled on, not able to stop herself. "I had a summer internship here between my second and third years of law school and was offered the job. So here I am." She shrugged in an effort to downplay her major and earthshattering career change.

She needed to escape, at least momentarily, so she

stood and walked to the door. Yet, she wanted to ask one more personal question before Peter joined them. "How is Carrie? I haven't seen her in a long time."

"Busy traveling with the Manhattan Ballet Company. She's been in Paris a few weeks, but she'll be back in New York to rehearse for their spring season, which starts in May. Carrie says they have some exciting new choreography. You should go see her."

"I don't know...I'll try." It was hard to breathe. Maybe that question should have remained unspoken.

Envy tore at her soul. Carrie enjoyed the career Ava had lived to embrace. Sure, she was a well-paid lawyer in a successful Park Avenue firm. But that was never her aspiration.

Ava slipped through the door without explanation and inhaled deeply as she went in search of Peter. What heavenly prankster had placed her in a conference room on the thirty-eighth floor overlooking Park Avenue with the man she had vowed to forget?

****

What a strange conversation, Brian mused as he waited for Ava to return with Peter. Her reaction to his news about Carrie was more than odd. Was she jealous of his sister? Surely Ava was engrossed in her career as a young lawyer at a successful firm, having eschewed dance years ago as an unattainable profession. Yet, talk of Carrie's world cast a gloomy shadow over her pretty features.

Maybe her confusing vibes had to do with something different altogether. Perhaps she was philosophically against representing a drilling company. Or was it more personal than that? Perhaps she was upset he didn't remember meeting her in the past. Whatever it was, she didn't come off as a warm, friendly person who had been best friends with his sister during college. He had no doubt she was smart as a whip and dedicated to helping her clients. And maybe that's all that should concern him.

Whatever Ava's issue, it wasn't his job to figure it out.

Before long, Peter returned with Ava and all talk turned to the business at hand. Brian's goal was to interject new blood into the running of the family business, and this was his chance to steer at least some of their legal business to a younger, more creative law firm—a goal he'd been pursuing ever since joining his father's company.

Although most of the conversation took place between Brian and Peter while Ava took notes, Brian's eyes intermittently strayed to her. She looked the part of a Park Avenue lawyer, with her navy pinstriped suit and hair pulled back in a bun. But he also observed that her pretty heart-shaped face was flawless, and her dark blue eyes, almost a deep purple, were fringed with long, black lashes. Her youthfulness was highlighted by her small frame—not that she was short, maybe five four—just thin, willowy.

It hadn't escaped his notice earlier that she glided instead of walked. Every movement, even something as benign as reaching for the doorknob, was graceful. And he ought to know. His sister moved the same way.

"Black spandex is not generally appropriate for tennis, but I'm sure the guys won't mind." Brian smirked as he took in his sister's get-up and that of her friend, as the three met in the downstairs hall of their

vacation home in Newport.

He raised a brow in appreciation as his eyes grazed over the lithe creature standing next to Carrie, dressed in black tights, black leotard, and black ballet slippers. He knew the uniform of the dancer. At his parents' insistence, he'd gone to dozens of recitals over the years, ever since his little sister became addicted to dance when she was five.

"Hello to you, too, big brother." Carrie attempted a scowl, but her grin broke through. No matter how hard she tried, she could never be annoyed with him for long.

Brian grabbed her into a bear hug and avoided his usual ribbing, given the presence of a guest. And a beautiful one at that.

"Glad you could make it for the weekend." He released Carrie and turned his attention to her friend. "Aren't you going to introduce us?" He zeroed in on royal blue eyes, an intense color he had never seen before.

"This is my roommate, Ava."

"Nice to meet you, Ava." He held out his hand and shook hers, noticing a gorgeous smile to go along with her gorgeous eyes "Have you ever been to our Newport house before?"

"No. This is the first time." Ava's voice was quiet, shy. "Carrie invited me to your graduation party weekend. I hope you don't mind."

An unfamiliar vulnerability surfaced on her expressive face. Not like Carrie at all, who was outgoing, charismatic, and the opposite of vulnerable.

"Since you two apparently aren't joining us, what are your plans?"

"We're working on our project for a summer choreography course we're taking. We'll be performing it for the showcase." The glint in Carrie's eyes told him she hardly considered it work. "We'll catch up with you later. Have fun."

Carrie pulled Ava down the hall to her very own hardwood floor dance studio, a gift from their parents on her thirteenth birthday. Now she had a friend to share it with. They may never emerge. Unacceptable. He would have to pull out all the stops to assure their presence—at least Ava's—at the different events over the weekend.

With his sights now set on her, there was no way he was going to let her slip through his fingers.

Brian blinked as Ava's sapphire eyes caught him staring. She angled her head as if to ask a very personal question.

"I'm sorry, Peter, can you repeat what you just said?" Brian had to get his head back into the conversation. Time was money.

But he couldn't seem to shake the odd feeling overtaking his brain. Was that a real memory from the lost weekend or just his injured brain playing tricks on him? Until this moment, he hadn't remembered a thing from that weekend, his last memory being of driving from Cambridge to Newport the Thursday before.

Brian got through the rest of the meeting by promising himself he'd come back to this disturbing recollection—real or imagined—when he wasn't paying six hundred fifty an hour for Peter's time and counsel. Upon agreeing on representation, Peter stood.

"It was great to meet you, Brian. I look forward to working with you." Peter pumped Brian's hand and smiled. "Ava, why don't you take Brian back to your office and go over the fee agreement and retainer requirements."

Brian nodded. "That works for me."

Maybe Ava was the key to that lost weekend.

****

No, no, no. Ava's mind screamed. This couldn't be happening. Just an hour ago, Peter dropped the name Stanhope on her as his next client, and from that point on, she knew her world was about to spin out of control. Now, Peter wanted her to confine herself in her postage stamp-sized office with the father of her child. Damn, damn, damn. This couldn't get any worse. She had enough trouble breathing and talking at the same time while meeting with Brian alone in the conference room. At least once Peter showed up, Brian focused on him and she was able to pull herself together—to a minimal degree. She must have wiped her hands on her skirt every five minutes, and she emptied her water glass several times, until there was nothing left in the pitcher. Just when she thought the meeting had come to an end and she'd be able to escape to her office to deal with the fallout, Peter sucker-punched her.

Now, she and Brian would be on top of each other, and she was sure she couldn't bear having him so close. But all she could do was agree. "This way, Brian."

Ava walked ahead of him, her face on fire and no doubt producing a lovely, sweaty sheen. Betrayed by her own features, she inhaled slowly so as not to let Brian in on the anxiety he caused without even knowing it. While in the conference room, she had surreptitiously taken in his movie-star looks while he responded to Peter's questions. She generally didn't go for men with blond hair, but his highlighted those aquamarine eyes to distraction. The eyes that had penetrated hers years before, convincing her of his ardor. Mesmerizing her. She sighed quietly, as she led him through several halls until reaching her turf.

"Come on in." Ava moved a huge file from her client chair to an already cluttered table in the corner. "Sorry about the mess. I usually don't have company." She gave him an apologetic smile and indicated the now-vacant chair. "Have a seat."

She could do this. The sooner she accomplished her task, the better. Just focus. From a drawer, Ava pulled out their lengthy fee agreement and, went over it with Brian, who had obviously seen one or two of these in the past.

"Where do I sign?" he asked, cutting to the chase.

She flipped to the last page and slid the agreement across the desk, knocking over a picture frame. Before she could grab it and toss it into a drawer, Brian picked it up and looked at it. He smiled. "Who is she? Cute kid."

Ava swallowed, dying to snatch it out of his hand. "My niece," she rasped as her voice deserted her.

He studied the photograph a little too long, and Ava struggled to come up with something—anything— to take his attention away from the blond-haired, blue-eyed angel who looked strikingly similar to him.

"I thought maybe she was yours," he said, beaming his eyes across the desk to hers. "She has your nose. And your smile." He cocked his head, still studying Ava, as if to compare the two. She lowered her lids to stop the comparison. "What's her name?"

"Briana." She held her breath, hoping he would

find nothing odd in her niece's name being a rendition of his.

Finally, he put the frame back on the desk and she nonchalantly placed it facedown before locking back into his eyes, which were focused solely on Ava.

"Are you married?" Not the question she was expecting.

"No."

"Entangled?"

He smiled. A very sexy, very familiar smile. Was he flirting?

Ava shook her head. "No. What about you?" The words fell out of her mouth before she had time to catch them, and she inwardly winced. "Never mind. That's none of my business."

"It can be. Especially since I'm not married or entangled either."

There could be no mistaking it now. His easy banter. The way he drew a person in with a direct and open question. The mating game, according to Brian. It all came back. The way he had enticed her before. So simple for him—the master. But she knew better than to fall for him a second time.

"We should stick to our working relationship." Ava hoped her regret in that decision didn't shine through. She picked up the signed fee agreement. "I'll have my secretary make a copy for you." She rose and moved around the desk. "How would you like to pay the retainer? Check? Credit card?"

Brian raised an eyebrow. "All business, I see." Yet, the hint of a smile tugged at his lips. "Check. Do I make it out to you?"

So playful. Like he'd been that weekend. If she

didn't keep her wits about her, she'd fall right down the same rabbit hole. "No. The firm. I'll be right back."

Out in the hall, she stopped to fan herself. The heat he generated should be captured for raw energy. No need to frack. She wiped away the smile inching over her lips. *Do not cave in. You'll only get hurt. Again.*

Reentering her tiny, airless office with his copy of the agreement in hand, she snapped into business mode. "Thank you so much for giving our firm the chance to represent you. You won't be sorry." She held out her hand to shake his.

He stood, following her lead. "I'm sure I won't."

She would have preferred to end their contact there, but she couldn't let him meander through the halls trying to find the exit. "I'll show you out." Avoiding further conversation, Ava led Brian to the reception area, just as Peter emerged from his office.

"Brian, I'll get back to you shortly, after I have a chance to review your documents." Peter clapped Brian on the back.

"Great," said Brian. "By the way, I have tickets to the Knicks game Saturday night. Floor seats. Would you and Ava like to join me?"

Ava's brain screamed no, as Peter accepted for both of them. Of course, he was a rabid Knicks fan and why would it cross his mind that a lowly associate would have better things to do on a weekend night than generate good will with a new client?

She gave a tight smile in assent, as she knew she had to, turned and strode straight to her office where she closed the door and bit her finger to keep her shriek from reaching the lobby.

Chapter Seven

The roar of the crowd reverberated in her chest as number seven threw the ball from half court and made the basket. Ava relaxed her squeeze on Brian's arm, as she screamed at top range with him and the rest of the fans, clapping so hard her hands stung. It had taken a while for her to get into the game. Peter had bowed out at the last minute, leaving her jittery and anxious about spending the night with Brian alone. But his casual charm and easy conversation calmed her enough to focus on the game.

No one advised her that sitting wasn't allowed during the last quarter of a basketball game. Not that she would have wanted to. The electricity sparked through her at high voltage, turning her into a crazed lunatic with the rest of them.

It was touch and go until the last two seconds when the Knicks scored the winning basket. Brian high-fived her in true sportsman-like manner. Then he slid his arm around her shoulders and hugged her to him, his smile blazing over his team's hard-fought win.

"So, what did you think?" His mouth was close to her ear as he held her tight, sending firecracker sparks through her veins.

Ava couldn't rein in her exuberance. "I loved it. Who would have thought?" Not knowing all the rules at first, she'd tried to keep her questions to a minimum so as not to interfere with Brian's dogged concentration. And also to keep in line with her rules for the night: no bonding over basketball. "You were so intense there for a while, I thought maybe you were one of their coaches."

Brian chuckled. "No. The unofficial coach role belongs to Spike Lee. I don't think the team needs more than one."

"How did you get these great seats?" Being so close to the action heightened her interest in the game. It didn't hurt that she could also celebrity watch. At time outs, Ava craned to get a better look at Beyoncé and Jay Z who were rooting for the other team. She also caught a glimpse of Howard Stern and his pretty wife, and of course Spike Lee, the movie director, who paced and yelled like a true coach. But the thrill of seeing stars at this close range couldn't compare to the thrill of sitting side by side, legs touching, with Brian. Not the reaction she'd wanted.

Ever since Peter accepted this invitation for her, she instructed herself to keep cool, distance herself from Brian's charm, and refuse him entry into her life. This was going to be a one-time thing. No connections would be made, no fun would be had. But as soon as they'd met at Madison Square Garden, Brian's effervescence fizzed around her, knocking down walls and streaming through fissures. She rationalized her time spent with him would be used wisely as a reconnaissance mission, to learn a little about the man who was her daughter's father.

They filtered out of the arena with the happy crowd, allowing their hallowed win to swirl around them like confetti. So this is what it felt like to be a fan, connected to a victorious team. At least she hoped that was the reason for her elation.

"It looks like I'm going to have to buy a Knicks shirt," she ventured. "You and I may be the only people here without one."

"I have a few," he grinned. "I didn't want to scare you off by wearing one—letting you think I'm some sort of fanatic or that I don't know how to dress." He steered her toward a kiosk with Knicks gear. "Pick one out. I'll get it for you. Then if you ever come with me again, you'll fit right in."

Those few sentences sent warning bells vying against the sweet strains of a violin. "You don't have to do that—"

"I want to. I want you to remember your first professional basketball game. And the great time you had. With me."

The violins won out.

Once outside in the mild May air, they searched for a quiet pub in the area, an impossible task, so they sacrificed the "in" spots for a hotel bar seeking calm over rowdy. With a vodka and club in front of Brian and a merlot in front of Ava, they toasted to their victory.

"So you don't generally attend sports events for entertainment," Brian stated. "What do you do in your free time?"

"I don't have much free time." Ava spun her glass, watching the wine creep up its sides. "I'm at the office until eight most nights. It's quieter after five, and I can catch up without the distraction of phone calls and client meetings." She kept to herself her secret indulgences of Saturday afternoon dance classes and

Sunday visits with her daughter. His daughter. The one person in her life who made her truly happy.

All at once the knowledge of her secret threatened to strangle her and a heavy weight sat on her heart, making it hard to breathe. Until this moment, she had compartmentalized her different lives, none of which included Brian. And now, here he was, being ever so smooth and gorgeous and attentive. Without a clue about their previous connection.

Out of all the law offices in New York City, why had he chosen hers?

And why was she out with him on a Saturday night?

Of course, deep in the recesses of her soul, she hoped he would remember her after spending some time together. But wishful thinking would not change the fact that his memory of her was permanently erased. She should run screaming in the opposite direction right now. Instead, here she was, having a glass of wine and making small talk with the father of her child.

His deep voice cut into her bleak thoughts. "Those kinds of hours can't be good for your social life. You must be disappointing young men all over the city when you choose work over them." Brian arched an eyebrow waiting for a response.

Ever the charmer. His accident clearly hadn't affected his ability to captivate. "Yes. I'm sure I'm frustrating most of the single male population here. Married, too." She smiled at her absurd statement. "But they'll move on and find someone else to ease their disappointment."

He chuckled over her teasing response.

"Don't worry," she continued. "I do get out of the

office on occasion." She couldn't let him think she was one-dimensional. "I go out to dinner with friends and attend fundraisers more than my salary warrants. When I get a chance on a weekend, I go to a play or museum." She traced the napkin under her glass as she searched for a plausible explanation for her bland routine. "Being a second year associate doesn't lend itself to much free time if you want to impress your employers." Maneuvering away from her life, she asked, "What about you? You must be putting in the hours to please your boss."

Brian smirked. "Yes. My father is a taskmaster. But I've learned how to deal with his difficult and workaholic ways."

"Really. And how is that?"

"Once I learned the business, I pushed to segregate the marketing, sales, and contract component from the hiring and oversight of the specific jobs. Then I convinced my father I should be in charge of the marketing team and he should manage the job sites and workers."

"You must work very hard and do a great job if your father ceded control of a major part of his company to you."

Brian grimaced. "Just because I run a division doesn't mean I'm not micro-managed by the boss." He shrugged. "But that's what I was born to do. Work in the family business."

"You sound…reluctant."

"You're being kind. You probably want to say apathetic." He grinned. "It's a good job, although I do work long hours. But I leave myself time to play. I just camouflage it by inviting clients or business contacts to games or the theater or whatever it is I want to do."

Disenchantment, ridiculous as it was, clawed at her chest. So she was a business contact, a write-off. "It's too bad Peter couldn't make it tonight. You would have gotten more networking points." She hadn't meant for it to come out so sarcastic, but there was no taking it back.

"I'm glad he couldn't." He put his hand on her wrist, spreading warmth up her arm. "I really wanted to reconnect. After I spoke to you at the office the other day, I phoned Carrie. She told me how close the two of you were at NYU. She was so happy to hear you're doing well. She'd love to get together. She also reminded me you and I spent time together during my graduation party weekend. While I don't remember, and I'm really sorry I don't, when I saw you at your office, I couldn't take my eyes off you. I would love to get to know you better."

While the words were right, Ava didn't trust his sincerity. She didn't know him, despite their instant connection years before. Had he changed since his college days? Then, he'd been a carefree player who had turned her naïve head. Carrie had warned her away from him more than once. But he had said all the right words that night, too. If he hadn't fallen from his horse, if he hadn't had a brain injury, would he have continued to see her once they were both in the City? Or had she been a clichéd one-night stand—someone new and different from his gaggle of friends—a woman he'd wanted to capture for the sake of the conquest, then discard with the spoils? She'd never know.

She withdrew her arm from his touch, requiring the space to say what she needed to say. "I had a great time tonight, Brian. It was really nice to see you again. Unlike you, I do remember the time we spent together." She bit her lip, regretting that last statement. "I know it's out of your control...the fact you can't remember." She shrugged trying to cover up any upset that might have escaped. "I don't think we should see each other. On a personal level, that is. I'm sure I'll see you at the office when you're meeting with Peter, although I won't be working on your contracts. I do environmental litigation."

Defeat etched his face. Surely he'd never been rejected before. And she just might be crazy to be the one rejecting him now. Any woman in her right mind would want to date this gorgeous, blond-haired, blue-eyed Adonis, who was not only striking, but successful, charming, and fun. The number of women who had looked him up and down as they walked through Madison Square Garden hadn't passed her notice.

But she couldn't take the risk. If they started dating, if things worked out in the beginning, she'd assuredly fall for him all over again. And while the last time their "break-up" had been the result of a traumatic head injury, she still felt the pain, even though his rejection was unconscious. She couldn't go through that again. Especially since this time it could be much worse. He might consciously reject her.

And what about the issue of Briana? If they saw each other, he'd soon know she visited her niece almost every Sunday. He'd ask about her, want to know why she had such a strong connection to a six-year-old living sixty miles away. He might even ask to accompany her on one of her visits. No, it would be better, for her and Briana, if she cut it off right now.

Yet, she was dying to know the person he was today. Maybe she could see him again, once or twice. Find the flaws. At least then, it would be easier to walk away and she would harbor no regrets or continuing fantasies about what could have been.

"I'm sorry if that came out sort of harsh." She smiled in apology. "I just don't have much time to spend with friends—or brothers of friends." She should just stop there. Mixed messages were lethal in the legal field, and she was starting to sound like a fool. Ava wasn't even sure what she was saying. Was she agreeing to see him again or not?

"Since you have so very little time, I better start getting to know you right now." His teasing statement lightened the dark mood she had manufactured.

"What would you like to know?"

"Where are you from? Where does your family live?"

A chill ran down Ava's back.

"Why are you looking at me like that?" His question snapped her from the past.

"It was a déjà vu. You asked me those same questions, right in a row, that first night in Newport. You had taken me away from your friends, and we sat at a table under an old oak tree. Just the two of us." She shook her head to dispel the weirdness of it all. Yet, as she responded to his questions, nothing in Brian's expression acknowledged he had heard any of this before.

Oh, so very strange.

****

At least she decided to stay. A few minutes earlier, Brian thought Ava was going to cut short their date and hightail it out of there. But why? She'd seemed to have a great time at the game, and they had been enjoying a nice talk at the bar. As soon as he suggested seeing her again, the curtain fell and Ava seemingly had a war going on in her head. Had he treated her badly that weekend in Newport? If only he could remember.

When he asked her questions about herself, she'd given a condensed version of her life. She grew up in Lawrenceville, New Jersey, with an older sister. When she was fourteen, she went to boarding school, followed by NYU for dance. In the beginning of her senior year, she switched paths, transferred to Columbia, then attended law school. Having interned at Calloway and Burnett, she was offered a permanent position upon graduation. All very matter-of-fact, as if she thought he'd be bored hearing about it. But what came from her telling was that she was a strong, independent woman, a woman who had succeeded without much guidance from her parents. Or so it seemed, since she barely mentioned them. What a different life she led from his.

"Your face really lights up when you talk about your niece. You must love children."

"I do. Well, I love Briana. She's beautiful and funny, and already showing signs of being a talented dancer."

"Just like her aunt."

A shadow crossed Ava's face as she studied her hand. "I loved dancing. It was my passion for so long. I hope Briana experiences that."

"I'm guessing you'll help foster that feeling." He took her hand in his. It was cold, so he warmed it. "Life takes us in directions we may not have anticipated."

She looked him directly in the eye. "Not you.

You've always known you'd work for your father's business. That you'd be the heir apparent. Even if you and your father disagreed about working on Saturdays."

"How do you know that?"

"I had breakfast with you and your family in Newport, and you told your father you wouldn't work Saturdays because you'd be more efficient during the week."

Brian chuckled. "I was obnoxious back then, thinking I knew how to run the company before I even started. I'm sure my dad wanted to clock me in the head, but he knew I'd find out soon enough that work didn't stop on the weekends. Not when you're running a successful company."

"So you fell into step and learned from the master?"

"I did. But at first, I was resistant. I wasn't sure the family business was going to be my long-term career choice. I knew I had to take my place in the company after college, but I figured I'd give it a year, maybe two. If I didn't like it, I'd leave." He shrugged. "I'm still there. Once I learned the business from the bottom up, I knew it could be even more successful if I could convince my father to make some changes. That was a real challenge, but so far it's working."

"Do you still hate big, formal parties?"

"What?" Brian looked at Ava, confused. Where had that come from?

"You told me you preferred hanging out with friends at the pool, like we did that Friday night, much more than attending over-the-top black-tie affairs like your graduation party on Saturday night."

"It's true." His brain throbbed trying to locate even

a snippet of that long-lost weekend. "I still prefer spending low-key time with family and friends."

"You're so close to your family. That's nice."

Given Ava's previous friendship with Carrie, she knew a lot more about his family then he knew about hers. Eerily, she also knew more about him. Apparently, he'd spent more than a little time with her that weekend.

Brian stood abruptly. "Why don't we walk for a while? It's getting crowded in here." And he wanted to be alone with her. It would be more intimate, even if they were walking in one of the most populated cities in the world.

She nodded her acquiescence, so he paid the bill, and led her onto the crowded sidewalks of 34th Street. They strolled past Broadway, then Sixth Avenue, then Madison. Holding her hand, they took a left on Fifth as the crowds thinned. It was just after midnight, but the City was still alive with cabs, buses, and limos transporting those who were heading home or maybe just going out.

"If you hadn't come to the game with me, what would you be doing tonight?" he asked, searching for another bit of insight into her life.

"I might have met a friend for dinner. By now, I'd be back in my apartment watching an old episode of *Friends* while falling asleep."

"Are you tired? Do you want me to take you home?" He certainly didn't want to wear out his welcome, but he also wasn't ready for this date to end. He might not see her again for a while.

"No, I'm not tired." They stopped in front of Lord & Taylor's window, and Ava studied the fashions.

"That gown is amazing. It probably has an amazing price as well."

The strapless, deep blue gown was molded to the mannequin's body. A slit ran up one side from the floor to mid-thigh.

"You'd look sexy as hell in that little number." He stared at the shape of the gown while pulling his collar away from his neck.

Brian felt confined in his Armani tux after spending the last few days in shorts or swim trunks. And he was certain the bowtie around his neck was cutting off circulation, but he smiled through the slow asphyxiation. This shindig at the Newport estate was in his honor, and he knew the drill as he stood next to his parents greeting the incoming guests and directing them to the bar after a few friendly words.

His friends would surely have a better time than him, at least for the first few hours while he schmoozed with his father's business colleagues and played the thoughtful graduate, responding to the same questions over and over. How does it feel to be out in the real world? Do you have any travel plans over the summer? When will you begin working at your dad's company? Or some variation on the themes.

He glanced over at the crowded bar staffed by two bartenders and patronized by his posse—already laughing and getting into the partying spirit. In a few hours, he'd be able to loosen his tie, discard his jacket and join in the fun. But until then...

His eyes locked on Ava and an involuntary smile took possession of his mouth. Wow. She looked like a Greek goddess in a white, flowy, one-shouldered gown that not only highlighted the tan she'd gotten over the last few days, but drew attention to her sculpted shoulders and incredibly toned arms. Her long, dark hair was loosely piled on top of her head, while escaping strands fell down her back—a back that was half bare. He swallowed as he wiggled his fingers, itching to run his hands through that luscious mane and over her smooth skin.

The hairs on Brian's arms stood at attention as the memory flashed through his brain. He studied Ava's profile as they stood in front of the store window: long lashes, deep blue eyes, tiny nose, wide mouth, slender neck. The same gorgeous woman who wore the white gown. He stared a little too long.

"What?" she asked.

Brian inched closer, eyes trained on those beautiful sapphires. Leaning forward, his mouth possessed her lips, soft, gentle, at first. But then latent desire broke free, and gentleness turned passionate as the power of attraction zoomed deep in his core. His fingers threaded into her long, dark hair, so silky and smooth to the touch. It didn't matter that they were standing on Fifth Avenue for all the world to see. For they were alone in a crack in space, their own little universe.

Her magnetism had pulled at him all night, and finally, thankfully, he'd given in to its force. Ava's warm body molded into his, and she slid her arms around his neck, sending currents down his spine. So much better than any first kiss he'd ever had. So sensual. So sexy. She pulled back slightly staring into his eyes, her fingers caressing his face, as if memorizing its planes.

She didn't speak but seemed to be transmitting thoughts through those gorgeous, serious eyes. He couldn't look away. If she was placing some magic spell over him, he was a willing victim. At that moment, he would have followed her into a burning building. Although, he'd much rather follow her into her bedroom.

Ava leaned in for another scorching kiss but backed away too soon. "That was nice." Her voice, velvety and low, underscored her words with the same desire he felt.

"More than nice." Brian reached for her hand to keep their connection.

The words screamed to get out. Let's go to my place. Or yours. Somewhere where we can do this naked. But he held them in check. She'd already questioned the wisdom of their seeing each other. He had to change her mind, to make her want to get to know him. Mystery and promise might work. Acting the caveman would not.

They began walking again. At Lexington Avenue an idea struck. "I have a friend who owns a club up here. He's always inviting me. Do you want to go?"

"A dance club?" Ava's eyes lit up, telling him his hunch was spot on.

"Yes. I think. I've never been to it. It's called Pure on Lex and Fifty-Sixth."

"Are you kidding? That's impossible to get into." Ava's smile split her face.

Brian grabbed her elbow and put on his New York City walk—a fast-paced stride meaning business. In no time they covered the twelve blocks standing between them and Paul Curtain's club. The line ran down the block, but Brian moved straight to the muscular bouncer dominating the entrance in black leather. After giving the gentleman his name and a password that Paul reserved for friends, the velvet rope was unclipped for their entrance. Easy.

The pulsating techno beat thrummed through his chest as he led Ava toward the bar. "Something to drink?" he yelled next to her ear.

"I'd rather dance." She looked longingly at the dance floor where bodies swayed and bounced to a Beyoncé song as lights flashed over the masses.

Of course she would. Isn't that why he had this brainstorm in the first place? Brian gestured for Ava to lead the way as the music turned to an Usher hit. At least he knew the song.

Ava started out moderately as she moved her hips from side to side smiling shyly at Brian. And then the music took over her incredibly sexy body as arms, legs, pelvis, and head swung, undulated, and popped with every discernible and not-so-discernible beat. She was a natural, and the music lived within her.

Approaching his sister's dance studio to the right, he heard a pounding beat, not at all similar to the classical music that fueled Carrie's usual dance practices. He stopped to watch through a small square window off to the side. Ava, dressed in a black leotard and tights, leaped and twirled through the air like a spinning top, set on its course around the circumference of the room while Carrie spun in a more confined area in the center of the room.

Brian's eyes sought Ava as her tight body coiled and released, coiled and released. Her arms were at once fragile and muscled, highlighting biceps and long, graceful fingers, sweeping through the air to mirror her legs. Her leaps were huge, with powerful extension and maximum air between her and the floor. No sooner would she land than she'd pull her limbs into herself and pirouette on her toes, spinning fast enough to make him question the physics of it all. This was no prissy ballet. This was fast and furious modern dance where you could feel the beat in your throat. Okay, maybe he'd experienced a little too much dance in his life, but this was definitely as good as anything he'd seen on the New York stage. Ava was even better than his sister.

What happened to the shy, vulnerable girl he'd just met? On the dance floor, she was a powerhouse. Full of confidence, energy, and magnetism.

When the music ended, he stood rooted to the floor, and his hands came up in a spontaneous clap.

"Who's out there?" Carrie flung open the door to reveal their intruder. "Brian, what are you doing here? I thought you were playing tennis."

"I am. I was. I-I had to come in for more balls."

He stared at Ava, with her dark brown hair pulled tight in a bun at the nape of her neck, drops of sweat beading on her chest just above the scoop of her leotard and above her full upper lip. Hot and sexy. He swallowed, fantasizing about licking the moisture from her mouth, her neck, molding that cute little powerful body into his.

"Then why are you just standing there?" Carrie placed her hands on her hips, challenging him to stop staring at her friend and walk away.

"I'm going." He backed away from the door, but couldn't seem to make his body turn and move down the hall.

Until Carrie slammed the door in his face.

Another memory from the lost weekend?

He cleared his head and focused on the Ava before him, her torso bending and stretching in an erotic movement that had her hips gyrating as she turned in a slow circle. Willowy arms extended over her head sending her powerful movements to the ceiling and back. Oh, so sexy, Ms. Harrington.

Brian could watch her all night. And did, until he could no longer keep up. After at least eight songs, he motioned to leave the dance floor.

"I need some air, water, and a chair," he yelled over his shoulder.

"You'll find no seats available in here," Ava yelled back, inspecting the crowded bar area. "Why don't we grab a bottle of water and leave?"

"Are you sure? I don't want to take you out of your element." He couldn't contain the smile that had started with their first dance.

She nodded. "I'm good."

He ordered two bottles of water, gave Ava one, and took a long swig from his before finding the exit.

Yes. She was good. More than good. Incredible, sexy, seductive perfection. He'd have fantasies about the way her body moved for a long time.

And that memory. Was it real or imagined? This was the third one he'd had. And only when Ava was around. Could she be the key to unlocking those shuttered memories from the lost weekend so long ago?

"That was so much fun." Glee overtook her shining eyes and smiling face. "Thanks, Brian. I can't remember the last time I went out dancing."

"Glad you liked it. I enjoyed it, too." An understatement of huge proportion.

As they walked north, they talked about their love

of the City, their favorite restaurants, plays, and museums. Brian stayed away from the subjects of work, families, and that weekend in Newport. He needed time to process those flashbacks. And hopefully they'd have plenty of time to learn each other's secrets. If he could convince Ava she had to see him again.

It was four a.m. when they finally stood in front of Ava's apartment building on East 82nd.

"We must have walked and danced at least ten miles tonight." Ava dug for the keys in her purse. "My feet should be screaming by now, but I hardly noticed."

"A true sign you had a good time." Brian faced Ava, hands on her shoulders. "I know I did. I can't remember the last time I stayed up until four."

Ava smiled. "I had a great time. Thank you."

She lowered her lids, not allowing him to silently plead to do this again. So, he'd have to beg out loud because there was no chance he could forgo more time together.

He scrambled for something she wouldn't be able to refuse, shamelessly using what he'd learned tonight to persuade her. "I know one of the producers of *The Book of Mormon*. It's been out a while, but if I could manage some house tickets this week, would you like to go?"

"I have client meetings Tuesday and Thursday nights."

That wasn't a no. "Then Wednesday it is. I'll see what I can do and call you at work." Pushy, yes. But hopefully not a turnoff.

"You know how to turn a girl's head," she drawled playfully. "But of course, I remember that about you."

The tease wasn't accompanied by a smile. Uh-oh.

What did she recall about him that he couldn't? "I hope I didn't do anything that weekend to offend you." Everyone in his life knew what *that weekend* meant. "If I did, I'm sorry." When it came to women, it was always best to apologize, even if you didn't know what you were apologizing for. "I was a bit of a player back then. Loving the challenge of the chase, you might say. But I'm sure Carrie warned you of the error of my ways. She was always very protective of her friends." He needed to stop talking. Now. Before he disparaged his own reputation and lost the advantage he'd gained over the last few hours.

"Yes. Carrie warned me." Her voice was low, maybe sad.

He lifted her chin to look into her eyes. There was a story there, he was sure, but one she clearly wasn't sharing tonight. He bent and kissed her, slowly and fully, trying to erase whatever memory clouded her impressions. But the sweet, soulful return kiss reawakened the passion that had surfaced a few hours earlier, and he intimately explored her mouth with his tongue, holding her tight, as if to never let go.

For this could be one of the few times he'd be able to experience the magic that was Ava.

****

The taxi ride to his apartment on the upper West Side passed in a blur. He tried to focus on that weekend, and what possibly transpired to make Ava sad. Had they shared the same kisses as tonight? Had he promised to call, take her to a play, see her again? Or had it been even worse? Given his penchant for sleeping around back then, had he seduced her, then moved on to someone else? His jaw clenched at that

78

possibility. But rationalization was his friend. If he'd been that despicable, surely Ava wouldn't have accepted the offer of another date. She might not even have come to the game tonight.

The angst lessened slightly. Even if something did happen between them, Ava knew about his accident. That he had no memory. Surely, she couldn't fault him for not following up on any promise. And if he'd led her on in some way, Carrie would have known and insisted he make it up to her good friend once he was better.

Pushing aside the bleak thoughts, Brian turned his concentration to the present and the strong attraction between them. A heady buzz swarmed through his veins. Bizarre, but kinda cool.

And the memories. They had to be real. They were so vivid. And they starred Ava, a woman he didn't know, but who clearly knew him—at least a little. At times tonight, he'd felt her intense focus, as if searching for answers to unasked questions. He could drown in those eyes while giving up secrets he didn't even know he harbored.

The only way to deal with all this craziness running around in his head was to see her again. Get to know her better. Convince her to open up more, for she guarded her privacy very skillfully. While sharing bits about her past, her family, and what drove her to become a lawyer, he couldn't help but notice she kept to the facts while shielding the emotion. She wasn't close to her parents, but she visited her sister almost every weekend and she adored her niece. And anytime he went near the topic of dance, some dark veil fell over her face, and she changed the subject.

Ava's world would be a challenge to crack, but he loved a challenge. At least now, he was mature enough to go after the emotional challenge and not just the physical, sexual one he chased before *that weekend.*

Would she let him?

Chapter Eight

The massive files on her desk, chairs, and credenza held her office hostage. Ava stood in the doorway, coffee in hand, surveying her crowded domain. Thankfully, she didn't have to share this peanut-sized space with another associate, like many of her law school friends at other firms. Real estate in New York City was at a premium, and she'd have to prove herself worthy before graduating to a bigger office. Worthy meant billing two thousand hours a year, making her budget, and bringing in clients. Incredible how one moment in time had altered her path from spinning on her toes and leaping through the air to drafting legal briefs and researching governmental regulations.

Ava maneuvered through the maze, careful not to spill her coffee, and sank into her chair. Glancing at the phone, she sent out her oft-repeated mental plea. Please ring. And make it be Brian. It was Wednesday morning and she'd been reiterating that same plea since Monday. Had she misunderstood his invitation?

She gazed off into space, allowing the pull from the past to monopolize her brain.

"Are you tired?" Brian slung his arm around Ava's shoulders and pulled her close.

"Yes. I think I'll head back to my bungalow." The half mile walk wasn't something she was looking forward to.

"I'll drive you on the golf cart," he said, as if he'd been reading her mind.

"That's okay. I don't want to take you away from your friends." Although she'd like nothing better, she had already monopolized his time tonight, and this was his weekend.

"They'll all start heading for their rooms soon. Besides, your place is the farthest away. I don't want you to walk alone."

"Might I get mugged?" she joked. Their many-acred property was not only fenced in, but a gate at the entrance was monitored by security cameras. This was clearly the high rent district of a high rent community.

Brian laughed. "Not by intruders. But maybe by me."

Tingles ran down her spine. Not bad tingles. But certainly apprehensive ones. Should she be so enamored with him? Carrie was always talking about her brother's latest girlfriend. There'd been a string of them. No one seemed to last.

And she surely didn't want to be one of them, left bruised and wondering why he didn't care about her, like some poor, pathetic outcast.

"Why so quiet?" he asked as they took off in the mini-car. "I hope my comment about being afraid of me isn't worrying you. It was a joke." He turned his dazzling smile loose. "I promise I won't hurt you."

Did he mean physically or emotionally? Of course, it wouldn't be the former. He was a gentleman and a lover—apparently.

"I'll hold you to that promise." She smiled back, hoping to lighten her mood. But of course, there was no way she could keep him from hurting her unless she

walked away from him—now.

And that wasn't going to happen.

He stopped the vehicle in front of her cabin. The flitting butterflies turned into stampeding horses. But he didn't get out and rush her into her temporary home. Instead, he reached over and caressed her face, so gently, his fingers felt like trailing silk. Then he leaned over and kissed her—a deep, soulful, delicious kiss that transformed the stampeding hooves back into beating wings. She dared to touch his handsome face, his golden hair. And when she did, she felt all hesitance drain away as she spun into his centrifuge, pressing against him, holding on as if for dear life.

She tasted his tongue, breathed his breath, felt his muscled arms around her. Surrendering to him would be oh, so easy.

But then he broke their kiss, their enchanted connection. Slowly she opened her eyes, still in his embrace, but now gazing at his handsome face. Everything she felt was surely displayed on hers.

"I have to go." His voice was deep, sensual. Caring. "There's a lot going on tomorrow. Sailing, horseback riding."

She swallowed her disappointment. "Thanks for the ride. Maybe I'll see you tomorrow sometime." She got out of the cart and gave a small wave as she stood in front of the guesthouse, unable to go in before he pulled away.

The electric motor hummed to life, and Brian eased the vehicle forward, glancing back with what Ava thought could be the same sadness she was feeling. When she entered her temporary residence, the sound grew softer and softer, as Brian headed away from her.

But his essence loomed large as it floated and immersed itself into her being.

Ava sighed. She'd wanted more then, and she wanted more now. Of course he'd made their plans tonight contingent on his ability to obtain house seats. But if he couldn't pull strings, wouldn't he call her to explain? He'd seemed so persistent the other night.

Finding a gap on her desk for her coffee cup, she picked up the transcript of a deposition she reviewed last night, before the words blurred and her comprehension waned. Ten hours of dry reading could do that to a person. But the trial in this particular case was scheduled for next month, and she'd been working with Max Spencer nonstop to get ready.

Their client, Tri-County Environmental Council, was trying to stop Brookstown Natural Gas Company from drilling near the Delaware River to prevent pollution for years to come. How could fracking even be allowed? Deep into her work, it took a few buzzes before she realized the phone was ringing.

She grabbed the receiver. "Ava Harrington."

"Hi, Ava. It's Brian."

Her thoughts scattered as relief, anxiety, and joy all crashed into each other. She needed calm. "Hi, Brian. How are you?" Normal sounding. That was good.

"I'm caught up in meetings near Scranton. I'm sorry, but I'm not going to be able to get back in time tonight to take you to the play."

Frustration careened through her being, but perhaps this was the better outcome. She'd been questioning the soundness of establishing a friendship with someone who couldn't remember her, along with their past.

"Are you there?" His voice broke into those bleak

thoughts.

"I'm here. That's fine. I'm really busy at work, too. I was here last night until ten and should probably do the same tonight." Sure, she was here late last night. So she could leave early tonight. But not a problem.

"Oh. I was hoping you'd pick up the tickets and take a friend. A female friend, preferably." She caught the humor in his tone.

She eased back into her chair, the angst disappearing. "You got the tickets?"

"I did. I really wanted to see you tonight." Sincerity punctuated his words. "I've been here since Monday, and thought I could wrap it up by this morning in order to be back in time, but we've run into some snags. It's a really promising property, but one of those No-Fracking groups has been in the owner's ear. He's making me work for my money." He laughed, and it sounded so good, even though she secretly rooted for the opposition. Not only was it dangerous to get close to him for personal reasons, she was not enamored with his company for destroying the environment.

Ava turned her focus back to the matter at hand. "I wouldn't want those tickets to go to waste," she said.

"Great. They're at the will-call window at the Eugene O'Neil Theater on 49th. Under my name."

"I can't believe you went through all that trouble and now you're going to miss the play." Regret over not seeing Brian was mitigated by the pleasure coursing through her.

"There are strings attached." His smooth voice sent chills down her arms. "You have to give me a scene by scene reenactment. On Saturday. I'll pick you up at two, and between scenes, we can walk around the

Village. Enjoy the sights or shop—whatever you want. I just need to make a quick stop to look at some furniture for my apartment. Can you make it?"

How could she not? He was giving her hard-to-get tickets which must have cost a small fortune. And he was inviting her to spend the day with him on Saturday. There was no downside. Except that she had a dance class on Saturday. She rubbed her forehead. Ava often switched classes at the last minute, given her schedule. "I guess I could rearrange my plans."

"Perfect." He sounded truly happy with her response. "Have fun tonight.

"Thanks. I really appreciate it."

She couldn't wipe the smile from her face after she hung up. While not spending the night with Brian came with disappointment, she knew she'd have a great time with Amy, her best friend from law school, who'd be ecstatic with the invitation. And in the wings was her date on Saturday, which would keep her enthusiasm at a high for the rest of the week.

She did a few pirouettes in her head, then a leap for good measure, before getting down to the business of law.

****

Ava's bed looked like the tables at the semi-annual sale at Barney's. Assorted jeans, pants, tops, and sweaters were strewn helter-skelter as she donned an outfit, took it off, tried another, and discarded it with the rest. After twenty minutes of attempting to find the perfect ensemble, she looked at herself in the mirror. Are you crazy? This is a casual event that shouldn't raise so much angst.

Exhaling slowly, she searched for her favorite

black jeans and paired it with a black cotton sweater and colorful scarf. In perusing the bed, she realized she hadn't changed her color scheme since college: black and white dominated. Classic, elegant, and easy to match. She introduced color with blazers, coats, scarves and purses. It worked for her.

The intercom buzzed as she dumped the contents from her black hobo bag into her favorite pistachio green satchel, bringing out one of the colors in her scarf. After one last survey in the mirror to check that there were no strays falling from her sleek ponytail, she grabbed her black leather jacket and ran to confirm the identity of her caller.

"I'll be right down." No need for Brian to see the disaster she'd left while fretting over what to wear.

As the elevator descended, the ever-present questions running around in her head threatened to ruin her high. If you're going to keep seeing him, are you going to tell him he's the father of your child? What do you expect his reaction to be? You can't really think anything good can come from this revelation. The niggling questions built up, and she finally told her conscience to *shut up* just as the doors slid open.

The smile that met her as Ava stepped into the lobby killed them off for good.

Brian gave her a warm hug and a kiss on the check before moving back. "You look beautiful."

Three words any woman would want to hear, but coming from Brian, they poured over her like honey. "Thank you, sir. It took me a while to decide what to wear, knowing I'd be acting out a play for you throughout the day. Missionary clothes didn't quite make the cut, but I thought black was close enough."

"You don't look like any missionary I've ever seen." He placed his hand on the small of her back and guided her toward the street. "I have a cab waiting. We're off to the furniture district first. A stop I'm sure will have you questioning my invitation." His facetious tone told her he'd rather walk through hot coals.

If he only knew. It didn't matter what they were doing today. She would have gladly helped sweep the streets if it meant being with him. She mentally thumped herself on the head. Where is this taking you? Didn't you learn you can't count on anyone but yourself to make you happy?

"So, how was the play?" he asked as they slid into the back seat of one of the City's finest, with its taped seats and overwhelming mystery scent from a dangling air freshener.

"Irreverent, satirical, and really funny. We loved it. Thanks so much for the tickets."

"Who is we?" he asked, an eyebrow raised.

"My friend, Amy, who also thanks you." Ava put her hand on his sleeve to punctuate her words, and he maneuvered his hand into hers. Warm and electric. Perfect.

"Will you be performing any dance routines for me today as you take me through the story?" His mouth twitched at his teasing question.

"Of course. What's a musical without big song and dance numbers? I don't have all the words down, and my singing isn't so hot, but…" Ava shrugged, buying into his joke.

Their banter went on, and before long, they were getting out of the cab on 19th Street and Broadway.

"I'm really sorry to drag you with me to do this,"

Brian said, "but the thought of buying furniture on my own had me procrastinating."

"What are you looking for?"

"A living room set." He took her hand and walked toward Gilberto's Home Design. "I hear this place has contemporary, edgy stuff."

"You don't have furniture in your living room? What do you sit on?" He'd been in the city for years. How could he have survived without a couch?

"I have furniture. I took some from my parents when my mother re-decorated their Larchmont house. It's definitely her taste. Not that it's awful. She has a very good eye for all that. It's just not me."

They entered the store's showroom and while Brian checked in—apparently you needed an appointment at a place such as this—Ava glanced at a price tag on a very plain, very modern sofa. Fifteen thousand dollars. Whoa! She wouldn't be shopping here any time soon. Pottery Barn and IKEA would have no worries.

For the first fifteen minutes, they had to deal with Chloe, the sales associate who preferred to be called a designer. She talked them through the different styles, fabrics, and accent pieces until Brian had had enough and asked if he and Ava could have some time alone to discuss their favorites. Chloe's mouth formed an O but she had the sense not to do an eye roll.

"I'll be in the design center when you need me," she said in a condescending voice, obviously thinking Ava and Brian would never be able to pull this off without her help.

Brian drew Ava to the opposite side of the showroom, out of earshot from Chloe. "What do you think of this arm chair?" He dragged his hand over the seat á la Chloe. "The craftsmanship is just superb. And the fabric is hand-loomed." He caught Ava's eye and laughed. "That way I could pay an additional ten thousand."

Ava finally let out her own giggle. She'd been so good, not knowing if Brian was mesmerized with Chloe's presentation or bored to tears. "Don't forget about the hand-carved ebony accents polished to a rich hue." Ava circled her index finger over the wood arms, also mimicking Chloe.

"Do you like any of this stuff?" He turned in a circle to survey the showroom.

"The question is, do you? You're the one who's going to live with it." Ava definitely didn't want to influence Brian's choices, assuming she wouldn't be around long enough to even see it delivered.

He turned to an ensemble with couch, loveseat, and two chairs. "I like this, but I don't like the color." It was a shade of beige, like most of the furniture in the store.

"Chloe said you could choose from a whole book of fabric. Why don't you take a look and see if anything catches your eye." Despite Ava's reluctance to get involved in Brian's home decorating, they had similar views on what they liked in both fabrics and colors, and Ava warmed up to the job after a while.

"What do you think of this pattern, darling?" he asked. "I think it would look great with our antique pieces."

"I agree. It would look especially lovely next to Aunt Martha's rolltop desk."

He whispered to her, his eyes crinkling. "Aunt Liz, not Aunt Martha."

"Oh. Sorry. I always get them confused."

They went on in that vein until they made their final decisions. Brian didn't seem to consider cost as one of the variables so neither did Ava. Spending someone else's money had its allure.

After finalizing the details with Chloe, who assured them they had made excellent decisions—as any good saleswoman on commission would—they walked out into the pleasant spring air of the late afternoon.

"That was exhausting." Brian exhaled in relief, glad to be out of the store. "It never occurred to me it could take so much time to make a decision about a couch. I thought we'd be in and out and onto our next activity by now." He draped his arm around her shoulders as they walked down the street. "I'm so sorry I put you through that. Who knew?"

Ava fell into step, happy to be in his embrace. "It was fun, once we got into it." And once she was able to fantasize about being a real couple with Brian, it wasn't exhausting at all.

"Shall we head to the Village?"

"Sure. It's only four thirty."

"I don't know about you, but I'm starving after all that work," said Brian. "I know it's early for dinner. Maybe we can sneak in on the senior citizen's specials."

"If we were in Florida, definitely. They start at three thirty there." She glanced at him, taking in his gorgeous smile. "I'm hungry, too. Where do you want to go?"

"I know of a great steak restaurant on Bleecker Street. How does that sound?"

"Good with me. I subscribe to the high protein

diet." Even if she didn't, she'd find something to nibble on while staring at his handsome face.

A half hour later, they were ensconced in a comfortable booth, not vying with the crowds who would come later. It wasn't awful eating so early. The waiter was attentive, the noise at a minimum, and the company exquisite. Who could ask for more?

"So tell me about your deal in Scranton." Ava wanted to sound interested, even though the work his company did, conflicted with every fiber in her body, as well as the work of the organizations she represented on a daily basis. She briefly wondered if she had subconsciously chosen this line of work to assure she would never end up with Brian. Interesting food for thought.

He zeroed in on her eyes, and she was dragged kicking and screaming, into his web. She swallowed, then scolded herself for giving him the chance to do this to her—again.

"I don't want to talk about work." His voice was low, sexy. "I want to talk about you. You've dealt with me, and my needs, all day." He reached across the table for her hand, and the heat nearly melted the ring she wore into her finger.

"What about me?" Her voice sounded hoarse, shaky.

"How did you get started in dance?"

Ava sipped her drink, reluctant to share this piece of herself. "My mother. She was a dance teacher, and she would take me to her studio while she taught, even before I could walk. Perfect day care for her, perfect training for me. I learned the ballet positions standing in my play pen. Then when I was five, I had my first ballet lesson." She laughed at the thought. "I insisted on wearing a tutu, even though the uniform was a black leotard and pink tights. My mother explained to the class that since it was my first day, she was allowing my indulgence, but never again. It became a ritual. On every little ballerina's first day, she got to wear the tutu."

Ava's reminiscence sparked memories of a joyful time when she and her mother were inseparable. But just as quickly the light died at the thought of her mother's desertion. "I'm sorry. I didn't mean to bore you with such a silly story." She lowered her lids, then turned her head, attempting to focus on something other than him.

"You didn't. I want to get to know you. Everything about you. You intrigue me."

He stroked her palm with his thumb. Startled at the tingling sensation, she looked into his eyes. A mistake, for they reached into her very soul.

Turning the conversation back to Brian for her own protection, she said, "I guess your passions are a little different than mine. Golf, tennis, sailing. Much more athletic."

He grinned, perhaps at her transparent ploy. "I don't know about that. I've watched Carrie hurtle through the air, drop to the floor, spring back up, and balance on her toes. Dance looks very athletic to me. And the training time she invests puts my efforts to shame. I'm guessing you did the same. When you danced." The knife twisted in her heart, but she smiled at the memory.

"This is a pretty ring." He inspected her finger.

"It was my mom's. She told me the intricate gold

swirls reminded her of the pattern of spins in a ballet."

Ava swallowed and inched her hand out of his.

"So you and your mom are close."

"We were. She was my dance teacher, my mentor, my friend. Her dreams for me became my dreams. I practiced most afternoons in her dance studio before classes started and she perfected my turns, my leaps, and my carriage. We went to every professional dance performance we could get to, whether in Philadelphia or New York. Then we dissected the choreography, the individual dancer's strengths and weaknesses, the costumes." Ava laughed at the memory. "You'd think we were critics from *The New York Times*."

"It sounds like the two of you have an incredibly strong bond. Does your mother still teach little ballerinas?"

"I haven't seen my mother in thirteen years." Sadness, heavy and suffocating, surfaced with a vengeance. Brian looked like he wanted to crawl under the table, but he couldn't have known the facts surrounding her mother, since he knew practically nothing about her.

"I'm sorry," he said quietly, covering her hand with his.

Ava shrugged, trying to minimize the effect this estrangement had on her. "It's okay. It was a long time ago."

"What happened?"

A lump grew in Ava's throat. After all these years, she still missed her mom terribly. Even though she hated her, too. But her mother had never looked back.

"If you don't want to talk about it, I understand."

Brian's voice enveloped her with sympathy. While

sharing this story would be painful, Brian had a way of peeling back her layers without ripping them off.

Ava inhaled for strength. "My mother moved to L.A. to work as a choreographer on a TV dance show." The anger and hurt hid just beneath her words. Even after all these years she couldn't keep the emotion buried. She despised her mother for what she'd done. How could she have left Ava when she was only fourteen?

Ava grabbed her water and took a sip, trying to swallow the bitter taste.

"That must have been awful for you. But I'm sure she wasn't leaving you. Maybe her marriage to your father wasn't working."

Ava appreciated the diplomatic rationale Brian presented, but she had no sympathy for her mother. A parent doesn't fly clear across the country to start a new life if she has an unhappy marriage. She should have filed for divorce and stuck around to raise her children.

"I'm sure their marriage wasn't good. They argued. A lot. Once my sister went off to college, I guess my mother thought she'd put in enough time. I know my dad was devastated, but he never said much. One night, I heard him crying. That was one of the saddest things I've heard. A grown man—who was supposed to be strong for his kids—sobbing. I never let on I knew."

"Have you tried to reach your mom?"

"No." The word came out too harsh. Too loud. But she would never call. Her mother left them, and Ava had no interest in ever speaking to her again.

"Did she ever contact you?"

"Not at first. She probably thought it would be too hard on us—at least that's what my father said. She called me a few times at boarding school, but I didn't want to talk to her. After a few attempts, she finally sent a letter. I never told my father. He probably would have demanded to see it, but that wouldn't have helped any. It was her explanation about why she left. She married too young. Had my sister at eighteen. She wanted to be a dancer all her life. Now was her big chance to work on a high-profile show. Get recognition for her talent." Ava's throat clogged with emotion. "I'm sorry. This is difficult."

Brian had no idea how difficult. Ava was blasting her mother for deserting her, when she'd done the very same thing with Briana. Of course, she rationalized she hadn't really left her. She stayed in constant contact. But how would Briana see it when they finally told her?

"Did your mother's desertion have anything to do with your giving up dance in college?"

The hairs on Ava's neck prickled. This conversation was getting too close to her hard limit. "No." She shifted in her chair. "It just didn't work out. Things changed." She looked straight into his eyes, willing him to know the real reason. But nothing surfaced.

Instead, Brian nodded. "I understand perfectly how a parent's dream could become yours. At least in your case, you had the same dream. In my case, I'm not so sure. I'm destined to work for, and eventually take over, my father's company whether I want to or not."

"You don't want to?"

"I haven't decided yet." He grimaced. "Ever since I was young, it was drilled into me that I'd be working for the company. As a kid, you don't question what your parents tell you you're going to do. When you're in college, you look around, see other options. They're intriguing, but you stay the path you think you chose, until one day you realize, 'Hey, that wasn't my dream. I'm in yours.'" He shrugged. "It's hard to get out of someone else's dream."

"Are you trying?"

"Not now. I've put so much time and effort in learning the business. And I'm good at what I do. I think I'll keep at it for a while. See what the future brings." He shrugged, seemingly at peace with his decision. "Back to you. You told me before you're from Lawrenceville. What's it like there?"

She just couldn't manage to keep this conversation away from her. "It's the next town over from Princeton. Nice as suburbs go, with a quaint little village. It's a historic town, but as a resident, you don't much care about that. There are several malls in the area, lots of offices, and tons of traffic during rush hour." She scowled. "I haven't lived there since my mother left— except for summers during high school. My father shipped me off to boarding school. Then I moved to the City."

"You didn't want to go to boarding school?"

"No. I was only fourteen. I wanted to live in my house, be close to my friends. But once my mother moved out, my father decided I should be gone too." Ava vowed to try harder to keep the bitterness from her words.

"What about your sister?"

"She was in her first year at Northeastern back then. Although we were close, those four years between us were a lifetime at that age. When she was into hanging out with her friends and dating, I was dressing

97

up in tutus and tiaras and pretending to be the Sugar Plum Fairy."

Brian smiled. "Carrie did the same thing. But I tortured her. Sometimes I mimicked her, ruining her fantasy. Sometimes I stole the crown right off her head and ran through the house making fun of her. Having a brother around was no picnic. At least you escaped that fate."

"Yes. But often I wished I had a sibling closer in age. I envied my friends who did. Even if they fought or teased each other once in a while." She paused. "Maybe if I had a younger sibling, my mother wouldn't have left. Of if she did, my father wouldn't have enrolled me in boarding school." What ifs, while necessary to indulge her illusions, were a waste of time.

"So, you and your sister are still close?"

Again, he was treading near dangerous territory. "Yes. And we became even closer over the past six years."

"Was it because she had a baby?"

Ava swallowed, her throat tight. "Briana is adopted, but yes." That's all she needed to say. No reason to expound.

"What about your father? Have you mended your rift?"

He had so many questions.

"Not exactly. I talk to him on the phone once a week. He calls on Sunday nights—like clockwork. That's when I fit into his schedule."

"I would have thought you and your father would be closer, having dealt with your mother's desertion together."

"My father worked all the time. Still does. He owns

two gas stations, and they're open seven days a week."

Although Ava spoke with indifference, the wound from her father's actions dove deep. Even deeper was the devastation over her mother's desertion. Her upbringing was so different from Brian's. His parents seemed involved in every tentacle of his life.

This time he didn't allow her to pull away when he took her hands. "You're a strong woman."

Then he smiled, a gorgeous wide smile meant just for her. A smile that touched her heart.

Not only could his smile and touch do real damage, so could his words. Lovely, sensual, caring words, that coming from any other admirer, would have her opening up like a flower. But with him, she had to keep her petals closed. At least for now. She hadn't prepared herself to tell him about that weekend in Newport, and all the choices she made as a result of it. She would have to tap dance around any searching question that delved too close to the truth.

Perhaps a teasing, flirtatious colloquy would keep him away from the facts better left for another time. So she smiled, as coyly as she could pull off. "No more about me. I need to keep at least some of my life a mystery, so as not to ruin the attraction."

"The attraction has been building with every little bit I learn about you." He laced his fingers with hers.

Lucky for her, their meals arrived. Hopefully, they could move onto other subjects to accompany their food. "This looks delicious. I didn't realize how hungry I was."

"It's hard work shopping for furniture. I may never do that again." Brian cut into his steak, chuckling over the experience.

While fawning over filet mignon and sweet potato casserole, Ava succeeded in steering the conversation away from her and onto more general subjects like the Grammy Award winners, current movies, the presidential primaries, and the state of the economy. Nothing too controversial, nothing too gossipy. But also, nothing too revealing. She had enough soul-baring for one night.

Brian went along with the conversation and thankfully, didn't revert back to the more personal details of Ava's life. Having no room for dessert, they decided to walk for a while, and headed toward Washington Square Park.

"It's still early," ventured Brian, as they skirted the park. "Maybe you'd like to see the current state of my apartment so you'll be able to appreciate the change I'm working toward."

Ava's heart somersaulted in her chest, making it hard to respond. "I'd love to," she rasped.

Of course he lived on Central Park West. What child of a wealthy family with homes in New York City, Larchmont, and Newport didn't? Ava mentally smacked herself for generalizing and scolded herself to give him the benefit of the doubt. But she couldn't help the question that came popping out as they rose to the twentieth floor of his apartment building.

"Did your parents buy this for you?" Ava tried to keep all judgment from her tone.

His sexy half-smile was becoming very familiar. "No. It's all mine. I bought it last year, after saving my bonuses over the first six years. Of course, I have a mortgage, too. My father doesn't pay me that much."

All relative. What may not be that much to Brian

was assuredly several years of her salary put together. She couldn't fathom saving enough of a down payment to qualify for a mortgage to live here. And what could those monthly payments be, once you figured in principal, interest, taxes, and co-op fees? All she knew was that she'd never, even after working for twenty years, be able to afford a place in a such a building. This was for trust fund babies or people with family wealth. Not those who only had an income from working for a living.

The insecurities that had plagued Ava in Newport came hurtling back. Even though she worked as a lawyer at a great law firm in the City, she would never be in the same league as Brian. Yet, why did it matter? People from different backgrounds met and fell in love all the time. Look at Kate Middleton and Prince William. Sleeping Beauty and Prince Charming.

Brian unlocked the door, and they entered his apartment. It was huge by New York City standards. The living room looked as big as a tennis court, and it had wide, long windows on the far wall overlooking Central Park. It was sparsely furnished in shades of gray, blue, and black with no other color apparent in the room. The walls were off white with no artwork or photographs vying to break up the expanse.

"Now you can see why I wanted to warm up this place." Brian switched on a few lamps.

The furniture he did have looked expensive, well made. "You could have added pillows, rugs, a different color paint," Ava said as she took it all in.

"Now you tell me." His self-deprecating smile eased her angst. "I need to find my own style, be my own person, and all that rot." His gaze scanned the room as if viewing it from a different perspective. "You're probably right about adding color."

"Well, your choices today will totally change the look. But you should branch out and buy accessories, artwork that you love. Maybe some area rugs, or you'll have the same problem with your new furniture." Ava walked over the hardwood floor, her heels echoing around the room. Although her apartment furnishings were mass-produced and came straight from the pages of a catalogue, she had added her own touches to make it warm and personal. She approached the window overlooking Central Park. "Amazing. Who needs art work when you have this view?"

Brian came to stand behind her, his hand easing around her hip. "It's even better sharing it with you." Warmth radiated up her spine and through her body. Ava was enjoying this too much. She should tell him about their child before this—whatever this was—went too far.

Leaning closer, he kissed her on the cheek, then moved to her neck. Ava slanted her head to give more access, for the flitting kisses sent hot, electric sensations zooming and crashing against each other. Sensations she never wanted to stop. She turned, and Brian moved into her space, assaulting her lips with a hot, erotic kiss that promised much more. She opened her mouth to mate with his, tasting lust and passion as if he was one of those fiery desserts. A temptation she should not partake of, but one she couldn't resist.

Tearing his mouth away, he held her face in his hands, gazing with an intensity so dangerous, it swept away all willpower and pulled her into his aura, as if she were a flimsy spirit, devoid of flesh and bones.

"I want you," he whispered, his voice husky, sexy.

Her body ignited, and her mouth moved without thought. "I want you, too."

Brian took her hand and led her through the apartment toward the back—his bedroom. Darkness enveloped it, but he turned on a small lamp on a corner table, away from the bed. It cast a low light, turning the room into a romantic boudoir with a king-sized bed covered in deep green and taupe stripes. Massive mahogany end tables and dressers gave the room a masculine touch while Post-Impressionist artwork toned it down. Surprising, but beautiful. The floor was covered in a beige plush carpet. Nothing of the cold and sparsely decorated living room transferred into this room. It was warm. Inviting.

Brian stood before her by the bed, then traced the contours of her face with his index finger. He brushed it over her lips, which involuntarily parted with his touch, then replaced it with his warm mouth. Slowly, sensually, he ignited each nerve, each synapse, with a slight caress at times and with insistent pressure at others. A master of seduction who obviously had perfected his moves over the past seven years, while she had shied away from intimate relationships.

For a brief moment, she flashed back to the guesthouse in Newport, to the night she had so willingly given Brian her mind, body, and soul. She'd basked in his touch, in his words, and believed they'd find a way to be together, into the future. But fate had stepped in with a freak accident.

She pushed it all away—the accident, his memory loss, her pregnancy, the adoption—all of it. Banished, at least for now. She wanted nothing to interfere with what she was experiencing right here, right now. She'd fantasized about reconnecting with Brian over the years, fantasized about this very night. And here she was, in his arms, being shattered with mere kisses.

Ava caressed his cheek, feeling the stubble of beard, the contours of his beautiful face. She pressed against him, molding tight to planes and muscles, feeling his strength…and passion. His hand slid down her neck, her clavicle, then brushed over her breast, eliciting a moan from deep within. With little effort, he glided her scarf around her neck, the silky material heightening senses already at high alert.

"We could use this later." Brian's husky voice broke through her haze as the scarf fell to the floor. Did he mean what she thought? Was he into kinky stuff? Yet, the thrill those words evoked surprised her.

Her shock must have shown, for he smoothed his fingers over her furrowed brow. "Don't worry. I'm not into S and M. I'd never do anything you don't want me to."

His words were like pure honey being poured over her body. The thought of Brian licking that honey from every pore sent liquid fire streaming through her veins. Maybe she wanted kinky.

Ava smiled at the epiphany but kept it to herself. Clearly under Brian's spell, she'd follow him into deep, dark territory under the guise of seduction. But once released, her conscience would prevail. And give her a talking to.

"That smile looks mischievous," he murmured between kisses.

Ava bit her lip to remove it. "No mischief here. I'm all yours."

"Good. Because we're just getting started."

He eased her top over her head, then released her hair from the band that held it in a ponytail.

"Beautiful," he murmured as he traced the black lace of her bra, sending wild stirrings to every erogenous zone possible.

She inhaled, secretly begging him to do more, to touch her all over. The sweet torture of delicate fingers grazing the curves of her breasts as he unclasped her bra had her whimpering for more contact.

"What do you want?" he whispered in her ear, before tracing the lobe with his tongue.

She could barely stand. "I want you," she breathed while unbuttoning his shirt, then pushing it over his shoulders, letting it fall to his feet. She ran her hands over hard muscle and tight abs, then burrowed into his neck, taking in his delicious scent. "All of you. Connected to me."

She pressed against him, hot skin to hot skin, tongue roaming. His sharp intake of breath evidenced her power over him, and she reveled in it. She moved her hands up and around his shoulders, losing her fingers in the softness of his hair as her mouth sought his, needing to be joined with him.

Brian's hand skimmed from her hip to the zipper of her pants, easing it down before sliding the confining material of denim and lace over her sensitized legs. His hot gaze scorched her already-burning pores as he stood before her taking in her naked curves. Quickly disposing of all remaining clothing, Brian pulled the comforter from the bed and guided Ava to join him between the cool, cotton sheets. His mouth covered hers in a breath-stealing, mind-searing kiss before trailing his tongue down her neck and teasing her nipples. She arched her back craving more contact, and he obliged by sucking the sensitive point until it was hard and peaked. He moved his mouth to the other breast as Ava writhed below him, losing her mind to the intensity of this feeling.

Brian's hand smoothed down her abdomen sending heat and sparks everywhere he touched. His finger massaged the sensitive nub between her legs before sliding in and out of her opening, spreading fire from core to extremities. Ava raised her arms above her head and spread them wide across the bed, as if some invisible restraint held them there as she did the same with her legs. Giving her body to Brian to do with what he wanted—what she wanted.

He braced himself over her, all corded veins and muscles, as desire darkened his eyes. His erection stood long and hard between them. Ava raised her pelvis to brush against him, making the invitation ever so clear. She'd wanted this for so long that it seemed more a dream than reality. Brian reached to his nightstand for a condom, sheathing himself before rubbing the head of his penis against her ultra-sensitive opening. A master of control, he eased in and out slowly, only giving her a little at a time, to ensure she was ready for him. But she was more than ready, and she bucked to take him in further, to take all of him.

It wasn't long before she reached the pinnacle and fell off the edge, a freefall of explosions and fire powering through her being, made even better by the guttural words emerging from Brian's mouth as he joined her. Their breaths came in gasps, and Ava could feel Brian's heart beating erratically next to hers. She closed her arms around him and stroked his back, holding on tight.

It had been a heroic effort to keep the bittersweet memories of their lovemaking seven years ago at bay, but any time a shooting flash had inserted itself, Ava buried it and found the present.

But now that the fevered passion had subsided and they lay with limbs entangled and only their own thoughts, Ava had a harder time. Things could have been so different if Brian hadn't fallen from his horse. Good different.

A tear slipped from her eye, and she brushed it against the pillow so Brian wouldn't see.

She was sliding into dangerous territory.

Chapter Nine

Ava stretched under the warm sheets of Brian's bed, basking in an erotic replay of the previous night, when Brian made sometimes sweet, sometimes passionate love to her. Just as he had in the guesthouse many years before. The aroma of frying bacon brought Ava back to the bittersweet morning she'd spent in the Stanhope's kitchen in Newport.

But she didn't want to ruin the joy that was hers right now. She and Brian were different people today. Ava had grown up quickly after that weekend, making difficult decisions that changed her life. She had a career in law, an apartment on the Upper East Side, and a child whose existence drove her every move. Brian had also matured. As Vice President of Stanhope Natural Gas, he took his responsibilities seriously and had settled down from those college days.

Ava reluctantly got out of bed and slipped into her panties and Brian's button-down shirt, barely reaching mid-thigh. She lifted the collar and breathed in his scent. Delicious. She found her way to the kitchen using the clattering sounds and wonderful aroma as a guide.

"Good morning." She entered the very small space. Who in New York needed a big kitchen anyway? "Smells good." Brian looked good too, dressed in worn jeans hanging at his hips, and nothing else.

"I was hoping you'd wake up." He came over and kissed her on the nose, then stood back and gave her an appraising once-over. "My shirt never looked so good." His casual words and easy smile sent Ava's heart twirling as if on toe shoes.

"Can I help with anything?" Another déjà vu. This was getting as dangerous as a minefield.

"Sure. You can set the dining room table while I finish the pancakes. The dishes are on the sideboard."

Ava squeezed her eyes shut, hoping to dislodge the video of breakfast at the Stanhopes'. Although that morning in itself was perfect.

"Good morning," she said to the small group who inhabited the kitchen, feeling a blood rush when her eyes found Brian leaning against the counter.

His easy grin and quick wink had her darting her head in the opposite direction so no one would notice her obvious blush. His kisses from the night before still scorched her lips and melted her heart.

"Can I help with anything, Mrs. Stanhope?"

"That's very nice of you to offer, Ava. Carrie may need help with the pancakes."

Carrie stood at the counter, whisking the batter in a huge bowl. She glanced over at Ava and motioned with her elbow. "Could you grab the ladle for me?"

"Sure." Ava handed the utensil to Carrie as Brian approached.

Before she could move out of the way, he slid his hand over her hip and butt. Electric sensations zapped through her body, and she jumped away from him so no one would see. But her skittish reaction knocked her into Carrie and sent the whisk with pancake batter clattering to the floor.

"I'm so sorry. I didn't mean to bump into you."
Ava could hear Brian's warm laugh through her
apologies. "Where are the paper towels? I'll clean it
up."

If her face hadn't been red before, she was sure it
was now scarlet. Any good impression she may have
made on the Stanhopes yesterday, was sure to take a
downturn this morning. Mr. Stanhope looked up from
his newspaper without expression, then immediately
resumed reading.

But Mrs. Stanhope shook her head and pursed her
lips. "Honestly, Carrie. You need to be more careful.
The floor was just washed yesterday."

Brian eased away from the counter, a grin still on
his lips. "It was my fault. I'll clean it up."

Ava's eyes followed him as he tore off a few sheets
from the paper towel holder and squatted to wipe the
offensive batter from the clean floor. The muscles in his
shoulders stretched and contracted under his blue polo
shirt as he worked at getting every last drop. When he
stood, he was just inches from her, and she longed to
reach out and touch him—any part of him, but Carrie
was right there. Probably watching her watch him.

His intense gaze—hot and sexy—kept her rooted to
the floor in front of him, unable to turn or even step
away. Sizzling electricity jumped from his being to hers,
sending her libido into overdrive—in the most
inappropriate of settings. It was bad enough he'd had a
starring role in her dreams last night—the leading man
flirting with her but never consummating their
attraction. Now, here he was in real life, just a touch
away, and she still couldn't have him.

Carrie broke the spell. "Can I see you a minute in

the other room?" She pulled Ava out of the kitchen and down the hall.

"Please don't tell me you're into him. Please?" Her voice begged Ava to deny the attraction.

All Ava could do was shrug. More telling than any answer.

"Oh, Ava. Don't make me feel sorry for you. Cut him off right now. If he's showing any interest, it's because he's enjoying the conquest. You'll get hurt. And I don't want that for my best friend." Carrie placed her arm around Ava's shoulders.

A heaviness centered in Ava's chest. She adored Carrie. She valued her opinions. But not this one.

Of course she'd ignored Carrie's advice and the whole wonderful weekend came crashing down around her, starting with Brian's accident. Should she heed that advice now?

Ava set the plates on the table, willing the memories back into hiding. Especially now that Ava was flirting with happiness. Brian had miraculously found her again. He had picked up the broken thread and tied it together.

Maybe this same scene would have played out seven years ago when Brian moved to New York, if he hadn't had the accident. Perhaps they'd still be together, she a dancer with a prominent dance troupe, and he in the same position he was in now, as VP of his family company. He'd be making breakfast for her before her performance this very evening. They could be living together, or even married.

Although she was forgetting one major complication. Whether Brian had the accident or not, she would still have been pregnant and would still have been faced with the decision about the baby. Would that have been the stake in the heart of their relationship instead of his lack of memory? Or would they be a happy family of three?

"Everything's ready." Brian breezed into the dining room with a plate full of golden-brown pancakes and another of scrambled eggs, jolting Ava's musings right out of her head. "The coffee's ready in the kitchen. Why don't you grab the pot and I'll get the bacon."

Ava followed his instructions and when they both sat down, a veritable feast lay before them.

"Are you having an emergency Board of Directors meeting?" Ava laughed at the amount of food taking over the table.

"When I cook, it's usually for my whole family. I guess I should have cut back." He shrugged. "Doesn't matter. I'm famished. You zapped all my energy last night."

Ava blushed at his playful words. "I didn't hear you complaining." She tried for coyness, but a tiny bit of ego slipped in.

"Who's complaining? I'm giving us sustenance so we can pick up where we left off." His sly smile inched over kissable lips, before downing a forkful of pancakes drenched in syrup. "Unless, of course, you have other plans. I don't mean to be presumptuous." His smile faded while waiting for her answer.

She swallowed a bite of scrambled eggs. Thankfully, Kim had called and said Briana had a birthday party to go to today, because she didn't want to think she would have blown her off to spend time with Brian. Even so, it was against her best interests to spend time with him. "I brought work home to get to today. I have a crazy week ahead of me and wanted to get a jump on it." She sipped coffee disappointed she pulled the work card.

"Then I'll have to entice you with something irresistible so I can be your priority today."

"And what might that be?" She arched an eyebrow, knowing deep down, any activity with Brian would trump work. Hell, it would trump dancing with Baryshnikov during his heyday.

"After breakfast, I propose we go back to bed. After we tangle in the sheets until you beg me to stop, we'll shower and get dressed, because Carrie's performing at three." He looked expectantly at her.

Ah, Carrie's performance. While his other suggestion had her full attention, this latter invitation sent her spirits screeching to a stop. Although she had followed Carrie's career with the Manhattan Ballet since she won a coveted spot with that prestigious dance company five years ago, Ava hadn't been able to convince herself to attend. She feared her jealousy and regret would color the experience, and there was no reason to put herself in a funk. Besides, their friendship had waned since Ava's transfer to Columbia and her refusal to get together with Carrie while she was pregnant. Carrie had no idea what had inspired Ava's cold shoulder, but after Ava gave Briana up for adoption, Ava did make a few half-hearted attempts to meet. On one hand she had wanted to reconnect with her best friend, and on the other, it highlighted all the negative consequences of the weekend in Newport. Given Ava's ambivalence over reuniting, the two of them went their separate ways.

"I haven't seen Carrie in years," Ava finally

responded. "Does she know you and I...have been dating?" Was that the correct phrase to describe their current relationship?

"Yes. And she's dying to see you." Brian's eyes flashed with anticipation. "So will you come?"

Ava would have no way of knowing whether Brian's interpretation of Carrie's feelings toward Ava were accurate. Had Carrie shared with Brian her take on Ava's coolness toward her? Of course, it would make sense that if Ava could ignore the negative connotations Brian unwittingly brought with him, then she should be able to do the same where Carrie was concerned. The huge difference was that Carrie was living the life Ava had craved.

Brian pushed his chair back from the table and gathered some plates. "I didn't realize my invitation would be so difficult for you to accept. If you don't want to go, just say so." A tinge of disappointment underscored his words.

"I'm sorry." Ava also stood and helped clear the table. "It's not that I don't want to see Carrie. The thought brings back so many memories. I really regret that she and I haven't remained close. We were inseparable at NYU. It would be wonderful to see her again." Ava loaded the dishwasher, while Brian stored the leftovers. "Since I need to go home and change, it would be better if I left now and got in some work. I could meet you at the theater at 2:30, if that works for you."

While she wanted to take Brian up on his invitation to spend the rest of the morning back in his bed, she needed some distance as well as time to get her head in the right place for a reunion with Carrie—and an up close and personal experience with the career she had left behind.

Chapter Ten

Ava's anxiety melted with the first few vibrant measures of a Count Basie classic, as several members of the dance troupe twirled onto the stage. Ava couldn't take her eyes off Carrie. This was no time to contemplate the past. Ava reveled in the present, so proud of her friend who covered the stage with powerful momentum at some points, and graceful control at others.

Clapping so hard her palms smarted, Ava was hardly the poised former ballerina in the audience. She had transposed herself into an avid fan. Waiting for Carrie to change, she and Brian stood near the bar in the basement of the theater until Brian steered her toward his parents.

Ava's heart beat a wild tempo. The last time she'd interacted with them was at Brian's graduation party. Before she and Brian had stolen off to the guesthouse.

"Mr. and Mrs. Stanhope. It's so nice to see you again." Ava's raspy voice surely gave away her angst. Although neither of the Stanhopes would have tied Ava to Brian back then.

"Ava, it's nice to see you, too." Mrs. Stanhope spoke for both of them as Mr. Stanhope nodded. "We hear you're a lawyer. Brian's lawyer. What a small world."

"Actually, one of the partners at my firm is Brian's

lawyer," Ava explained. "I work with the litigation group, not the corporate department." She didn't want the Stanhopes to think it a conflict of interest for her to get together with Brian socially.

"What happened with your interest in dance?" asked Mrs. Stanhope. "We thought for sure you'd be up there with Carrie, taking the world by storm. You were such a dynamic presence on stage."

Ava swallowed. "Thank you for your kind words. Things changed for me." She shrugged, hoping that vague statement was enough to satisfy their curiosity for her career switch. "I'm happy doing what I'm doing." Not much conviction penetrated her words, but it was the best she could do.

Mr. Stanhope perked up and took over from his wife. "Very practical, Ava. You have a career that will last you a lifetime and give you financial security. Dancing is hardly a long-term career path."

"Now, now, Glenn," Mrs. Stanhope said. "Carrie is doing very well, and we did support her choice."

Mr. Stanhope's frown told Ava he may not have been in on that decision, but Ava remembered they gave Carrie much more leeway than Brian in choosing her ultimate profession.

Out the corner of her eye, Ava saw a striking young woman kiss Brian on the cheek. She couldn't focus more on the incident while chatting with the Stanhopes, but she also couldn't ignore the intimate way the stranger touched Brian's arm or how she stood close enough to be considered in his space. She also looked vaguely familiar.

"Ava!" Someone called her name from an open door in the corner and when she looked up, she saw

Carrie's beaming smile.

Ava nearly flew to meet her friend halfway, throwing herself into Carrie's arms. They laughed, cried, and talked at the same time, barely taking time to breathe. Given their past, Ava had been so worried about their reunion, ever since Brian had invited her today, wondering if Carrie would be cool or distant. But the minute they saw each other, the years dropped away.

"Carrie, you were phenomenal up there. I've never seen you leap so high. It was as if the air was your partner and helped you defy gravity. And your pirouettes—you did so many, and so quickly, the perfect lines of your form blurred for those few seconds."

"Coming from you, that praise is like a stellar review in *The New York Times*. I can't believe you're here. And with my brother." Carrie hugged Ava again, allowing Ava to finally relax about their first encounter in years, as well as the fact she was with Brian on what might be considered a date.

Carrie and Ava stood off to the side, catching up on part of the seven years they'd been incommunicado.

"How's the practice of law? I hear you've got a great job at a Park Avenue firm."

Ava nodded. "It's good."

"I'm glad you found what you were looking for. Although back then, when you transferred to Columbia, I was traumatized by your decision." Carrie laughed it off, but Ava could still see the hint of sorrow in her eyes. Surprising after all these years. "I felt lost without you. I had no one to share studio time with, no one to dance with in the showcase."

"What about Lisa or Colleen?" Ava pulled the names of their classmates from her brain.

"None of them compared to you. You pushed me to be a better dancer because you were so good. Since I didn't want to embarrass myself, I practiced more. Harder. You were my inspiration."

Ava's throat constricted. "I had a hard time, too." Carrie would never know how hard. "But law was a field where I felt I could succeed."

"I still can't believe you dropped out. We could be dancing together today."

Ava's heart broke at her words. Maybe she should have told Carrie the real reason for her defection. But what would that have accomplished? And she couldn't tell her now—not when Carrie's brother still didn't know.

The web was strangling her.

Carrie nudged Ava playfully. "So what's going on with you and my brother?'

At least this was a conversation she could have without suffocating. It even brought a smile. "He showed up at my law firm one day, and we've seen each other a few times since then."

"I don't know what you two have going on, but he's a great guy. It makes me happy to see my old friend and my brother together."

Ava considered whether to raise the past, then went for it. "When we were at NYU, you always talked about him being such a player. When I was at your house in Newport the weekend of his graduation, you warned me more than once he wouldn't be good for me."

"Brian did play the field, as they say." Carrie rolled her eyes and grinned. "Things changed after the accident. For the better," she added, clearly not wanting Ava to believe anything negative about her brother at this time.

Ava glanced over at Brian. "Who is he talking to?" she asked with a casualness she didn't feel.

She and Carrie had spent at least ten minutes in their own little world, and Brian was still ensconced in a conversation—or perhaps even an argument—with the woman who had taken him aside.

"Oh. That's Terri." Carrie's wary expression didn't give more away.

"Terri from Harvard? Brian's friend who was in Newport that weekend?" How she pulled that information from the air, she didn't know, but when it came to Brian there seemed to be little she forgot.

"You have a great memory. Yes. She and Brian dated for a few years."

"A few years?" Ava's voice cracked and the joy that had invaded her moments before dissipated. "When did they break up?"

"Just after Thanksgiving last year." Carrie might have shared more, but her parents chose that moment to come over and congratulate her.

"We hope we gave you enough time to catch up with Ava." Mrs. Stanhope handed Carrie a huge bouquet of roses. "You were wonderful today, honey. We're very proud of you." Mr. Stanhope gave Carrie a hug and voiced similar praise. "The two of you look like long-lost cousins," Mrs. Stanhope continued. "It's a shame it's been so many years since you've seen each other, but maybe now that you're both settled in your careers, you'll get together once in a while."

Carrie slipped her arm around Ava's waist. "I'd

like that."

"Me too." Once she told Brian about Briana, would Carrie change her mind?

Ava forced a smile while she watched Brian and Terri.

The few times they'd been together, she and Brian hadn't talked of past relationships. At first, Ava had assumed Brian still had his player tendencies—to date many with no ties—until she got to know him a little better. When they first met, she had counted on that, believing he would lose interest before she cobbled together the nerve to tell him about their child. In direct contrast, she secretly hoped he had changed and they would fall madly in love, he'd adore Briana just as she did, and they'd live happily ever after.

What a ridiculous vision. Although she contemplated telling Brian the truth, she predicted anger, incredulity, wrath, and a myriad of other negative emotions, which would drive a stake into their budding relationship.

Neither scenario had the happy ending she craved.

"Ava," Brian cut in, "I'd like to introduce you to a friend of mine." His hand held Terri's arm, and they both smiled sweetly at her. "This is Terri Cartwright. We went to college together."

Ava put on her own sweet smile and held out her hand. "Hi, Terri. I think we met at the Stanhope's Newport house many years ago."

Terri's eyes widened. "You were Carrie's friend. The dancer."

Ava nodded. Interesting how women's memories of the competition never fade.

"Well, I better be going." Terri gazed at Brian.

Perhaps she was waiting for an invitation from him to get together later. Did she know Brian was with Ava today? Would Brian tell Ava about his and Terri's relationship?

When Terri finally left, hopefully without a rendezvous place and time, Ava's inner spirit sagged. The emotions of the day had zinged all over the place exhausting her from trying to keep up.

Brian turned to Ava. "We're all going to Café Antonia's for dinner. I hope you're hungry."

Ava's stomach bunched. She couldn't possibly sit through a Stanhope family dinner with her mind clambering to sort through the past, present, and future. "I'm sorry, but I really need to go home and work. I've put it off long enough today. Thank you so much for inviting me." Ava's tone was stiff and formal, not at all like the conversation she contemplated having after spending last night in Brian's bed.

"Is everything okay?" He looked into her eyes, searching for the answer she might not form into words.

Ava swallowed. "Good. Everything is good."

He looked at her skeptically. "Would you prefer the two of us go to dinner alone?"

Of course she would. But she'd never admit it. "No. No. You go with your family. I'm sure Carrie would want you there." She glanced at Carrie, whose adrenaline was still pumping, as she talked animatedly with her parents. "Let me just say good-bye to her and then I'll grab a cab."

Ava hugged Carrie and promised they'd get together soon. She had reconnected with her best friend—a friend she missed terribly. But hanging over their happy reunion was Ava's secret. She shook hands with Mr. and Mrs. Stanhope, giving her apologies for not being able to join them for dinner. Then Brian walked her outside and hailed a cab.

She would love to duck into it without having to say more to Brian. She feared unwanted tears would pool in her eyes, and she'd be unable to explain the reasons for the emotions. She wasn't sure she could even explain them to herself—so many jumped to be the winner. Envy over Carrie, insecurity over Brian, jealousy over Terri, conflicts over her own desires—not to mention Briana.

What a day!

****

"Carrie, did you invite Terri to your performance today?" Brian's non sequitur stopped the dinner conversation between his parents and sister and his mother pursed her lips at his rudeness.

Carrie sipped celebratory champagne. "Of course not. I was as surprised to see her as you were."

Brian's usual camaraderie while in his family's company deserted him. Ava's excitement at seeing Carrie was a wonderful sight, but Terri had diverted his attention. He hadn't seen her in months, and frankly, hadn't wanted to see her after what she'd done.

It wasn't until she cornered him today, that she confessed to giving him some time to get over his anger, hoping they could at least get together and talk.

Now she wanted to talk.

Their conversation had gotten heated when he noticed Ava taking it all in.

Although he didn't introduce Terri as anything more than a college friend, the flash in Ava's eyes told him she knew something had been omitted.

"Did you tell Ava that Terri and I had dated?"

"Dated? Is that what you call it?" Carrie's smirk did not go unnoticed. "I told her you'd been together for a few years. Why?"

"Ava seemed…surprised. Or something. I don't know. I thought she would come to dinner with us. Maybe I'm reading too much into it. She said she had to work. Of course, that's all it was."

"I'm sure Ava doesn't think you've been a monk for the past several years. When we were roommates, I used to tell her I felt sorry for all your girlfriends—if you could call them that—because you were such a player."

Brian's uneasiness over Ava's sudden departure grew. "Do you think she remembers that?"

"Of course. We talked about it today. But I told her you'd matured. You have, correct?"

Carrie's dry wit usually made him chuckle, but something about the short scene when he introduced the two women didn't sit well. "Do you think she believes you?"

"Why wouldn't she? Although she may have some questions about your relationship with Terri. Like any woman would."

"Did you tell her we lived together?" Brian's anxiety increased with his tone. He had wanted to ease into discussions with Ava about his last relationship and the reasons for its failure, but at a time he thought appropriate. Especially since Ava seemed very careful, almost guarded around him.

"No. But you may want to mention that to her. Along with the fact that it's definitely over. After seeing Terri swarm all over you today, Ava may have some reservations."

"She wasn't swarming all over me." Now he was getting defensive. He hated that.

"It's all in the eye of the beholder."

"Carrie," her mother broke in, "stop agitating your brother. Let's have a toast to your spring program. It's absolutely beautiful, dear."

"Thanks, Mom."

They toasted Carrie's successful season, but Brian couldn't help the uneasiness growing that Ava might have taken away the wrong impression. If he wanted any chance of seeing where their relationship could go, he had better straighten out any misconceptions, sooner rather than later.

He had tried to get his family to hurry it up through dinner, but they languished over coffee and dessert, telling stories and otherwise conversing as if they hadn't seen each other in a year. Every time he glanced at his watch, trying to give them a hint the hour was getting late, Carrie threw in a snide remark that he always had somewhere more important to be. She reiterated tonight was her night, and she wasn't letting him off the hook—a masterful way of getting him back for all those years he had tortured his little sister.

It was almost nine before he finally escaped. Brian stood outside Ava's apartment building, considering whether to call, have the doorman announce him, or maybe just go home.

He finally opted for the doorman route and breathed a sigh of relief when Ava okayed his visit. When he knocked on her door, it took more than a few seconds for her to open it. And when she did, her face was pale and strained.

"Come in." She lowered her lids and motioned to the living room.

"What's wrong, Ava?" His heart tightened at the thought he may be the cause of her unhappiness.

He pulled her into him, indulging in the feel of her body against his. He kissed the top of her head and breathed in a mixture of wild flowers, the scent of her shampoo. "I missed you tonight. I couldn't get my sister to shut up so I could leave."

She laughed into his shoulder as he still held her tight.

"Did you get your work done?" He looked into her drawn face.

"Not much." She moved away and pulled him toward the sofa. "Sit down. We need to talk."

Uh-oh. Those words were never good. But he did as she asked and waited for her to say what she wanted to say.

She swallowed as if the words were difficult. "Are you and Terri still seeing each other?"

So, it was all about Terri. "No. We broke up last November. I hadn't seen her until today."

Ava stared at her hands, twisting her mother's ring. "Do you still care about her?" Her sapphire eyes bored into his, making him want to lose himself in her kiss.

"No. Not at all. That's over."

"I was surprised to learn you'd been in a long-term relationship so recently. Not that we talked about it. You just never gave any hint. When did you start dating her?"

Brian stroked her hair, needing the connection before sharing his very personal, and in the end, very painful story with Ava. But he would do it so they could move forward.

"After college, after my accident, Terri helped me a lot. We both lived and worked in New York. We'd been friends at school and remained friends for a few years, but I knew she wanted to be more than that. She put up with my dragging leg and stuttering speech. She was my biggest cheerleader, pushing me to go to my therapies when I would have blown them off for not seeing immediate results. She was smart, very career-oriented, and we had a lot in common. And, of course, my parents loved her."

Brian took Ava's hand. "Is it okay to tell you this?"

Ava nodded, but worry creased her brow. He didn't want to be the cause of that worry. He and Terri were over. Best to get the whole story out as quickly as possible.

"After a while, we became more than friends. We moved in together and talked about getting married."

Ava stiffened. "What happened that you didn't?" she rasped.

"We were on two different paths. I wanted to have kids. She didn't. She was moving up the ladder quickly at her company and didn't want maternity leaves, or children, to interfere with that." He kept the bitterness over her choice well hidden. "We grew apart."

"That's why you broke up?"

The question hung between them for a while, before Brian answered. "Mostly," he finally said.

Ava looked at him puzzled.

"In November, I learned she'd had an abortion a week earlier." His voice cracked and he inhaled to keep calm. "She never told me she was pregnant. She never asked my opinion. Of course, she knew I'd want her to have the baby. And she didn't want me to interfere with her decision." His jaw ached as he ground his teeth together. "I would never have found out if the nurse hadn't left a message on the answering machine at home asking if she'd had any problems after the procedure. To call if she had any questions or complications." Brian swallowed the bile in his throat. "When I confronted Terri, she tried to get around it. Lying to me that there was a problem with the fetus and she had no choice. But in the end, she finally confessed. That was the last time I saw her. Until today."

Ava's throat constricted. "I'm so sorry, Brian."

He stroked her cheek, then leaned over and captured her lips. He hadn't meant to—it just happened.

What started out as a need for connection ignited something in his soul, and he slid his hand around and cupped Ava's head, bringing her closer. His lips devoured hers, parting them and seeking her tongue, entwining them, inflaming him. He had come here to explain his prior relationship, but just the sight of Ava, looking sad and vulnerable and young, made him want her more than he should.

He slid his mouth to her check, her neck, her shoulder, tasting the sweet-salty combination of soft, creamy skin. He struggled to bring himself back. "I'm sorry you were upset today, but now you know there's nothing to worry about," he whispered before circling her ear with his tongue. She shivered. "Is there anything else you'd like to talk about?"

"Not right now." Ava looked directly into his eyes. A sexy smile and tantalizing gaze gave him permission to follow her to the bedroom, with all thoughts of Terri vanquished forever.

Chapter Eleven

He must be dreaming. But his eyes were open, staring at the ceiling of Ava's room as she breathed softly next to him, asleep.

Ava opened the door of the guesthouse, the white gown draped provocatively over one gorgeous body, her beautiful dark hair pinned on top of her head with strands falling around her lovely face.

Brian drew her into his arms and whispered, "You look like an angel tonight. I couldn't stop searching you out, just to get a glimpse." Then he placed his hands on either side of her face and lowered his lips to hers. Covering her mouth, he kissed her with a hunger and need, so surprising in its power that it took only seconds to transfer those carnal desires to the woman in his arms. He threaded his fingers into her hair, removing the combs that held it on top of her head, allowing rich, shiny tresses to tumble around her shoulders.

He stepped back, surveying his handiwork. "I've been wanting to do that all night." A smile escaped. "Gorgeous, beautiful Ava." He brushed his hand down the length of her arm from sculpted shoulder to delicate wrist, feeling the silkiness of her skin while a magnetic force moved through his fingers and up his arms.

He closed the door, then pulled her toward the bed, setting in motion more fireworks within.

"I brought one of the horses from the stable," he said. "I thought we'd go horseback riding later. When all the lights are off and just the stars are out. It's an incredible sight when the night sky is really clear. Like tonight." He knew what women liked. They liked romance, and he had the tools to pull out all the stops.

"That sounds wonderful."

Ava placed her hand on his cheek, tracing the planes down through his jawline. Then she leaned in and kissed him.

His hands roamed over her body, possessing her, igniting sparks within him. And those sparks started a slow burn that shut down his mind and inflamed his senses. He slid her gown over silken skin and tossed it on the floor. A fantasy he'd yearned for all night. He stood while he tore at his tuxedo shirt and pants, discarding them in seconds, but not before pulling a condom from his pocket. He tore at the wrapper with his teeth and rolled the latex onto his erect shaft. He knew he was rushing it, but up until now, he'd tested his patience to the limit. Rejoining Ava on the bed, Brian wound his arms around her, his chest brushing the tips of her breasts, before crushing their bodies in a passionate embrace. Rolling on top, his hips pushed against hers as his hardness stroked the entrance to her body. He moved her legs further apart so he could ease in, hoping she was as ready for him as he was for her.

As he glided in and out, stroking her inner walls, Ava's hands wandered up and down his arms, pulling his focus back to her. She locked into his eyes, hers blazing with desire and smoldering with passion. So powerful in their depths.

He grabbed hold of her hips and thrust into her

harder, pushing her to her climax as his took hold and exploded into a kaleidoscope of color and sensation cascading in and around his body. He called out her name while plunging one final time.

Ava's breath came in gasps as she inhaled. Still joined together, her fingers splayed across his back and she dragged manicured nails over his shoulders, extracting another moan of pleasure from him. A beautiful smile of pure happiness erupted over her features as she gazed into his eyes. Brian slid out of her, quickly disposed of the condom, and lay down next to her, his leg draping over her, his arm keeping her in a tight embrace.

"That was amazing," he said, pulling her even closer as she laid her head on his shoulder. Then he kissed the top of her head before his eyes closed.

While his heartbeat settled, he stroked her hair. "How'd you like to go for that horseback ride I promised?"

"Seriously?" Joy bubbled over, and Ava scrambled from the bed. "Let's go."

She rummaged in her suitcase for a pair of jeans and a T-shirt while Brian scrounged for his tux pants.

Leading Ava outside, Brian helped her onto the horse and after he mounted in front of her, she wrapped her arms around his bare chest, holding tight. They rode through the field to the edge of the Stanhope property, away from the dim lights of the main house. The night sky glittered with stars, and Brian pointed out the Big Dipper and to the left of it, the stars that make up the summer triangle, Deneb, Vega, and Altair, along with their constellations. And between them all and a little to the south was Scorpius the Scorpion with its bright red star, Antares.

As he studied the night sky with Ava embracing him, an odd sensation skittered through his being. This was one of those moments in time he knew he'd never forget. It was one of those moments where fate and luck collide into a perfect reality.

He gently shook Ava awake, but his words were more urgent. "Did we make love in the guesthouse?" Brian's heart galloped as he waited for Ava's response.

In the dim light seeping into the bedroom from the living room, he saw her eyes, huge and round.

"Seven years ago, the night of my party, did we?" The memory was too real to be a dream. There was too much texture, too many details.

"Yes," Ava breathed. "It was a wonderful, romantic night."

"Why didn't you tell me?" Confusion pulled at his brain.

"There wasn't any point. You didn't remember me." Sadness punctuated her voice.

He pulled her closer. "These last few weeks, while spending time with you, I've had a few memories. At first, I didn't think they were real—just some trick my brain was playing on me. But just now, it was so real—so intense. Was that the only time?"

Her eyes found his. "Yes. I had hoped we'd get together once you moved to the City, pick up where we left off. But when I came to see you at the rehab facility, you looked right through me. Nothing I said brought back any memories of you and me together that weekend. And I didn't want to say too much in front of Carrie because she didn't know we had gotten together—like that. She'd warned me to steer clear of you. But I couldn't. You were everywhere. And that's where I wanted to be."

Brian closed his eyes while stroking her back. "So, we have a past."

"I suppose you could call it that." Ava's tone was off. A hint of resentment poked through her words. "Two days. Only two days. And then it all came crashing down." Tears clogged her voice.

"I'm so sorry, Ava. I didn't remember anything of that weekend until I ran into you again. That first night after the basketball game, when we were standing in front of a store window, the gown in the window snapped something in my brain. Then when we were dancing at the Club, I pictured you spinning and leaping through the air in Carrie's studio in Newport. I thought it was some crazy illusion. But tonight… It was so tangible."

Ava's skin was cold to the touch, and he rubbed her arm, her back to warm her. "You're my good luck charm. My key to the lost weekend." He kissed her brow. "You must have done a number on me back then for these memories to be only of you." He smiled at the thought before finding her lips and covering them in a passionate kiss that awakened the craving he had only for Ava.

Then he made love to her again with his body and soul.

****

Ava laid her head on Brian's shoulder as they lounged in bed, clinging to the euphoria that enveloped her. She played with the hairs on his chest, relishing their closeness. "I'm so glad you came over tonight. I needed to see you."

Brian kissed her head and entwined his fingers through hers. "I needed to see you, too. I knew you were upset when you left the theater, but you wouldn't stay to talk to me."

"I couldn't sit through dinner with your family. There were too many emotions spinning around in my head. My reunion with Carrie. You and Terri." She left it at that. "It was a surprise, learning about that today. I remembered her from Newport."

But Ava could say no more. Like how insecure she'd felt around his Harvard friends that weekend long ago, or how ecstatic she'd been when he'd chosen her over them. She even remembered that Terri had found them kissing under an old oak tree. Ava had been sure Terri was looking for him for her own pleasurable purposes.

"Thank you for telling me." She burrowed her face into his neck.

He hugged her close. "So what about you? What's your deep dark secret?"

Ava's heart thudded to a stop and her head spun. "What do you mean?"

"What crushed your relationships? I'm sure you've left more than one lover in the dust. What was your breaking point?"

Ava breathed in slowly, sending oxygen and hopefully calmness to the organ now unrhythmically thumping in her chest. "I haven't had any close relationships. At least not any in which hearts were broken."

Brian looked at her as if she had two heads. "I don't believe that. You're beautiful, talented, smart. It would be impossible for you to reach this stage without having been in love."

If he only knew. "I've been busy, I guess. Law school was difficult, and I had to work nights and weekends to help support myself. Once I landed the job, I needed to become indispensable. So I still work nights and weekends." She chuckled, hoping to minimize the reality of her less-than-exciting life.

Brian's brow furrowed. "That sounds like an excuse. If you wanted a relationship, you'd have one despite your busy schedule."

Annoyance filtered through her at his presumptuous and simplified analysis. "Relationships aren't as easy for me as they apparently are for you."

"Ouch," he winced. "Don't get upset. I'm not faulting you. If you didn't want someone special in your life, that's your choice. I'm just surprised, that's all. Most women want a relationship, marriage, kids. Men too, once they get past their idiotic stage." He smiled, clearly trying to lighten her mood. "Maybe you're different. It's not important to you. But I hope I can change your mind."

Of course she wanted that. And she'd wanted Brian since the first day she met him. But once she told him she'd given their baby up for adoption, he'd hate her—for the secret she carried with her for seven years—for the lie of omission in not telling him once they reconnected. And for allowing the adoption to go through without his knowledge and consent. This could never go well.

His jaw tightened. "What's going on in that head of yours? I've never been good at reading women. You have to be direct, open." He lifted her chin to connect with her eyes. "You play it very close to the vest, not sharing too much of yourself. We could have had dinner alone tonight and discussed what was bothering you. Instead, you flew out of the theater, and we both had awful nights. If you want us to work out, and I hope you do because I'm crazy about you—" he kissed her lightly on the lips, "—you're going to have to be more direct, more open."

"I'd love to be able to trust in people and move forward. But I can't."

"In people, or in me?"

She lowered her lids. There were so many answers to this question.

"I get it. It's your protective armor and all that. Especially given your parents' desertion. Maybe I can help you bury your memories by creating new ones." He cupped her face in warm hands.

Brian's words strangled her heart, making it very hard to breathe. She wanted him desperately. Always had. Since the day they met. He was the reason her relationships didn't work out. She compared everyone to him. Or at least to the memory of him. And now that he was here, everything she remembered, all those fantasies, paled in comparison to reality. Her world had turned sunny, for she'd fallen in love all over again.

She had to tell him the truth. Everything about that joyful, horrible weekend and its aftermath. But the words caught in her throat. Ava moved away from Brian and sat up. "I need some air," she finally blurted. "Would you take a walk with me?"

"Now? It's after midnight." He tried to pull her back into bed. "Come here. Forget what I said. It wasn't meant to upset you."

"You didn't...I understand...I just need to move."

Heat prickled her skin from the inside and her nerves jumped and danced, screaming to be released. She tried again. "Please come with me. I need to tell you something. It's important." She moved around the room throwing on her discarded underwear, jeans, and sweater. As she came upon his clothing, she tossed it to him.

His confused expression kicked at her gut. She felt sorry for him, sorry for her. But she had to do this now. And she had to do it outside, where there was extra oxygen, extra space. Not that it would help the aftermath, but at least it would aid in the delivery.

Brian mumbled as he put on his clothes. "I don't understand why you can't tell me here."

She headed for the front door the second he had his shoes on. He followed her into the elevator, where the silence echoed in her ears. How should she start the conversation? With a history of their time together in Newport? With a play by play?

When they were finally outside, Ava directed him away from her building, not wanting the doorman to witness her destruction. She practically ran to the corner, pulling Brian along, before she stopped and turned to him.

"My niece, Briana, is really my daughter." Ava blurted it out in a rush with no thought as to the political correctness of it all. "She's your daughter, too."

Chapter Twelve

The words slammed against him but he couldn't comprehend. What was Ava talking about? Had she gone off the deep end?

Tears poured down her face as she studied him while wringing her hands and bouncing from foot to foot. "Did you hear me?" It was almost a scream.

Brian felt the stares of passersby, but their presence drifted to the fringes of his consciousness.

"Brian?" This time her voice was calmer, quieter.

He grasped for a response. But too many questions bombarded his fuzzy brain. "Could you repeat that?"

"You just remembered we made love the Saturday night of your graduation weekend. Then you had the accident. I learned a few weeks later I was pregnant." Ava's face transformed with anguish as her voice broke.

He shook his head. "That's not possible. I'm sure I acted responsibly. I always use condoms."

"We did." Her voice was flat now, some of her angst seguing into disgust. "Condoms aren't one hundred percent effective. I hope you don't think I should have done something more to prevent a pregnancy." A steely anger entered her watery eyes. "You were the only one I was with. I hadn't been seeing anyone. And when I met you, I-I…" She inhaled, perhaps to give her time to find the right words. "I fell hard for you," she whispered.

He closed his eyes. Given his recollection tonight, he'd felt something special for her, too. But this was insane. Impossible. He dug deep for words, any words.

They were still standing at the corner, cautiously facing each other, several feet apart, as if waiting for the bell to signal their next round.

"Why didn't you tell me then?" He was still holding onto his uncertainty like a shield. Still hoping to ward off the enemy.

But Ava wasn't his enemy. Until a few minutes ago, he'd been ready to admit he was falling in love. Trying to get her to open up to him and maybe even tell him the same thing. But this confession wasn't what he'd hoped for. Now he needed room. And air. And whatever the hell else Ava had dragged him out here for. Unable to stand still, he walked up the street.

She called after him. "I tried."

He turned and walked back. "When?" He couldn't keep the resentment from his voice.

"When I visited you at the rehab center. But you didn't remember me or anything from that weekend. Yet, I wouldn't let it go. I thought if you saw me, if I could remind you of the things we did—"

"Does Carrie know?" Panic segued into his brain.

"No. I didn't tell anyone except my sister and her husband."

The sorrow in her eyes convinced him he was injuring her beyond reason with his reaction to this confession. He needed to leave, to give himself some space and time to process it all. "I'm sorry, Ava, I have to go." He couldn't conjure up any warmth in his words, the shock overtaking all emotion.

She paled and reached for his arm, before pulling back. She bit her lip and nodded. "Okay." Her raspy voice suggested vulnerability. And hurt.

He should have felt bad about leaving her there, but his empathy had disappeared with her words. He had a child. A child with Ava. And he never knew. Never even knew he and Ava had hooked up seven years earlier until that memory came back tonight. He shook his head as if to unscramble irrational thoughts

Then he gave her one last look and walked away.

****

Ava stood on the corner in a daze as pedestrians sporadically angled around her to cross the street. Her eyes blurred with tears, but she couldn't take them off Brian's retreating back. Her stomach heaved, and she dashed for the trashcan, vomiting up what little there was, since she hadn't eaten since breakfast.

Seven years earlier, the day she learned she was pregnant, she'd meandered aimlessly around the Village wondering what to do. Alone and frightened, the thought of telling Brian—who at the time lay in a hospital bed with a traumatic brain injury—was the scariest part of all. She had been nauseous then, too.

Her head swam as she straightened up. Inhaling to steady herself, Ava blinked back the tears. She needed to get to her apartment before hysterics robbed her of all decency. Purposefully placing one foot in front of the other, she moved toward her building, only a half a block away, but not sure her wobbly legs could handle the task. She admonished herself to avoid all thoughts of Brian until she surrounded herself with the security of her four walls.

Reaching the apartment was a herculean effort, but

once inside, her skin itched and burned in the stagnant air. She threw open the windows in the living room, needing a blizzard to blow through, but all she got was a hot, humid breeze. She stood in the middle of the room, almost paralyzed, for she couldn't go into her bedroom knowing the sheets were tangled and the pillows indented from her and Brian's recent foray into passionate waters. Less than an hour ago they had made love with a hunger that suggested they couldn't live without each other.

A sob escaped, and she held her hand to her mouth. She'd known her revelation would lead to their undoing. Yet, it was no small secret that could be flitted away. Briana was a person, a growing child, who he had fathered. A six-year-old he had never met, who now had other parents raising her.

He'd walked away from Terri after spending years with her because she made the unilateral decision to abort their child. While Ava didn't have an abortion, the bottom line was the same. She'd effectively eliminated his chance to be a dad, something he apparently wanted, without giving him the right to weigh in on the ultimate decision.

They needed to talk about it more. He needed to understand the adoption was for the best. And she couldn't allow him to second guess that decision. Not now. How could he just walk away? How could this be happening again?

Ava covered her face with her hands and sank to the floor, her sobs turning into uncontrollable weeping. Every part of her body ached, inside and out, and she hugged herself to keep from disintegrating. The torture was so familiar, so devastating. Yet, she'd always known the truth wouldn't pave the way to their bliss.

If he was going to break up with her because of her choice seven years ago, then she didn't need him. She was better off alone. Just as she'd been when her mother left, when her father sent her to boarding school, and when Brian lost his memory.

She had survived it all, and she would survive again.

****

Brian sat in his office overlooking Fifth Avenue, a pile of phone messages begging for attention. But his mind couldn't focus.

His father poked his head through the door. "You were certainly anxious to end dinner last night. How was the rest of your evening?"

A disaster, he thought. "Fine."

"Did you meet up with Ava?" A glint in his father's eyes told Brian he wished he was young and single again.

"Yes." *But it didn't turn out as great as you're thinking.*

"Guess you're not in the mood to talk." His father honed in on the obvious.

"Not right now." *Maybe not ever.*

"I'm in the office this morning. Then I'll be out at the Fishkill site this afternoon."

Brian nodded. He and his father were close. Closer than most fathers and sons. They saw each other every day, talked about the day-to-day business of their company, and courted prospective clients at dinners and sports events. And of course, his dad knew more than most about his love life—pre-Terri, during Terri, and post-Terri. Maybe a little too much. But this new

142

explosive news was way beyond what he was willing to share. He needed to sort through the jumbled thoughts bombarding his brain on his own.

Although he'd like nothing more than a redo of yesterday, minus the news he was a father, he had to accept what Ava had shared so painfully last night and deal with it. While all he could feel when she'd first told him was a simmering anger over the fact she'd kept this huge news a secret for seven years, he had mellowed since then. Marginally. He could accept that she couldn't tell him while he was in rehab, since he didn't even know who she was. That had to be awful for her. But why didn't she tell Carrie? They were best friends. Carrie could have reintroduced her to him, given him information about that weekend.

Instead she'd kept it to herself, dropped out of NYU, given up her dance career, and had her sister adopt their child. There were so many questions surrounding those decisions. But what had kept his anger up was reestablishing a relationship with him while maintaining her secret, never once letting on she had been much more than a guest at his weekend graduation party.

If he hadn't remembered they had made love, would she have told him the outcome? How could she be so deceitful? True, he had invited her and her boss to a Knicks game, which had started the whole ball rolling. True, she hadn't pursued him, and if he studied their interactions over the past few weeks, he might see that she tried to keep her distance, at least for a little while. Maybe that's why she wouldn't have dinner with his family last night. Maybe Terri was a convenient excuse. How could she face them all, knowing what she knew?

He massaged his forehead, then raked his hands through his hair.

The photo of Ava's "niece" flickered through his brain. Blonde hair, blue eyes. Briana. How could he have not seen the similarities in appearance and name? But at the time, he had no idea he had ever met Ava before. In analyzing that meeting in her office, she had been jittery. He'd thought it was the insecurity of a new associate signing up a client. When she took the photo from his hands, she'd turned it over on her desk instead of putting it back in its place. She then rushed through an explanation of the ten-page fee agreement and seemed relieved when she ushered him out of her office and back to the lobby. In hindsight, she'd been poised to refuse his offer of basketball tickets before Peter had signed her on.

Had she been hoping to never see him again? Or had she orchestrated this whole thing, so she could get to a point where she could finally tell him? The questions were excruciating and unending. He needed to talk to Ava to get the answers, but he wasn't ready to have a rational, coherent conversation. The host of emotions playing through him assured they'd end up arguing instead of discussing.

Perhaps a conversation with Carrie would help. She knew Ava better, and she also might give him a clearer understanding of what happened that weekend. How much she knew was still a mystery and if she didn't know he and Ava had slept together, maybe he shouldn't let her in on it. At least not yet.

But niggling at him was the quest for information. He dialed Carrie hoping to catch her at home. Luck was on his side when she answered. "Do you have a minute?"

"Sure. I don't have rehearsal until this afternoon. What's up?"

"Do you remember my graduation weekend in Newport?"

"Of course. We had a blast—until the accident."

"I still can't remember most things, but I've started having memory flashes. They seem to come when I'm with Ava. Did I spend a lot of time with her?"

"Hasn't she talked to you about that?" Carrie sounded apprehensive. Did women have a code of honor, too?

"Yes. A little." But not enough.

A sigh floated over the line. "You were quite taken with her. But then again, you were taken with most gorgeous females. She was enamored with you, too. I did my best to warn her away. If you didn't have the accident, the two of you may have hooked up in the City after that. Who knows?"

So, in Carrie's mind, they didn't hook up. Brian spoke cautiously. "Was I nice to her?"

"That's an odd question. What do you mean?"

"Did I treat her…respectfully or did I act like an ass?"

Carrie laughed. "You may have been a player, but you always treated your women very nicely. You never dated Ava, though. What's with all these questions?"

Brian quietly sighed. His sister knew nothing important.

"Ava said she came to see me at the rehab center. I can't believe I don't remember that."

"Since you didn't know who she was, there's no

reason for you to remember her visit. She had come to see me for a weekend and stopped by the center before we went to the house. She wasn't there very long. You were having trouble with your speech and your memory."

"Thanks for filling me in." Although he learned nothing of significance.

"Is everything okay between you and Ava?"

He rubbed his free hand over his face. "It's fine. I just had a flashback. It…confused me. I thought you might be able to shed some light, but I'll talk to Ava." He hung up disappointed Carrie couldn't help.

Yet, what did he expect? That Carrie would know intimate details of his time with Ava? He sat back in his chair and stared out the window. Even if Carrie had seen them together, she wouldn't have known how Brian felt about Ava. And that's what was really bothering him. Had he fallen for her, or had she been just one more to add to his stable of sleek fillies? He had been a player, relished it. In looking back, he wasn't the man he could have—should have—been. He didn't treat women with the respect they deserved, and he feared he might have treated Ava poorly as well.

Her words from last night barreled back to him, threatening to take him down. *I fell hard for you.* Right about now, he hated himself.

During the past month, he had gotten to know her. She was funny, smart, gorgeous, and independent, but she was also a loner. She had broken off her friendship with Carrie. Now he knew why. She wasn't close to her family, except for her sister and Briana. Now he knew why. She kept a tight lid on her emotions, which sometimes played out across her face, ever so briefly, before being wiped away. Now he knew why. She'd had his child, which ruined her ambitions, and she hadn't even had him to share her burden.

Brian picked up the phone and called Ava's cell. Of course she'd be at work, and a conversation about any of this would be impossible. He went directly to voicemail.

"Call me. It's Brian. Let's talk." He hung up feeling even worse, if that were possible.

Chapter Thirteen

Ava covered the circles under her eyes with concealer, yet nothing could erase the hollowness that permeated her being. She worked on an appellate brief, hoping the research would take her mind off that horrible scene with Brian, but not even challenging legal arguments could win out.

She read the same paragraph over and over, with not one word registering. At least she could hide out in the library, a little used room at the firm, since most attorneys did research on their office computers.

She'd slept on the couch, if you could call it sleep. Her eyes burned today from the tears she'd shed well into the morning. She'd fallen for him, again. When would she learn that she and Brian weren't meant to be?

It was only ten o'clock. She'd never get through the rest of the day. She'd have to feign illness so no one would question her departure. But she couldn't go back to her apartment. Besides, she needed to talk to Kim, to alert her that Brian now knew he was Briana's father. While she didn't expect him to do anything crazy, like hire a lawyer to vacate the adoption, Kim should know in case Brian showed up on her doorstep. She rummaged in her purse and found her cell phone, which she had turned off. A rare occurrence in her life. As soon as she turned it on, it advised her of a message. From Brian.

Her heart kicked at her ribs as she listened to the voicemail. "Call me. It's Brian. Let's talk." Six words said with no emotion. She listened again hoping to hear some warmth, some apology. Nothing.

She dialed Kim and tried not to alarm her. "Hi. It's me. I was thinking about coming down to see Briana, since I missed her this weekend. Are you around?"

"I'm off today. But it's Monday. She's at school until three. Don't you have to work?"

Ava paused, searching for an acceptable response. "I work almost every night until eight or nine. I thought I'd give myself a break."

"Great. How will you get here? Train or rental car?"

"Car. I should get there around twelve-thirty, maybe one." She thought it best to have the distraction of driving as opposed to wallowing away the time on a train.

"Are you staying over?" Kim sounded hopeful.

"No. I have to work tomorrow. But I can stay for dinner if that's okay."

"Briana will be thrilled. See you later."

Ava hung up and called the rental agency a few blocks away. Now that she had a destination, the sooner she got there, the better.

****

It had taken Ava longer to get to Kim's than expected, and as soon as she arrived the questions started. "You look ill. What's wrong? Are you okay?" Kim ushered her into the living room and Kim gingerly seated herself on the sofa, motioning for Ava to join her.

"You're not looking so great yourself." Ava hoped

for some preliminary chitchat before getting into the distressing reason for her visit.

But Kim's radar, along with her troubled eyes, prompted an upfront and honest response. "I told Brian he's Briana's father." Her statement came out in a whoosh, flying right at Kim and into the atmosphere beyond.

"What do you mean?" Her brow creased as the confusion tripled. "Where did you see Brian? Why would you tell him that?"

Of course, Kim wouldn't comprehend her confession. Ava hadn't told her she'd reconnected with Brian after all these years. She kept that bit of information to herself for several reasons, not the least of which was that their relationship would never last. Hence, there was no need to come clean. Besides, when Ava visited on Sundays, she focused on Briana. And since her sister and brother-in-law were also focused on Briana, as any good parent would be, there was little divergence from their script.

During these last few weeks, Ava naively imagined that if she finally shared the story of her and Brian's reacquaintance, it would be a happy tale. Instead, it had turned ugly. Ava felt the nausea return as she replayed their blissful time together, ending in last night's trauma.

Kim remained silent during Ava's recitation, then she stood and started pacing. "I don't understand. Why did you tell him? This was something between us. We promised to not even tell Dad. Why would you dredge up the past to a person who has no recollection of the event? Why tempt fate?" Kim's tone edged up the anger scale as she spoke. "This was settled between us seven years ago. He had nothing to do with it. He should have nothing to do with it now." Kim stopped pacing, her hands on her hips, her posture tilted to the right as she glared at Ava.

Although Brian may have had a little something to do with it, Kim's statements actually seemed rational as Ava sat here in her living room. Yet, last night, when she and Brian were in bed together and he talked of trust and opening up, there was no way she could possibly keep this information from him. It seemed the anchor of their relationship. Secrets had to be disclosed. Hearts opened.

But to what avail? As soon as she disclosed her secret, he walked away.

"I had to tell him." A suffocating sensation strangled her throat. "It was getting serious between us. How could I have a relationship with Brian based on a lie?"

Kim pointed her finger at Ava as anger spurred her on. "You should never have started a relationship with him. He was the past. You lived through the grief of his memory loss, of having his baby, of throwing away your dream. How could you even look him in the eye at this point?"

Ava stood and rounded on Kim, pointing her finger right back at her. "I am living my life as best I could. I'm sorry if the person I chose to love doesn't fit into your plan."

Kim's astonishment at her words punctuated her face—her mouth agape, eyes open wide. After several tense seconds of absolute silence, Kim's body morphed from warrior pose to chastised sister. "You're in love with him?"

Ava nodded, not able to speak for several moments. "I know it's crazy. I never thought I'd see Brian again. But we ran into each other at work. He's a client of the firm's. At first I was cautious. But I was dying to know what the father of my baby was like now." She swallowed. "I thought it would be a one-time thing. Satisfy my curiosity and we'd each go our own way. He still didn't know who I was."

"Then what happened?" Kim whispered through her clogged throat.

"He wanted to see me again. I couldn't resist. All those feelings from seven years ago resurfaced with a vengeance. I tried to push them away. I tried to convince myself this was a bad idea. It didn't work."

Ava stood rooted in her place. So much angst had built up since she'd reconnected with Brian. Trying to determine if or when she should divulge her secret had been hell, but also wreaking havoc was her fear of telling Kim about her relationship with Brian. Finally voicing her secrets gave her some relief. A lifting of the lid to let out a burst of steam.

Yet, she still had to deal with the fallout.

"I know it doesn't sound like it, but I'm happy you're in love." Kim attempted a smile. "I just can't believe there's only one person out there for you."

"I'm fairly certain Brian isn't in love with me at this point." Ava tried for sarcasm, but the heartache was just under the surface.

Kim sagged onto the couch, massaging her back. "Now what?"

"What do you mean?" Kim's question caught her off guard. She expected a soothing hug, words of empathy.

"What if Brian wants to vacate the adoption?" Kim put her head in her hands.

So this is where she wanted to go now. "He can't. I signed all the papers. You legally adopted Briana."

An ache started at the base of Ava's skull and wound its way to her temple. She had slid a small lie into her certification for the adoption proceedings. She swore, under oath, she didn't know the father's identity. And she rationalized that she really didn't. Brian was no longer the person with whom she had made love. He didn't know her. If she had put his name in the papers as the father, he would have been served. He would have had to consent to the adoption. There was no reason to advise him about the product of their amazing night together—a night he couldn't remember, with a woman who had no place in his life.

"He won't interfere." Ava's words weren't as convincing as she needed them to be.

"How do you know? Did he say that?" Kim's question demanded an acceptable answer.

"Yes." Another lie. But necessary.

Glancing at her watch, Ava noticed it was almost two-thirty and Briana would be home soon. She looked at Kim who was still rubbing her back.

"What's wrong?"

"I pulled something when I was lifting a patient. It's time for another pain pill." She stood and headed for the kitchen.

"Did you go to the doctor?" Ava called after her.

"Yes. I'm seeing someone from pain management."

"It doesn't look like it's working."

"The pills help." Kim came back into the room

with a glass of water.

"I'll go outside and wait for the bus." It would give the pill some time to work and Kim some space to assimilate the information Ava just dropped on her.

It would also give Ava some much-needed breathing room to figure out how to keep Brian from looking too closely into the adoption proceedings.

****

As soon as she saw Briana, Ava's mood lifted. It helped when Briana shrieked her name the moment she stepped off the bus. Her exuberant chatter continued as she skipped down the street holding Ava's hand.

"Mom!" she yelled when they entered the house, as if Kim weren't standing right there, "Aunt Ava's here."

"Yes, honey, I know. She missed you so much she took off from work today to see you." Kim's eyes still held the telltale signs of their emotional discussion.

"Aunt Ava, let's go to my room and make up a dance."

That's what they always did soon after Ava arrived. It was their special time together, and it transported Ava back to her own childhood when she and her mother did the same thing.

"Don't you want a snack first? Maybe something to drink?" asked Kim.

"No. I'm good." Briana motioned to Ava.

"I'm going to lie down for a little while since you two will be busy." Kim headed to her bedroom, slightly hunched over.

"Sure. We'll try not to make too much noise."

Ava followed Briana into her ballerina-themed bedroom, with dancers leaping on the wallpaper, her lamp's base made from toe shoes, and an open chest filled with tutus, boas, beads, and pieces of colorful satin they used to make costumes—or play dress-up.

"Who do you want to be today?" Ava moved to Briana's bureau, and searched through the old music CDs they had accumulated.

Briana paused mid-room and placed her finger on her chin. Such a little actress.

"I'm not sure if I want to be Cinderella or Giselle." She rummaged through the costume chest throwing the top garments on the floor in search of the perfect outfit.

"You were Cinderella last time. Let's do Giselle." Ava popped the CD into the player and perused the back cover for a song Briana would like.

Within seconds, Briana had added her school dress to the pile on the floor, and held up a white leotard and long white tutu. "Is this the right costume?"

"If you want to be one of the Wilis. I thought you'd want to be Giselle."

Briana stroked the white mesh. "No, we'll both be Wilis today."

Ava reached into the chest and found a long, tulle skirt. Being a ghostly spirit who'd been deserted by her lover seemed about right. She had discarded her suit jacket when she arrived, and had on a white blouse and beige skirt. "I'll put this over my skirt. It'll work."

Once dressed, Briana stood next to Ava in first position. "Okay. I'm ready. Teach me a new dance."

For the next hour, Ava choreographed a dance simple enough for Briana to learn, incorporating some of the steps and leaps she'd taught her in the past. They started and stopped the music dozens of times while adding more and more to their dance, until it was finally finished.

"Well, are you ready to perform for your mom." Every time Ava said that word, her heart froze and she said to herself, *I'm your mom and always will be.*

Briana jumped up and down. "Yes, yes, yes. I love this dance." She was so full of joy and such an adorable ballerina. Maybe she'd be the one to make it. In fifteen years, Ava could be sitting in the audience in a New York City theater watching her on stage.

Unexpectedly, a bitter jealousy stirred inside. "Why don't you go wake up your mom," she said, needing the time to pull herself together.

As they did every time Ava came to visit, she and Briana put on their show to the adoring accolades of Kim. Sometimes Kim even videoed their performance so Briana could watch long after Ava left. Although today, Kim seemed a little less enthusiastic, almost lethargic. Not surprising, given their earlier conversation.

"It's almost time for dinner," said Kim while hugging Briana and looking over her head toward Ava. "You're still staying, right?" Kim looked hopeful, clearly worried that after their talk, Ava might change her mind.

Briana disengaged herself from Kim's arms and ran to Ava. "Please stay." Briana wrapped her arms around Ava's waist and held her close. Ava returned the hug.

"I can stay for dinner, but then I have to head back. Unfortunately, I have to work tomorrow. Lucky, you get to go to school." Ava rumpled her hair. "Let's go clean up your room while your mom gets dinner ready."

The time flew by, and Ava worked to push aside her misery over Brian, at least while she interacted with

Briana. Dan came home right before dinner was served, so he didn't have time to talk to Kim about the reason for Ava's visit.

Dinner went as smoothly as possible considering the elephant in the room. With emotions held in check, they kept it together for the most important person in their life: Briana.

****

When Ava arrived home at nearly ten, she was exhausted and depressed. She always hated leaving Briana, and Briana didn't make it easier when she hung on her and begged her to stay over.

Checking the answering machine, there were eight messages from Brian. Initially, they were short and curt. "Call me when you get in." But as the night wore on, he seemed worried. "Where are you? I called the office. They said you took off for the afternoon. Please call as soon as you can."

The last message, which was just a half hour earlier, seemed more desperate. "Ava, if you're screening your calls, please pick up. I need to know you're okay." Then there was silence for a few seconds. "Ava? Please don't ignore me. I really need to talk to you." Silence again. Then he sighed and hung up.

She kicked off her shoes and rid herself of her suit. It had been a long, emotional day from morning till night. She didn't have the strength for a discussion with Brian tonight. But she needed to let him know she was fine—or if not fine in the emotional sense, at least in the physical sense. She tapped out a short text message to assuage his fears.

Tomorrow would be another day.

Chapter Fourteen

An incessant buzzing cut into her dream. Ava peeked at the clock on her bedside table—7:55—an hour later than she usually arose. Jumping up, she attempted to defog her brain and clear her eyes. The buzzing continued. Why was the doorman disturbing her so early in the morning?

Ava stumbled to the intercom adjacent to the front door and spoke. "Yes. What is it, Jeremy?"

"Mr. Stanhope is here to see you," came the formal response. "He says it's very important."

Damn. She closed her eyes, concentrating on an excuse to provide, but none came. "Ask him to come back in a half hour, please." Maybe she could escape between now and then. Although, he'd probably be waiting outside her building on the off chance she did try such a cowardly tactic.

A plan. She needed a plan. Forcing the dust bunnies out of her brain, Ava called work advising her secretary she had the flu. What did she care if it wasn't the season? Next, she got the coffeemaker going, then headed for the shower—her initial goal to wake up, her ultimate goal, to come up with the right words to keep Brian from doing what Kim feared he would.

After donning a pair of well-worn jeans and a white tank top, Ava dried her hair, and banded it in a ponytail. With no time to primp, the buzzer rang. She cursed uncharacteristically and sped to the intercom.

"You can send him up, Jeremy."

Too soon for her druthers, he was at the door. "Hi," she said as she ushered him in.

He nodded, moving past her and into the living room.

His familiar scent swarmed her senses and Ava briefly closed her eyes, craving more. She closed the door, but didn't move toward the seating area where he stood, favoring the distance for her own sanity.

"Where were you yesterday, last night?" A hint of accusation colored his words.

Her mind answered, "What do you care?" but she convinced her mouth to be civil. "I went to see Briana."

He studied her face as if deciding whether to believe her. "Can I sit down?"

"Sure."

"Will you please sit as well?"

Ava contemplated that request, not at all sure she could be still or have a calm conversation with the person who had walked away from her thirty-two hours earlier. But manners won out. At least temporarily. Ava sat on a barrel chair opposite Brian, noticing his pale face and tired eyes. Even sleep deprived, he looked model handsome.

This was his meeting, so she regarded him without speaking.

"Aren't you going to work today?"

Not the question she anticipated. She shrugged. "That was my plan. Until you showed up. What about you?" He also had on jeans and a polo shirt, but maybe he dressed like that in his business once in a while.

"I can't concentrate. I need some answers. More

than I got the other night."

"You mean more than you got before you walked away?" As much as she wanted to be the bigger person, she feared it would be impossible given the circumstances and his reaction. "Maybe you think the child isn't yours?"

"No. I would never question you." He sighed, then dragged his hands through his hair. "I'm sorry I reacted that way. I was in shock. You have to at least give me that."

She wasn't sure she had to give him any leeway, but she decided not to respond with sarcasm. "So, what answers do you want?"

"Tell me about that weekend. About how we met, what we did." He swallowed, visibly uncomfortable. "Tell me how I was with you. What you thought about me."

Ava inhaled. He wanted not only facts, but emotions. The former were easy. The latter would only make her more vulnerable, for what did she know of Brian's feelings that weekend? Only how she interpreted them.

She sat back and hugged her knees to her chest, knowing no matter the outcome, he deserved to know.

Then she told him the story of Brian and Ava—and its epilogue.

****

He let her tell it without interruption. Any questions could wait for later. She actually smiled through some of the telling, like when he spied on her and Carrie in the dance studio or when he surreptitiously grabbed her in the kitchen causing a whisk full of pancake batter to fall on the floor. She touched on their meeting in the gazebo and while horseback riding, going straight to the next scene as if she didn't want to divulge any chemistry they might have been feeling. She spoke animatedly of the first night after her arrival, with just his friends, playing croquet and water polo, again with little talk of any alone time they may have shared. Although she did relay that he brought her back to the guesthouse on a golf cart and then left. He surmised they must have at least kissed, for it wasn't like him to waste an opportunity with a beautiful young woman.

The dinner party he could almost picture. His graduation celebration wasn't the only over-the-top event his family hosted at their Newport residence. She remembered most of his friends' names and reported how nice they'd been to her, even though she was a stranger in their midst. He had to chuckle at that. All his guy friends were probably vying to get into her pants. Unfortunately, he'd been the one to succeed.

"The night before the dinner party, did we steal away and talk?" Although he thought he knew.

Her brow furrowed, but she responded. "Yes. I'd been listening to your friends, and you grabbed two margaritas from the bar and pulled me away, joking that they must be boring me. We went to sit at a table under an old tree. We must have talked for an hour."

A picture of Ava floated across his brain, her long ponytail so shiny and dark, swinging back as forth as she denied something he said. But his eyes were riveted on her long, gorgeous neck and sexy shoulders. He teased her about Carrie abandoning her, and she gave him a shy smile while defending his sister. He tried to hold that snapshot, but it faded, then evaporated,

161

leaving his mind in darkness and confusion.

"Was your hair in a ponytail? Did you have on a halter top?" He held his breath, waiting for her answer.

"Yes." Her deep blue eyes widened. "Do you remember?"

He clawed for another memory. Nothing. "I pictured you for a moment. Then it vanished. Just like before."

Her lids lowered, trying to hide the same disappointment he felt.

She continued. "You were so…smooth. Saying all the things I wanted to hear. I hadn't had much experience. I was so taken with you. You were handsome, of course. And smart and funny. A real leader with your friends. But I also saw a vulnerability. I guess I related to that. Or at least that's how I saw it. Wanted to see it. You seemed trapped by your family, by their ambitions for you." Her eyes met his, as if searching for confirmation. "You had this great, close-knit family, one that I would have sold my soul for, yet, you clearly held some rebellious thoughts about working for the family business."

How had young, naïve Ava seen all that in him in the course of one short weekend? Maybe he had fallen for her. Maybe they were soul mates—although he hated that expression. He searched her face, her eyes, for the answers to his unspoken questions. For how could he ask if he'd been truly interested in her or if she was just one of his conquests—the forbidden fruit? She obviously assumed he was being genuine or she wouldn't have made love with him. Her expression, not his.

He scrubbed his hands over his face, trying to wipe

away the hound-dog image he had of himself and replace it with Ava's "man-in-love" vision: that sweet, sensitive guy who met the woman of his dreams and swept her off her feet. Nausea swirled through his body, and he laid his head back against the cushion and closed his eyes.

"Are you okay?" she asked, concern in her voice.

He sat up. "Why did I have the horse when I came to the guesthouse?"

"You brought it so we could go riding later, after all the lights were out. You said the stars would be incredible."

So he had remembered it correctly the other night. At least he hadn't used that line on anyone else. "And they were."

She nodded. "Yes, it was so amazing. I sat behind you and held on. You wore just your tux pants, no shirt. You pointed out some constellations. It was breathtaking. Then we went back to the guesthouse and made love again before we fell asleep." Her smile faltered. "The next thing I heard was a siren." Ava's whole being caved with the weight of her words. "I threw on my clothes and ran outside. You were already in the ambulance. I begged Carrie to let me go to the hospital with her. I was freaked, devastated, scared. I don't know how many emotions washed through me in those moments, in that day, in all the days that came after."

Ava told him about her dozens of conversations with Carrie, of her trip to the rehab center. She stopped short of baring her feelings for him, but it was evident. Tears glistened in her eyes at reliving those days. He wanted to take her in his arms and hug away the anguish, but he couldn't move from his seat. He had to hear it all. And he did.

Picturing her the morning she fainted during ballet class kicked him in the gut. Hearing the doctor's words telling her she was pregnant, stomped him in the head. He trudged the streets of the City with her as she analyzed her options. Her ultimate decision to have the baby, give her up for adoption, and quit dance so she could help support their child, kneed him in the groin.

Although the pain Ava experienced dealing with all this on her own must have been excruciating, he was now suffering some version of it seven years later. He had a child he didn't know about, a child who missed out on knowing her real father.

"I want to meet her," he blurted out. "She should know her birth father."

Ava's head snapped up in response. "What? Why?"

"What do you mean why? I have a child." His voice escalated with anger at her imprudent question. "Briana should know her natural father. Know he didn't desert her. Maybe I need to get a lawyer involved. Find out my rights."

Ava propelled herself off the chair and hovered over him, her hands balled in fists, as she shouted at him. "So, this is all about you? About how you want to be perceived? The good guy who was kept in the dark." Ava's ire sparked with sarcasm. "What about what's in Briana's best interest? Don't you care about how she'll take this? She doesn't know I'm her mother. She believes Kim and Dan are her parents. They *are* her parents. How could you even think about ruining her safe, loving world?" Dismay strained her face as she berated him, now pacing around the living room.

The mother lion protecting her cub.

She was right. He wasn't thinking about how Briana would react to all this. He hadn't had time to think it through, even though he'd done nothing but think about the fact he had a child since the words rushed out of Ava's mouth the other night.

Before he could retreat, Ava stepped back into the ring to pummel him some more. "I thought you were a better man than that. I always did." She choked back a sob. "Since the first day I met you, even though Carrie warned me about you, about your selfish ways, I saw something different—better. While I may have been naïve back then, when we reconnected, I thought you were amazing. A man with principles, strength, loyalty. I guess I can't trust my instincts." She hung her head, and bit her lip, staring at the floor as a deep sadness took over her whole body.

Dozens of responses zigzagged through his brain. He didn't know where to start.

"I am a better person, Ava. I'm in a place right now that I don't recognize. I'm responding irrationally. Emotions are getting in the way of common sense, but I can't seem to rein them in." He sighed. "You've had time to process all this, make decisions. I've just been thrown into it. I know I'm not dealing very well. You might even say deplorably. But I can't help it."

"Did you tell your family?" she asked, refusing to look at him.

"No."

Something close to relief washed over her face. Of course she would think it was bad enough dealing with him without the whole Stanhope clan weighing in.

"How did you manage to keep this from Carrie back then?"

"She was in Newport at the hospital with you, then the rehab center all summer. When I found out I was pregnant, I transferred to Columbia so Carrie wouldn't see me. Once I dropped out of dance, I wasn't likely to run into her in the City since I wasn't auditioning or taking outside classes."

Brian leaned forward, his forearms on his thighs, hoping to force blood to his brain. "I can understand why you had to stop dancing while you were pregnant. Why didn't you just drop out for a year, and then pick up where you left off? Especially since you decided to give the baby up for adoption."

"I wanted to save money for her college, or whatever else she needed. No matter who adopted her. But once my sister agreed to the adoption, I really needed to help with the finances. Kim and Dan had a lot of debt at the time. I had to make sure Briana wasn't a drain on them. That meant putting my toe shoes away and pursuing a career in which I could earn a decent living."

The weight of her decision bore down on him. She had given up her lifelong goal so their child would be financially secure. All the while knowing that if she had told him about the baby, even if he had brushed her aside as she assumed, he would at least have paid child support. Then she could have been free to pursue dance. Surely she would have been a member of one of the esteemed dance companies in the City given her talent. But she'd given it all up for their child. And that's why she broke off ties with Carrie.

"So your friendship with my sister became a

fatality because you feared you'd resent her for living what should have been your life?"

"Congratulations." The sarcasm was back. "You uncovered my secret."

He flinched at the arrow she zinged. "You're full of secrets."

He was no longer angry, just overwhelmed with the revelations that sprouted from a weekend in Newport. Ava had done what she felt was right, cutting off all contact with her best friend after experiencing first hand Brian's memory loss. The suffering she went through, all alone, tore at his heart.

"I'm sorry for what you had to deal with for the past seven years. But now that I know, I can help. Are there any more secrets I need to know about?"

He had meant to lighten the mood with his question, but a raw and primitive grief took hold and haunted her eyes. "That secret tentacled into many areas of my life. It affected my career, my friendships, my family, and my relationships with men. Everything I did from the day I learned I was pregnant I did because you didn't know who I was. My life changed that weekend when you were injured as much as yours did. No...much more. You eventually healed and went on with your life plans."

Brian pushed his hands through his hair. Frustration and sympathy pulled at his soul. She should have come to him and told him what had happened that weekend, whether he knew who she was or not. Carrie, or one of his friends, would have backed her up, even if he'd acted like an ass and claimed his innocence. Someone must've seen them together flirting with each other. As bad as he might have been in those days, he never hopped into bed with a woman without charming her first. Back then the chase had been just as thrilling as the ultimate conquest.

He stood and went over to her, gently placing his hands on her shoulders as he looked into her glistening eyes. "I'm sorry, Ava. If I hadn't had that damned accident, things would have been different. I can honestly say I don't know if they would have been good different or bad different. But you wouldn't have had to carry all the responsibility and decision-making that came with having my child. You wouldn't have had to bear all the financial responsibility either. Unfortunately, we can't change the past." A lead weight pressed on his chest. "Let's both take some time and think about how to deal with the future."

She nodded, sadness evident in her beautiful eyes as the emotions of the last few hours clearly took their toll.

He kissed her on the forehead wanting desperately to keep a glimmer of hope burning between them. Their relationship had held such potential two days ago. He was falling in love with Ava. But her devastating secret blew up inside him, numbing his heart and soul first with anger, then frustration, then a searing burn as he searched for the right thing to do. His choices were few, but his decision could mean a horrible death for their once-promising liaison.

With no more words left to say, Brian turned and walked to the door, slipping out, as if just a shadow of the man he'd been only days before.

Chapter Fifteen

Ava passed through the lobby on her way to Peter's office, holding a letter from the court setting trial dates in the Delphine matter. Glancing at a client sitting in the corner of the reception area, she froze as her heart hammered. "Brian." His name sprang forth without thought.

His head snapped up, and his jaw muscle clenched signifying what, she didn't know. She swallowed, wishing she'd kept moving instead of calling attention to herself.

"Are you here to see Peter?" She hadn't noticed Brian's name in their computer calendar today, but maybe it was a last minute appointment.

Brian shifted awkwardly in his chair. "No. I'm meeting with Diane Grayson."

Ava stopped breathing. Diane did estate planning. And family law. Was Brian here to try to vacate the adoption? She closed her mouth and tried to inhale, but her heart blocked her lungs. She needed to respond and move on. Now. She nodded, unable to form even one word as her throat clogged. Damn. "Oh," she whispered before darting across the lobby and directly to her office.

Once inside, she closed the door, leaning against it for support. Let's not jump to conclusions, unreasonable ones at that. Brian came from a wealthy family. He could be here to do a will. Putting his affairs in order through an estate plan was not out of the question. Even though he was only twenty-nine. Still, what twenty-nine-year-old thinks of death? Maybe one who could have died seven years earlier.

She refocused on their last conversation. He wanted time to think about how to deal with the future. She'd thought he meant them—as a couple. She hoped giving him the time and space he needed would allow them to get back together. And move forward. Three weeks had passed; waiting for him to work through all this had been excruciating. She ached with the pain of possibly losing the man she had fallen in love with—again.

Over those weeks, the emotions morphed from anger to sadness and then to despair. Trying to ignore it all and move on, Ava worked on her cases until she was bleary eyed. She exercised at the gym until sweat drenched her T-shirt and she could no longer move her rubbery legs. Every night she fell into bed only when she knew exhaustion would render her unconscious, unable to think or even dream. Dreams of Brian acted as her enemy, thoughts of him her destruction.

Tears leaked out of her eyes, unchecked, and splashed onto her suit jacket. Pushing away from the door, she yanked open several drawers looking for tissues before finding a stash of cheap napkins. She blotted her face while attempting to calm down. This was insane.

Talking herself through it, she took some deep breaths. But the thought of Brian taking legal action to vacate the adoption could not be exorcised from her mind. She should have called him. Should have insisted they get together and talk more.

How could he be so callous, coming to her law firm for representation on this very personal matter? Hundreds of firms in the city could have done this apparently necessary piece of legal work. Brian must have at least considered the possibility he'd run into Ava. What an ass! Was he that much of a sadist that he wanted to rub her face in it?

Ava stayed behind her closed door for the next several hours, working to distraction, before a knock interrupted her self-imposed confinement. She cleared her throat, then pinched her cheeks to bring some color to her face. "Come in," she rasped.

Diane Grayson poked her blonde head in. "Are you too busy to chat for a minute?"

Oh. Here she was. Ready to divulge the details of her meeting with Brian. And most likely dying to ask questions burning on the tip of her tongue about their child and the adoption. Ava couldn't bear it.

"I'm sorry, but I'm really busy right now. I have this trial memo to get out by tomorrow." Ava rummaged through some papers, trying to look harried. "Maybe I can catch up with you at the end of the week."

"No problem." Diane shrugged. "I just wanted to thank you for referring Brian Stanhope to me."

"I didn't." Ava's terseness couldn't have been mistaken for anything but anger and she warned herself to tone it down. But she of all people would not have referred Brian to her. "I mean, I didn't know he had an appointment with you until I saw him in the reception area. Maybe Peter gave him your name."

"He wants to set up a trust for the child of a

friend." Diane emphasized the word "friend" as if putting air quotes around it, but Ava ignored the insinuation and focused on her first sentence.

"What? He's not questioning the adop—What did you say?"

"He's doing some estate planning. Although it seems strange. If this trust is for a child he fathered, maybe he'll come around and marry the mother. Who knows? We didn't talk about that. He made it clear he wanted to fund a trust for the health, education, welfare, and support of a child by the name of Briana Reynolds."

Ava's ears buzzed as Diane continued. "Briana is probably his child given the name similarity. Besides, why else would he put a million dollars in trust for a friend's daughter if that daughter weren't his?"

Ava lost her ability to speak as Diane's words collided in her brain. Brian wanted to not only pay for the needs of their child, but assure she would want for nothing. He hadn't come to the office to overturn the adoption. Pure joy bubbled through her, and she had to clasp her hands in her lap to keep her excitement from spilling forth.

Diane's words cut into her celebration. "Are you okay? You look odd."

"Odd? What do you mean?"

"You have this peculiar smile on your face, like you know something." Diane studied Ava while Ava molded her features into a more normal façade.

"No. I didn't know anything about Brian's wish to set up a trust."

"Well, he's naming you as trustee."

"Me?" Ava burst out. "He chose me to be the

trustee?"

Diane nodded. "I would have thought the two of you would have had a conversation about it. But maybe he wanted a lawyer to do it from the firm and decided you were the one, since you and Peter are representing him in his business dealings."

"I'm not representing him. Peter is."

Diane shrugged off her statement. "Just so you know, I did suggest he use a financial institution since it will always be in existence, even if it merges, but he insisted he wanted you." Diane paused, then squinted at Ava. "Do you know the child?"

"No." Ava's voice reverberated around her tiny office. Then she repeated her denial at a more level tone. "What did you say her name was again?"

Diane repeated it, scrutinizing Ava's demeanor, before she continued. "He wanted to see you when he was leaving, but your door was closed. I thought you had a client, but when your door was still closed hours later, I realized you had holed yourself up to get something done. You might want to give him a call to discuss this when you get a chance."

Ava barely nodded. Diane thankfully took Ava's catatonic state as a cue to leave. "I guess you want to get back to your memo. Good luck." Diane gave a half wave and left Ava's office without closing the door.

Oh my god.

Ava rose and rotated her shoulders, feeling stiff and achy. The roller coaster emotions of the day had taken their toll, and a pounding headache pushed itself front and center. She massaged her forehead and closed her eyes. Confusion made it worse. Did Brian have any ulterior motives for doing this? Was he still considering a discussion with a lawyer about vacating the adoption? Maybe he was attempting to soften her up, to make her so grateful that Briana would be taken care of that she wouldn't fight against him if he decided to take legal action.

Fear took root and spread. Ava cautioned herself to slow down. She had already jumped to the wrong conclusion about Brian being at the office. It was unwise and unfair to assume his generosity masked an ulterior motive. Yet, sitting here speculating would only lead to misinformed assumptions. And make her crazy. She had to speak to him. Ava grabbed her purse from the drawer and headed out of the office.

Needing time to formulate her words, she walked the twenty blocks to Brian's building, hardly aware of her surroundings or the oppressive humidity. After locating Stanhope Natural Gas on the marquee next to the elevator, Ava rose to the thirty-third floor in seconds, questioning her judgment the entire ride; she didn't even know if Brian had returned to the office after his meeting with Diane. She shouldn't have acted so impulsively.

Cloaking herself with confidence, she strode to the reception desk as if she had an appointment. "Brian Stanhope, please."

"Your name?"

"Ava Harrington."

"Is he expecting you? He's in a meeting right now."

Damn. Yet, what did she expect? That he'd be sitting in his office waiting for her to show up unannounced?

"Is it possible to interrupt him? It's very important

that I speak with him."

The receptionist looked at her warily, as if she were some stalker. Maybe she was.

"Have a seat and I'll check." She pointed to a sofa in the far corner of the reception area.

Ava moved to the area, but couldn't sit. Nerves bounced around her body like they'd been flung with slingshots.

She jumped when she heard her name, spinning toward the familiar voice. Swallowing her angst, Ava croaked out her request. "Can we talk? In private?"

Mr. Stanhope appeared behind Brian, a concerned look on his face. "Is everything all right?"

Brian never took his eyes off Ava. "Fine, Dad. I'll come by your office later to finish our discussion."

"Good to see you, Ava," said Brian's father, in a friendly, but formal voice, as he turned to leave. *What did he know? Had Brian told him anything? Everything?*

"Let's go to my office." Brian's tone couldn't be considered warm, yet it wasn't frosty. He had to know she'd hunt him down after learning about the trust.

She walked in his trail down a long corridor, the entire time tamping down the moths wreaking havoc on her insides. They finally reached their destination, a corner office with a view of eastern Manhattan. But she couldn't appreciate it at this moment. The words running helter-skelter around her brain screamed to get out.

Brian closed the door, and she leaned against it for support. He stood inches from her, his clear blue eyes trained on hers, sending a searing heat over her skin.

She felt her lips part, and a word escaped. "Why?"

He closed the minute gap between them and covered her mouth with his, kissing her so softly, so tenderly, a gasp of surprise seeped between them. He broke the connection without backing away, as if to ask her permission to continue. Her scrambled brain shot warnings to her heart and even voiced an opinion. *Protect yourself. Don't go there again.* But her heart rejected the counsel as Ava kissed Brian back, surrendering to the exquisite feeling of his lips against hers, his tongue intertwined with hers, his breath mingled with hers.

Coming to her senses, Ava disengaged from him, then closed her eyes and inhaled for the strength she needed. "We have to talk. My emotions are so close to the surface right now. I need some space." She slipped out of his circle and moved toward a seating area with a couch and two chairs. "Is this okay?"

"Of course." Brian followed as they took a chair catty-corner to each other.

"Diane told me why you were meeting with her. I have to be honest. I thought you were there to find out your rights with regard to the adoption. It just about killed me." Could she make herself any more vulnerable?

"So that's why you looked so pale. And so eager to get away." The muscle in Brian's jaw worked overtime. "I hoped you and I would have had a chance to talk at your office. But you were so skittish before my meeting and unavailable after."

He took her hand and massaged her palm with his thumb, sending flashes of fire through her veins.

"Thank you for setting up the trust for Briana." Ava eased her hand from his, immediately regretting the disconnection but needing the space to continue on. "But I'm still confused. Have you decided to attempt to vacate the adoption? Is that why you set up the trust?"

Shock etched his face. "You think I would go behind your back?"

"Brian, I haven't seen or heard from you in three weeks." Her voice escalated with her distress. "Why would I think you would include me in your decision, especially if that's the route you were choosing to take? I've been on pins and needles just waiting for the tearful call from my sister that she'd been served." Ava stood and started pacing, unable to find the calm she promised she'd exert once in Brian's presence.

As she passed by Brian's chair, he grabbed her wrist, then stood to face her. "I didn't realize you don't trust me." His piercing gaze held anger and hurt.

"You disappeared from my life twice already. While the first time it was through no conscious act, the cut was deep. The second time you twisted the knife. How much do you think I can take?" Tears stung the backs of her eyes, but she refused to release them. She refused to cry in front of Brian. "What would make me trust you?"

"My feelings for you." The words were murmured like a prayer, quiet and reverent. They floated and danced around Ava like a beautiful ballet.

Yet, the big question taunted Ava even after, or perhaps despite, his surprising declaration. And she had to ask, without accusation, without anger. "Why didn't you call?"

He shook his head, as if to deny the fact. "I had a lot to work through, and until I did, I knew I couldn't expect you to deal with me. I had to wrap my head around the past and what happened that weekend. What happened after that weekend. What I was like, how I handled my dating relationships, or maybe more accurately, my non-relationships. I tried to picture—recreate—our meeting. How we interacted. I dug deep to try to find us back then." Brian sat and tugged on Ava to do the same. "My memory wasn't kind. I asked Carrie about that weekend. My father, too."

"Oh my god! Did you tell them about Briana?" Ava's stomach plummeted and she felt nauseous.

"No. Although we're not secret keepers in our family, I wasn't ready to share this with them. I wanted you to be on board. You and I need to be on the same page about moving forward."

Ava sagged with relief but knew it was temporary. "Were they able to help you remember?"

"While I reconnected with some of our time together, I also remembered other dates, other conquests. I'd like to blame my actions on my youth back then. I did come to the realization that if you had told me about the pregnancy, I would have begged you to get an abortion. I would have been kind and doting, and of course I would have paid for everything. Even taken you on a vacation to heal. But with as much as I'd like to think I would have stepped up to the plate and stood by your side with whatever decision you made, I don't know that to be true."

Brian glanced at Ava, embarrassment clear in every muscle of his face as he continued. "From that realization, I had to jump ahead to now. I heard you loud and clear that morning in your apartment. How Briana only knows your sister and brother-in-law as her parents. What it would do to her security to find out something different before she was ready. I knew you were right." He loosened his tie as if to finally relax a bit. "I believe you when you say your sister is a good mother. I trust your judgment. As long as Briana is safe and happy and cared for, you have my word I will do nothing to interfere. Assuming that to be true, I still needed to do something to acknowledge my paternity and to take care of this person who is my responsibility. Every thought I had over the past few weeks was colored by what you did, your sacrifices, what you went through, how you handled it."

He now looked straight into Ava's eyes. "You're an amazing woman. Strong, focused, and committed. Since I respect you, I respect your decisions. I will continue to respect them and won't do anything to undermine them. You have my word."

Ava tried to swallow the knot in her throat. "Thank you" was all she could manage as the tension of the last three weeks began to unravel and ease.

"While I was analyzing my life, my choices, I thought it best to keep you out of it. I worked nonstop." A small smile played across his lips. "Not seeing you worked wonders for our company's bottom line."

Ava raised her brow in question.

Brian took both of her hands in his. "I never want to work that hard again." His smile bloomed into one of her favorite features. "Unless it's with you."

Chapter Sixteen

Ava cautiously agreed to a date on Saturday, and Brian had to respect that. He knew her fear was grounded in experience: two excruciating experiences involving him. In an effort to keep it simple and free from recent memories, he omitted the ballet, the theater, sports, and home goods shopping.

He chose a tiny Italian restaurant in Tribeca where the ambiance was far from upscale, but the food was excellent. She'd chosen to meet him there, a clear indication Ava was still skittish about accepting his invitation.

Brian waited outside, scanning left then right, before spotting her in the distance walking, no…gliding, toward him. She still had that ballet poise, that ballet walk with her toes turned out slightly, even though she wore heeled sandals instead of dance slippers. A photo flash of a younger Ava in a black mini skirt and white halter-top imposed itself on his brain. His heartbeat quickened as he struggled to expand the memory, to feel the excitement of that long ago flirtation, to keep it alive.

Brian placed his hand on Ava's back as they walked across some uneven terrain toward the east yard. Carrie stood in the middle of the croquet green contemplating where to place the rest of the white wire hoops she held in her hand.

"Great. You started without me." Brian strode toward her and directed where the rest of the wickets should go.

"It's about time you got here."

"I was playing the good host to your friend. Showing her around the property, so she wouldn't get lost." He showcased his innocent smile, not needing to advise Carrie of his not-so-innocent thoughts where her friend was concerned.

Carrie turned to Ava. "I hope Brian was a gentleman."

Ava blushed. "Of course. He's been very nice." She glanced at Brian and those gorgeous almost-purple eyes sparkled. *"Can I help with anything?"* She moved away from Brian. Probably a good thing so Carrie couldn't detect any stray electricity bolting between them.

"No, thanks. I'm just about done."

Brian picked up a mallet and ball. "Come over here, Ava. I'll give you a quick lesson, so you won't feel like a novice when the tournament starts."

She glanced at Carrie before strolling over to him. He gave her the mallet, then stood behind her, placing his arms over hers, cocooning her against his body as he demonstrated the swing. The slight hint of flowers tickled his nose, and he turned his head toward hers to breathe in more.

Delicious.

Attempting to hide his unmistakable lust, he let her go. "Try not to dig up the grass," he teased, giving her a friendly chuck under her chin. Although he wanted to do so much more.

"Hi, Brian. Are you okay?" she asked. The two

Ava's melded into the one standing in front of him.

He blinked to focus, took her hand and brought it to his lips. "Hi." He felt his smile take over his face. While younger Ava was gone, the feeling wasn't. It was deeper, stronger, all encompassing. "I'm great, now that you're here. Thanks for coming tonight."

Her sideways glance as they entered the restaurant, told him she was questioning his odd greeting. But he didn't want to reveal his memory flash given his immediate attraction to her that long ago weekend. It would only punctuate his penchant for going after beautiful women upon first sight.

"Brian, how good to see you." A chef, in his mid-fifties, came from behind the counter dividing the restaurant from the open kitchen. "Where have you been?"

"Tony, it's great to see you. Unfortunately, I've been busy with work. Not eating out much." Brian turned to Ava. "This is Ava Harrington. Ava, Tony Calabrese, the owner of this place, along with his wife, Nina."

Ava smiled warmly and shook hands with the man, who welcomed her just as enthusiastically. After some small talk, Tony described the evening specials, making every one sound like nectar from the gods. They were seated by the window and fussed over like long lost family members. A pitcher of water, a bottle of wine and a basket of warm flaky bread appeared without request, and even though Tony had asked for their order, he then recommended putting their meal together to give them a taste of several entrees. Who could argue with that?

Perhaps this wasn't the restaurant to go to if Brian

had any thought of winning Ava back through scintillating conversation. "Maybe, I should have chosen a more anonymous place for our date tonight."

"This is perfect." Ava sipped her wine. "It's charming and warm and family oriented. Just like you." Her beautiful eyes sparkled with her words.

"Wait till you taste the food. It's better than anything you've experienced outside of Italy." A fleeting conversation passed through his head during which Ava told him she had never travelled to Europe but hoped to someday.

"Have you been to Italy yet?" Perhaps she'd had the chance to experience the amazing food, people, and culture of his favorite European country during the last few years.

"No. I never had the money. I have student loans and I'm saving for Briana—in case she ever needs it."

"Now that she has a trust set up for her, maybe you can take a well-deserved vacation."

A shadow fell over Ava's face, removing all light. Uh-oh. What did he say to produce that reaction?

"I really appreciate you're making sure Briana is financially secure, but that doesn't rid me of my obligation. I want to contribute to her needs as well and I will continue to do it, as I have in the past, despite your generosity."

An icy blast accompanied her words. Not good.

Brian reached across the table and took her hand. "I didn't mean to imply you would or should turn your back on Briana. I just thought that since I now know about her and I'm able to help you share the burden, it would free up some of your funds to do something you couldn't do in the past."

"Taking care of Briana is not a burden." Mama lion's eyes locked on his as she pulled her hand away.

This wasn't at all going as intended. "I misspoke. An unfortunate choice of words." He held his hands up in defeat. "I'd been hoping to have a nice dinner, re-connect, stay away from flammable topics. But you seem bent on finding fault in everything I say."

Her rigid back relaxed, and her eyes softened. "I'm sorry." She shook her head. "But it bothers me that you could just plop a million dollars into a trust account for our child and think, presto, she's taken care of. I've been saving as much as I could afford, each week since she was born, and there is little to show for it."

Money was never a good topic for discussion, even under the best of circumstances, and in this instance, it forewarned of a disastrous end to their already-shaky reconciliation.

Brian put on his best face. "Let's start over. We'll have a nice conversation about the weather, or recreational activities in the park, or something else non-threatening. Then we'll build up slowly to more controversial subjects, like politics or sports. Maybe we can wait for our third or fourth date to start sparring over money."

Ava chuckled. It was almost a laugh, and Brian's mood soared.

"You're on," she said. "So what do you think about this weather? It's hot and humid. Perfect for August."

Brian's ego gave himself a high-five. He'd managed to turn it around, at least until the following minefield. For the next hour, they ate wonderful food, interacted with Tony and Nina, and laughed about last week's episode of *Saturday Night Live*.

"Are you going to your sister's for the Labor Day weekend?' he asked, holding his breath that this was an acceptable topic.

"I don't think so. I'd rather spend time with Briana when no one else is around. On holidays, my father is there. Sometimes Kim invites neighbors."

"What do you do on holidays if you don't spend them with your family?"

Ava bit her lip. "Nothing much. If my friend Amy is around, maybe we'll go to the movies or a museum."

"I don't get it. I mean, I know you're not close with your father, but he is your dad. And you are close to Kim, Dan, and Briana. Why would you hang around the City when you could get away for a day, maybe even a weekend, and enjoy it?"

Ava twisted the ring on her finger. "I don't want to spend time with someone who abandoned me." She bent her head down, shielding her eyes.

"Have you ever talked to your father, as an adult, to find out why he did what he did?'

"No. We don't really talk. Other than to say hi or engage in small talk, which means nothing. The only time I see him is at Kim's, if I'm there visiting Briana, and I generally spend most of my time with her. Alone."

"He's never asked you why you're giving him the cold shoulder after all these years?"

"No."

How could a family live like that? His family was just the opposite. They had to talk everything out, whether you wanted to or not. If Brian showed up for dinner with a frown on his face, they would question him to death until they learned about the problem, dissected it, and solved it. Ava's family was the complete opposite. Presumably, if you didn't acknowledge the problem, it didn't exist. No wonder Ava had been so secretive about Briana after they re-connected. She'd been raised to keep everything in, no matter how traumatic.

"I'm going to Newport. Would you like to come?"

Ava held up her hand. "Oh, no. Never. I don't think I could ever go back there."

Sadness twisted in Brian's gut. "Why? That's where we met. Where we..." Could he dare say it? *Where we made love, conceived our child?*

"My most distinct memories start with sirens and end with your memory loss. Of me." She shook her head. "Maybe someday I'll be able to shut them out and replace them with the good times I had...we had, there."

He hadn't thought of that. "I could stay here in the City. We could do something."

"No. You go. Be with your family. That's nice." Ava nodded her head, trying to convince Brian, or maybe herself, that he should go and she should stay.

For the second time tonight he realized, embarking on this relationship with Ava would be much more difficult than he imagined.

"So, you won't spend Labor Day with me. Is there any chance you'll agree to accompany me to the Manhattan Ballet's Gala in a few weeks? My parents bought a table and expect me to be there. Preferably with a date."

Ava raised her brow. "How many dates have accompanied you to your various social events over the past three weeks?"

Brian sighed. Another minefield. "One or two. No one I cared about."

Ava lowered her lids, refusing to allow Brian to see the disappointment in her eyes. "I guess you didn't really work nonstop."

Nothing he could say would make this better. Of course, running a major facet of his father's company demanded he make appearances at charity events and invite business associates to sports venues. Even so, none of that required a date.

"If I showed up alone at the Aids Gala or the Opera Ball, I would have been fair game for every attending single woman or mother trying to match-make. It was easier for me to take one of our unattached female employees or a daughter of one of our business contacts. They knew I was unavailable. They knew they were just a shill. I never asked anyone to come with me more than once, so as not to give the wrong impression. Ava, I never once thought of any of them as a date, in your sense of the word."

"Given your history, it's hard to imagine you wouldn't fall back into your bad boy ways given half a chance."

"I told you when we first met—re-met—that I've come a long way from those days." While he hated to bring up Terri, he felt the need. "I'm clearly a monogamist. I dated Terri for almost four years." He held up his hand. "I know talking about Terri may not be the wisest thing either, but I'm trying to make a point here."

She connected with his eyes, allowing several very long seconds to pass. Then a slow smile inched over her lips. "You're sweating."

He finally exhaled, returning her smile. "You're killing me, Ava."

Back on even ground, if not yet solid, Brian and Ava bantered back and forth, at least now in a teasing way. They finished their wine, passed up dessert, and Brian feared their time together was coming to an end.

"Before we got derailed, I had asked you to come with me to the Manhattan Ballet Gala. Will you? Please?"

"As a date or a shill?" Ava's eyes sparkled with mischief.

"A shill, of course," he teased. "Carrie would love to see you again. She's been in my ear about where you've been."

"What did you tell her?'

"That you work a lot. That it was hard for us to find time to get together."

Ava's eyes clouded. "A great excuse. I use it all the time."

"You don't accept invitations for dates?"

"Not usually. It seems a waste of time. Guys aren't looking for relationships. They're looking to get laid."

"That's a very negative conclusion to draw, Ms. Harrington. So, do I understand from that comment you want a relationship?"

"Yes." She looked straight into Brian's eyes as if daring him to get up and walk away. "I've been on my own for a long time. I'd like to share my life with someone special. Someone who has the same goals and dreams."

"Which are?"

"To work hard, but to enjoy life. Take advantage of the museums and theater and ballets. Experience the arts as they were meant to be experienced. To travel. See the places I've only read about."

"What about having children?" While worried about the emotions this question would generate, he needed to know the answer.

"Yes. I want children. That I could raise. Not right now. But in a few years."

He breathed a sigh of relief. "I believe our goals and dreams are in alignment. Perhaps, you shouldn't write me off so quickly."

"What makes you think I'm writing you off? I'm here, aren't I?" Her lips quirked, showing the tiniest bit of amusement.

"Yes, but with one foot out the door. You didn't want me to pick you up tonight. I'm sure it's because you have no plans to spend the night with me. You still haven't answered my question about coming to the Gala. You seem very suspecting of me, even though I've tried to put your fears to rest."

She sighed. "Yes, I will come to the Gala with you. Just to assure you don't take an employee or daughter of a business colleague. I don't have anything to wear though. I assume it's black tie."

"Yes. We can go shopping tomorrow. It should be easy to find something for you. You'd look great in a potato sack." Some angst slipped off his shoulders.

"I am not going shopping with you. I like to shop alone." At least she smiled with her statement.

"Fine." He glanced around. "We're the last ones in here. Can I convince you to come back to my place? We can continue our conversation about our symbiotic goals and dreams."

"Do you have ulterior motives, Mr. Stanhope?"

"Of course. I want to slip that pretty top and skirt off your incredible body and make love to you. For hours." The teasing cadence left his voice. "I miss you, Ava. I want to sleep next to you and wake up with you and spend time with you."

She seemed to consider his plea as she studied his face. Then she bit her lip, a familiar trait that bided her time to wrestle with her response. "I brought work home to do tomorrow."

Ah. The work card. "Okay. We can go to your place then." He gave her his most engaging grin.

She rolled her eyes. Adorable. "Fine. Let's go."

Triumph rained over him. At least tonight, he broke through her armor. He'd have to work doubly hard to ensure she didn't shield herself in it again.

****

Although he had been in Ava's apartment before, Brian had never really noticed its eclectic mix of ruffled femininity, sleek modern edges, and dance memorabilia. A bookcase contained photo books of some of the greats: Rudolf Nereyev, Mikhail Baryshnikov, Martha Graham, Gelsey Kirkland. Interspersed were fragile porcelain figurines of willowy ballerinas striking dancer's poses. The walls were painted in a tannish-pink color making the living room warm and inviting, despite the clean, stark lines of the furniture dominating the center of the room. Modern art and ballet prints graced the walls with not one family photograph amongst her possessions. At least not in view.

Until he noticed one small frame almost hidden behind a stack of books. Ava…in toe shoes, one pointed foot holding up the rest of her body, the other

190

defying gravity behind her, raised almost to her head. She wore a white leotard and tutu, looking ever the professional ballerina. Stunning.

"When was this taken?"

She grabbed it from his hand and placed it back in its spot. "At NYU."

"You look beautiful. Almost ethereal. "

Ava blushed. "Carrie took it at one of my performances. It's the only photo I kept from back then."

She moved away and started fluffing the pillows on the couch. "Would you like something to drink?" She hurriedly tidied the living room of a few stray items of clothing, clearly uncomfortable with him seeing a snapshot into her past.

He pulled her toward him. "Stop. You don't have to clean up for me. And I don't want anything to drink. I just want to hold you. For now." He hugged her to him, feeling her warm body fit against his—interlocking pieces to a puzzle. He breathed in her familiar flowery scent. "I missed you." He closed his eyes, wanting only to experience Ava in his arms.

She whispered against his chest, sliding her arms around him. "I missed you, too."

He smiled, as his lips grazed her head. "Was that hard for you to say?"

She nodded. "I'm very vulnerable, where you're concerned."

He pulled away enough to lift her chin, needing to look into her eyes. To let her see into him. "I'm vulnerable too, you know. We've had two beginnings and two ends. Although I never intended to end this with you when I walked away a few weeks ago. I just needed some time and space. I'm done with that. I hope you can learn to trust me again. Trust me not to walk away. I know you have issues with your parents. How devastated you are by their actions. And I've compounded that grief not only once but twice. I need you to give me another chance, Ava."

Her gaze clouded but her voice was clear. "Yes, I was hurt by my parents. It's made me stronger. Our issues—yours and mine—are different. I understand them. But I have to reenter this relationship with caution."

He nodded. "As long as you're willing to try again, that's all I can ask."

She bit her lip, and he smoothed his thumb over it, hoping to release the tension that small habit signified. Then he lowered his head and did what he'd wanted to all night, kissing her with all the pent-up passion he'd stored since their last encounter. Ava was his drug, and although he'd gone through the worst of his withdrawal during the past three weeks, being back in her arms spiraled his addiction to new heights.

Breaking the kiss just long enough to lead her to the bedroom, he found her lips again, allowing his tongue to explore every inch of her delicious mouth as his hands trailed over the silky skin of her arms and shoulders. Needing to feel more, he grasped the hem of her top and eased it over her head before tossing it on the floor. A white lacy bra diverted his gaze, and he brushed his fingers over the tops of her breasts, mesmerized by the sexy contours of her creamy skin spilling out of the delicately etched material. Delicious.

He bent his head to flick his tongue over her taut nipple, which strained against its confines. He sucked it through the material, while he fondled the other. Ava's moan sent erotic signals to his shaft, turning it to granite. He wanted—needed to be inside her. Now. With deft fingers, he reached around her back and tugged on the zipper of her skirt, letting it fall to the floor at her feet. Thankfully, Ava's fingers flew over the buttons on his shirt before flashing over the closure on his pants, disposing of them, along with his briefs, in a miraculous minute.

He snapped the front clasp of her bra, and slid the straps over her arms, before sliding her bikini panties down those toned, shapely legs. When he stood, Ava molded herself to his body, her breasts pressed to his chest, his erection against her belly. Her skin was so hot it burned, yet her hands felt cool as they roamed over his shoulders and caressed his neck, heightening the pleasure in every nerve ending until it blended with a delectable pain. He grabbed a condom, rolled it on, and pulled her to the bed, no longer able to withstand the sweet torture. He moved over top of her, then dipped his mouth to possess her, mating with her, loving her.

Ava opened her legs, a carnal invitation. He seized her hips and raised them, the tip of his penis throbbing against her opening, before easing into her, filling her. Total ecstasy. A gasp escaped parted lips as her walls imprisoned him. He drove hard and fast, willing her to come quickly for fear he couldn't keep control much longer. And she did. Her spasms convulsed around him as she called his name, sending him to the same place. He held her close, needing to drink in every inch of his vice, while satisfying the craving that sprang deep in his heart.

Chapter Seventeen

Ava slipped into the royal blue strapless gown that had hijacked her attention that crazy, wonderful, thrilling night she'd spent walking the streets of New York with Brian. Made of silk with a chiffon overlay, it was gathered in the back and fanned out to the floor and beyond. She had studied every inch of the fabric decorated with a modest amount of Zvorski crystals on the bodice allowing it to shimmer in the light. She recalled that Brian liked it. Or said something to the effect she would look good in it. Was this gown right for the gala? Or was it too over-the-top?

She inched her feet into silver strappy heels and grabbed her clutch just as the doorman buzzed the intercom. Waiting for Brian's slow ride up in the elevator, Ava paced her living room, the filmy train rising with her movement and floating behind her like butterfly wings. She felt beautiful, elegant, rich.

The knock on the door sent her stomach somersaulting. She held her hand to her abdomen and fought the mixture of anxiety and excitement as she gave herself one last look in the hall mirror before opening the door.

Brian gave a soft whistle confirming she'd made the right decision. "Do you like it?"

He swallowed, his adam's apple working above his black tie and white collar. "You look amazing. That's the dress we saw in some store window on our first date, isn't it?"

"You're very observant for a guy." She smiled. "I struggled with whether to buy it or not. I wasn't sure what people wore to the Ballet Gala."

Brian chuckled. "You are going to turn heads, mine included. Every man there will be jealous of me."

Fireworks exploded around her as he kissed her on the cheek and led her out of her apartment. On the elevator, he whispered against her neck. "Beautiful." Just one word, but it sent delicious shivers down her spine.

A limousine waited for them at the curb, and Ava slid in. He sidled close and slipped his arm through hers. "Thank you for agreeing to come tonight. It means a lot."

It meant a lot to her as well. Brian was inviting her into his world despite the thorny issue of her recently revealed secret. She glanced at him, and his smile melted any trailing angst. He lifted her chin so their eyes locked. "I adore you, Ava." He lowered his head and brushed his lips against hers, slow and seductive and teasing.

These thrilling words and caring actions had her spinning under his spell. She threaded her fingers into perfectly layered thick blond hair and increased the pressure as she drank him in, mating her tongue with his. A soft moan escaped, and Brian gradually pulled away.

"If we keep this up, I'm going to ask the driver to head back to your place instead of going to the Gala."

"You can't," she said. "You have to at least let me wear this dress for the evening."

He arched an eyebrow. "All night my hands will be itching to slide that thing off you."

"I like where your mind is. It proves I'm not just a shill." Ava couldn't help the smile that took over her mouth as she teased him.

His eyes darkened, and his expression grew serious. "I wish you knew what you mean to me."

Brian's declaration speared her heart and entered her soul. The words "I love you" sat on the edge of her tongue, but if she spoke them out loud, she'd open herself up to him—again. She just couldn't put herself out there. Instead she took his hand and kissed his fingers. "I'm glad we found each other again." If it could only work this time.

Entering the Waldorf's Grand Ballroom, Ava's eyes darted in every direction, taking in the theme of an evening in Paris. Lights twinkled in the ceiling made to look like a starry night above projected images of the Eiffel Tower, Notre Dame Cathedral, and the Palace of Versailles. The tables were covered in navy tablecloths with silvery overlays, and the centerpieces of lighted tapers and white peonies made the room look elegant even though it was huge.

Brian perused the crowded venue and quickly homed in on his family as if he had a tracking device. Carrie was the first to greet them.

"Ava, I'm so glad you could make it." She hugged her, then stepped back and studied her appearance. "You look amazing. Where'd you find such a gorgeous gown?"

"Me. Look at you." Ava took in Carrie's stunning aqua strapless sheath, which enhanced the color of her eyes. "No one can compare to our Prima Ballerina."

Carrie glowed. "I've missed you so much. Who would have thought when we were at NYU together, we'd be dressed in designer gowns celebrating a new dance season at the Waldorf?"

A jabbing barb pricked her soul, but Ava inhaled to lessen its sharpness. Their plan at NYU encompassed both of them headlining major dance companies, not just Carrie. But Ava couldn't ruin Carrie's night. Instead, she smiled at her friend. Carrie had been born to attend galas at the Waldorf and dress in Valentino. Yet, she never made Ava feel like her poor relation. Time hadn't changed Carrie, even though now she was one of the guests of honor at an important event.

"I'm so proud of you, Carrie. You accomplished what you set out to do." While the sentiment sliced at her heart, she was truly ecstatic for Carrie's well-deserved position in the renowned dance company.

"Thank you. That means a lot coming from you. And I can't tell you how happy I am that you're dating Brian. It will assure I'll see you once in a while." She linked her arm through Ava's. "It's such a lark that Brian brought us together after all this time. As soon as the season is over, let's plan a weekend together. Maybe in Newport. I want to hear all about our lost years. Even if it makes me cry."

If she only knew. Ava kept a smile pasted on her lips and agreed to get together, although she wasn't at all sure she'd go through with it. Especially in Newport. Only time would tell how Brian wanted to deal with this news and share it with his family. She shuddered to think how Carrie would react. His parents were a whole different story.

After saying hello to Mr. and Mrs. Stanhope, who

greeted everyone with the same conservative enthusiasm—after all, they were huge benefactors of the Manhattan Ballet and had a little something to do with its star performer—Ava happily settled into the role of Brian's date. He introduced her to some of the other members of the ballet company, business acquaintances, and friends.

"You know a lot of people."

"It comes with running a business. You never know where your next client is going to come from, so we spread our antennas in every direction."

"Is that why you're out so many nights?"

He nodded. "I try to choose wisely. But there are dozens of events a month among the different Chambers of Commerce, business groups, and charitable organizations. I'm lucky if I get to spend one or two nights at home." He wrapped his arm around her waist and pulled her in close, whispering against her ear. "Of course, if there's a chance of spending the night with you instead of attending some networking event, I'd be happy to send my regrets."

He lingered at the side of her neck, sending shivery tingles through her body. A spontaneous smile erupted, and she turned into his embrace, wanting nothing more than to imprison his lips and enjoy a long, seductive kiss. But they were in the middle of a ballroom filled with people—people Brian knew.

She arched her eyebrow. "I intend to test you on that offer."

"You don't believe me?" His eyes sparked with mischief.

"Let's just say I believe you thrive on the social scene. But I'm not beyond bribing."

"With sex, I hope." The sparkle in his eyes turned to fire, and Ava felt the heat sear her skin.

Just then the chairwoman of the event tapped on the microphone and invited everyone to take their seats.

Brian blew out a breath. "Don't think this conversation is over." His husky voice betrayed barely hidden lust, promising more than mere chitchat later on. And frankly, she couldn't wait.

They sat at a table near the front with Brian's parents, Carrie and her latest beau, and two other couples who were good friends of the Stanhopes. The conversation was lively. Ava participated as much as possible, while Brian distracted her with his hand floating up and down her thigh. He had clearly orchestrated their seating arrangements, since she sat to his left, while the slit of her gown was on the right. And on more than one occasion she swallowed a shriek as warm fingers found their way beneath that slit.

Barely breathing, she grasped his hand from traveling any further, then whispered in his ear. "If you keep that up, I may just have an inner-body experience."

A coy smile moved over his lips. "Is that a possibility?"

"If you don't stop teasing me, I can't be held responsible."

He groaned under his breath. "Let's leave now."

Ava chuckled at his impatience. And she was right there with him. "I wish we could. But the live auction is starting in a few minutes. Maybe we can escape after that."

With twenty items on the auction block, it didn't appear they'd be released anytime soon, but the spirited bidding was catchy, and bidding wars over simple items like season tickets to the fall performances raised thousands. The last item was a sapphire and diamond necklace, and Ava's heartbeat increased at the thought they'd soon be on their way. She barely paid attention to the bids until Brian held up his hand to enter the fray. Surprised he was interested, she kept her comments to herself. He obviously wanted to support his sister's dance company and drive up the price. He surely wouldn't outbid the bald-headed gentleman in the back who wanted the necklace for his model girlfriend.

Until he did.

When the auction chairperson brought the necklace to Brian, he handed her his credit card. While he waited for the receipt, he opened the velvet box, took out the necklace and placed it around Ava's neck. In front of everyone.

Mrs. Stanhope's brows nearly disappeared into her hairline, and Mr. Stanhope grinned awkwardly. Carrie's eyes widened as did her mouth.

"What are you doing?" Ava asked through a tight smile.

"I'm giving you a necklace, since it won't look good on me."

"You can't do that."

"Why not? It goes perfectly with your gown." A confused look shadowed his eyes.

Unable to continue the conversation in front of his family and friends, whose bewildered countenances belied their polite congratulations on his purchase, Ava suggested as calmly as possible that they leave.

Brian quickly came up with a plausible excuse that he had an early morning tennis game, giving Ava the impetus to stand and say her farewells. "It was so nice to see you all tonight, and I hope to see you again soon." She went around the table and either kissed or shook hands with each guest as appropriate. "Carrie, congratulations on helping to raise so much money for your company. I can't wait to see the new season." They hugged one last time, and Ava took hold of Brian's arm as they exited.

"You shouldn't have done that," she reiterated, fingering the pendant that graced her neck.

"What? Bought you a necklace?"

"Yes. It's too expensive. I can't accept it."

"I don't understand why you can't accept a gift gracefully." Annoyance punctuated his words.

"I don't mean to be difficult. But I feel I'm being manipulated in some way. First the trust for Briana, now this. You're overwhelming me." She glanced at Brian to see if her words had been too harsh.

His jaw clenched, but he kept his eyes straight ahead as they neared the limo.

"I've been independent and self-supporting for a long time," she continued. "I don't need anyone to take care of me."

Brian followed her into the back seat of the car and gave instructions to the driver before slamming the door. "You really can't trust anyone, can you?" His eyes flashed in barely hidden anger, but he kept his voice even. "I bought you a necklace at a fundraiser that I thought you would love. I am not going to apologize for giving you a gift. I am hardly taking care of you." Brian threw up his hands and his piercing gaze challenged her. "And how you can bring the Trust into this is beyond me."

She shook her head and swallowed. Brian was right. He homed in on her issue as soon as he began talking. "I do have a hard time with trusting others." The words stuck in her throat but she willed them to come out. "But I also noticed the expressions on your parents' faces. Even Carrie. Like they couldn't believe how much money you just spent on me."

"I don't give a crap about my family's expressions or whether they approve or disapprove of my spending. I'm a grown man. I work hard for my money, and I can do with it what I please."

Ava's voice escalated in frustration. "Everything you do, you do to get their approval. You work for your father's company, you have lunch with your mother once a week, you go to all Carrie's performances in New York."

"And you have a problem with any one or all three of those things?"

She grimaced at her own complaints. "No. You're lucky to have a wonderful family whom you adore." Could she really be calling him out on that? "I'm just not sure how I fit in, or even whether I do. They loved Terri. You told me so yourself. I'm a stranger who definitely doesn't come from the same background."

"You're a lawyer, for god's sake. A respected professional. Why would you think you wouldn't fit in with my family? You were one of Carrie's closest friends in college. You're hardly a stranger. She's dying to reestablish that friendship."

His words punctured a hole in her misplaced anger, fueled by insecurities. She sighed, hopefully releasing whatever tension still remained. "What do you think they'll do when they find out about Briana?"

"So that's it. That's what's bothering you. It's not the necklace."

She turned her head and stared out the window as they inched up Broadway. Brian grabbed her hand and squeezed it. That small gesture allowed the knot in her gut to loosen.

"They won't do anything. They will follow our lead and bow to our wishes."

She placed her hand over the necklace. "Thank you for this." Her throat tightened. She needed to get back to a good place with him after going off the deep end the last half hour. "Brian...I love you." The words slipped out unchecked, but she didn't care. She needed to say them, even if he didn't reciprocate.

His head snapped around, and the hard lines of his face softened. A slow smile curved his lips. "Are you just saying that so I'll forgive you for your irrational behavior?"

He was giving her an out, but she didn't want it. "No. I'm saying it because it's true." She allowed him to see the honesty in her eyes, in her soul.

He caressed her cheek with trailing fingers and penetrated her gaze with his. "I love you, too."

His words wound around her heart while his lips moved over hers in a demanding crush that had her seeking more. She'd never get enough of his kisses, and she claimed more with her mouth until his became hot and insistent, pulling her under his spell. His tongue danced with hers before feathering kisses across her face, then tracing her sensitive ear lobe. Tingles shot to her extremities, eliciting a moan that could probably be heard by the driver despite the privacy shield. His tongue travelled down her neck sending wild sensations to all her erogenous zones. He found his way back to her mouth before disconnecting his lips from hers. "I think we've been in front of your building for a while. Let's go upstairs and get naked."

Ava closed her eyes and inhaled, attempting to rein in her hormones, at least for the few minutes it would take them to get from the seclusion of the limo to the privacy of her residence. "I'm ready."

As soon as the elevator doors shut, Brian cornered her in an embrace and backed her against the wall, imprisoning her with his hard body and insistent lips. Fireworks shot through her system as she sought his lips, devouring them with untamed ardor. Brian pulled her into him, hugging her while assaulting her mouth with a primal passion that built within. His hands were everywhere, in her hair, caressing her shoulders, stroking her arms, brushing against her breasts. Warmth rose from her core spiraling outward and bathing her in lust. Her hands roamed beneath his tuxedo jacket, feeling his hard chest and pumping heart.

Thankfully, when the doors opened, no one was there to witness their out-of-control make-out session. Ava dug in her clutch for the keys and handed them to Brian, unable to stop her jumping nerves in order to perform this simple task. Brian chuckled at her ineptness.

As soon as they gained entrance, Ava reached for his bow tie and tugged it loose before sliding his jacket from broad shoulders. With focused haste, she unbuttoned his dress shirt and splayed her hands over his hot skin as she kissed his neck. Inhaling his musky scent, she followed his jaw line to his lips, where she paused to savor his beautiful mouth.

Brian's hands smoothed over her shoulders and down her back before releasing the zipper of her gown. The shimmery fabric slipped down her body and pooled on the floor around her feet. Because the bodice was fitted, there'd been no need for a bra, and Ava stood there in her navy lace panties, strappy sandals, and the sapphire necklace. Brian helped her step out of her dress, his gaze never leaving her body. Smoldering desire burned in his eyes as he discarded the remainder of his clothes.

"Follow me," she rasped, heading for the bedroom.

"Anywhere," he breathed.

Ava pulled the comforter from its resting place in one tug, and Brian playfully grabbed her around the waist, slid off her panties, and tossed her on the bed.

"I finally have you where I want you," he growled, following her onto the bed before capturing her lips with his mouth.

What he could do to her with just a kiss.

But after the exciting night of foreplay, she was more than ready for him. Ava ran her hand down his back, then around to his front and cupped his shaft in her palm before stroking it from base to tip, then sheathing it in a condom. Primal need roared through her being as the muscles between her thighs clenched in anticipation.

Brian moaned with pleasure, driving her to dizzying heights. Pushing him onto his back she crawled over his body before rubbing her mound against his rigid erection. Then she positioned it at her entrance and lowered herself, filling her body with him. Pleasure rippled through Ava as she quickened the pace, no longer willing to build slowly toward her goal.

She wanted it. Now. The pressure had her wild with desire, and she threw her head back as an amazing orgasm spiraled through her like a rocket before exploding. Brian's fingers dug into her hips as he drove fast and furious, racing to meet her at the top. And in seconds he joined her.

Gasping for more oxygen, Ava collapsed onto his chest, her heart beating hard against his. Brian's arms encircled her, and he held on tight as their breathing slowed and their bodies relaxed.

Warmth and love surrounded her, and Ava never wanted to move from this bed.

****

Ava awoke to Brian's gaze as he lay on his side, watching her. "How long have you been awake?" She smiled at the handsome man inhabiting her bed.

"Fifteen, twenty minutes."

"Why didn't you wake me? It's already ten-thirty."

"You need your rest." He wiggled his eyebrows teasingly.

"Oh, really. For what?"

"I thought we'd go out to breakfast, take in the Picasso exhibit at the Met, maybe stroll through Central Park. Then come back here and get more exercise." His smile lit up the room.

"Don't you ever relax on a Sunday? Lay around in bed, read the paper, watch a movie, order in?"

"I could do that. I could do anything with you." He stroked her arm as his words curled around her heart.

"Great. I am going to teach you to loosen up, to chill." She grinned at the skeptical look on his face.

"So how do we do this?"

"First, we put on jeans and a T-shirt—oh, you

don't have anything with you but a tux. I'll get dressed and run downstairs to the deli to buy the paper and bagels. You stay here in bed."

He put his hands behind his head. "I'm liking this already. As long as you remove your clothes the second you come back."

"Oh, I will. I won't even wear underwear." Ava tossed him what she hoped was a seductive look, then disappeared into the bathroom.

When she came out, Brian was standing by the window in his tux pants, looking out.

"You're supposed to be unclothed and in bed," Ava stated, her hands on her hips.

"I can't let you go out alone. Especially with no underwear." His blue eyes twinkled, but the set of his mouth told her he wouldn't back down.

"Okay. Put your shirt on. There's an extra toothbrush in the bathroom. Hurry up. I'm starving."

Brian was ready in two minutes, and they left the apartment to accomplish their errands in the least amount of time possible.

"Do you want to stop by your place to get some clothes?" Ava asked before they entered the elevator.

"I'll go later. Right now I want to eat, read the paper, and make love to you," he whispered. "Not necessarily in that order."

Unfortunately, there were others on the elevator, so Ava couldn't respond to his sexual comment. They moved to the rear, and Brian slid his hand into the back of Ava's jeans, palming her nude butt. She jumped at the unexpected invasion but held her squeal. Alerting their co-riders wasn't in her best interests.

Brian ignored her glance, staring straight ahead as

he massaged her lower back, then grazed a more private area. She tried to pull away, but his hand tightened on her hip. "You are in so much trouble when we get out of here," she whispered.

He had the nerve to chuckle. "I look forward to it."

Brian held her prisoner until everyone else exited the elevator. Then he nonchalantly released her and led her out. Trying to defuse the blush heating her face, Ava waited until they arrived on the sidewalk before stopping him in his tracks. "You are incorrigible." She underscored her words by shaking her finger at him as if that would put him in his place.

He engulfed her disciplining hand in his, kissed her fingers, then drew her into him, covering her mouth with his. Unbridled pleasure pooled between her legs and rampant desire jumped into overdrive. How could he have so much power over her?

By the time he ended the kiss, she was panting.

"I'm not the only one who's incorrigible." His eyes burned into hers, the planes of his face set into a serious mask. Gone was the teasing foreplay and in its place hot, hard lust. It bounced from Brian to her and back again as they stood locked in each other's embrace in the middle of the sidewalk.

"Where's the deli?" His non sequitur had her furrowing her brow. "We need to get what we came out here for, so we can get back to your place. As quickly as possible." The seriousness in the set of his face, along with his words, snapped her to attention.

"At the next corner." She motioned with her head.

Brian released her from his arms and practically pulled her up the street. "In a hurry?" she asked playfully.

"More than a hurry." His husky voice accentuated his carnal need.

They purchased the bare minimum: newspaper, two bagels, cream cheese for him, butter for her. She had preserves in her refrigerator. Within minutes they were heading back to Ava's apartment. Forewarned, she stepped to the other side of the elevator away from Brian, with others in between. He smirked at her, and she smiled sweetly in return.

No sooner had she closed her front door when Brian shed his shirt and pants and helped Ava do the same. Their discarded clothes evidenced their trail into the bedroom and they frantically fed their starving libidos, without so much as a thought toward their growling stomachs.

****

The weekend passed by too quickly, and Ava found herself daydreaming about it at her desk on Monday afternoon. Giving into her desire to speak to Brian, she picked up the phone and dialed his work number.

"I was just thinking about you," he said with the hint of a sexual undercurrent.

"I've been thinking about you all day," Ava admitted.

"What are you doing after work?"

She sighed. "I'll be here until at least eight. I have a motion due tomorrow. I'll probably get takeout on the way home and collapse in front of the TV. Why? What's on your busy schedule tonight?"

"Making dinner for you. Come over as soon as you're finished work."

"Are you serious?"

"I'm always serious."

"Wow. This is too good to be true. Are you trying to spin me into your web so you can toy with me before eating me alive?" She'd meant it as a joke, but the silence on the other end of the line, advised her Brian hadn't heard it that way. "I'm kidding. Really." The silence expanded. "I'm sorry. I've just never been treated so well. It scares me and when I get scared, I try to be funny. Unfortunately, you're not laughing."

She heard his pained sigh through the line. "If we had dated seven years ago, you might have been right. Because of our past, your words hit close to home. I'm not like that anymore, and I don't want you to believe I am. But when you say things like you just did, I feel as if I'm fighting an uphill battle with you. I'm not sure you'll ever trust my motives."

Ava bit her lip, searching for the right words to dispel the tenseness coming through the phone. Deciding to avoid the issue that led them to this strained point, she opted for a direct and honest response. "I would love to come to dinner tonight. What can I bring?"

"Just yourself. And a vow we will leave the past where it belongs. We can't go back to make things right. You and I still have a lot to work through in dealing with Briana. But I want you to know that I love you. I am not in your life to toy with you. I need you to trust me, just as I trust you."

Ava's throat constricted, trapping the words she needed to say. But the words, "I trust you" wouldn't form on her lips. All she could manage was "I love you, too."

Chapter Eighteen

Brian answered the door in faded jeans and a tight navy T-shirt that stretched across one amazing chest. Ava's mouth watered before she even had a chance to sniff the wonderful aroma emanating from the kitchen.

His eyes roamed her from head to foot and back again as if she had on the sexiest outfit ever, instead of a conservative black business suit.

"Hello, beautiful," he breathed, before ensnaring her mouth in an erotic kiss that zoomed straight to her toes.

"I could get used to this," she murmured as he escorted her into the living room.

His slow and very seductive smile empowered her to take more of what she wanted, and she stopped him, leaning in to steal another hot, powerful kiss.

"I can live on those," she sighed, allowing the stress of the workday to fall away.

"I promise you that and much more. Later." His eyes locked on hers and sealed his promise. "Take off your jacket and get comfortable. Would you like a glass of wine, or something else?"

"Wine is good." Ava examined the living room and nodded. "Your new furniture looks great. And I love the paint color you chose."

"It's coming together. There's a piece of artwork I have my eye on in a gallery on 72nd Street. But I'd like your opinion before I make such a big investment."

Elation fizzed through her blood. Brian was including her in his life, and she wanted nothing more.

He drew her to the sofa. "Have a seat. Relax." A plate of cheese, crackers, and grapes sat on the coffee table. He moved in beside her and clinked her glass. "So, what keeps you at the office until eight every night?"

"We have a trial coming up soon. Max Spencer and I. He's the lead attorney and has a great reputation in representing plaintiffs in toxic tort cases. I'm just the lowly associate, but I've been helping him prepare for trial, getting all the exhibits organized, doing the first draft of direct and cross-examination of witnesses. I'm learning a lot."

"Do you like litigation work?"

"It's interesting. Obviously it's more cost effective for our clients to settle. Although they don't always see it like that. Once they dig in and take a position, it's difficult to move them toward a compromise. But trials cost a lot of money, not only in attorney's fees but for expert witnesses as well." She was amazed at how quickly their client's bills skyrocketed once they started preparing for court. "Once we know the case can't be settled and we're going to trial, we're all vying to be involved. Most lawyers want to get in front of a jury, at least once in a while, to perform."

"If you can't perform dancing on stage you'll perform talking in a courtroom?"

Ava glanced at Brian to see if he was teasing. He wasn't. "Interesting way of putting it. I never thought of it that way."

"Will you get a chance to examine any witnesses,

or will Max take over once you do all the work?"

She laughed. "He's doing the work, too. But yes, I'm in charge of the direct examination of a few witnesses. It's a great way to get my feet wet in the judicial arena."

"I'm sure you'll be brilliant."

She smiled at his faith in her. "Thanks for the vote of confidence. But let's not talk about work. Can I help with anything in the kitchen?"

"No. Everything's under control. The chicken's in the oven and will be done soon."

"Do you like to cook?"

"I love it, when I have the time. Being out so much at night, I'm a happy man when I can come home after work and make something simple but good. On those rare occasions, I like to go to the organic market and mill around. I end up buying way too much for one person, but everything looks so fresh and good."

"Interesting." Ava sipped her wine and studied him.

"What?"

"Nothing." She smiled, keeping her thoughts to herself.

"No, you don't. Something's going around in that head of yours. What is it?"

He clearly wasn't letting her off the hook. "Okay. I'll spill, but don't forget you asked for it."

He nodded. "Go on."

"For a guy who makes a living from environmentally questionable means, I'm surprised you shop at an organic market." She smiled to take the edge out of her words.

He nodded. "Those are competing interests, aren't

they? I guess I never compared the two. So, which one should I give up? Eating healthy or earning a living?" Ava was about to respond when he held up his hand. "No, don't tell me. I'm afraid you'll try to convince me to leave my company. And given how persuasive you can be, I might end up in the unemployment line."

"I suppose that wouldn't do," she admitted. "You then might have to sell this amazing apartment with the fantastic view."

His jaw clenched, and Brian set aside the teasing banter. "Does it bother you what I do for a living?"

This topic headed into dangerous territory. How could she condone fracking when there was proof it was poisoning underground water and affecting the lives of the people who lived near the drilling sites? The people who her nonprofit clients represented. On the other hand, Brian and his father were in the natural gas business, a business that supplied what people wanted and needed. What they demanded.

"That's a difficult question to answer," she hedged. "You have a right to be involved in an enterprise of your choosing. This is a free country. A capitalist society. You've become a very successful businessman and there's a lot to be said for that."

"Spoken like a true lawyer. That's not who I want to hear from. I want to hear from Ava, the woman I adore."

She inhaled the heady importance of his words. "When you say it like that, I'll say anything you want to hear." She reached over to caress his face. "But if you really want to know my views, I'll share. I worry about the children. The future. What's good for some people, whether it's making money off their land to lease the rights to drill or for people who own the drilling companies, isn't good for the people who live near the sites and end up with polluted ground water in their drinking systems. Personally, I would err on the side of the innocent people who get nothing from the drilling except illness."

"That's the answer I expected from you. The one I didn't want to hear. But given your career choice, it's really a no-brainer."

"Brian, I would never ask you to leave your company or change your business. We all find our way to a career. Sometimes it finds us. I know I represent nonprofits who would like to put you out of business. I didn't exactly chose this field. I needed a job and interned at the firm after my second year in law school. The work is interesting, and I like what I do. I'm not a crusader, unless I have to be in court. I'm not out at nights and weekends picketing natural gas drilling sites. I guess you could say I'm content with what I'm doing, but I'm not passionate about it. Hopefully, it will never come down to me against you." She gave him a wan smile. "I would never let it."

"Thanks. For being honest and open." He chucked her under her chin. "Dinner should be ready. Let's eat."

A change of scenery and subject could only be a good thing. The conversation had gotten too heavy, too fraught with political, legal, and idealistic views.

They sat at the kitchen table, a small, intimate space Ava liked a lot better than the formal dining room. They talked about other subjects for over an hour, never finding the conversation lagging. Finally, Ava pushed her chair back. "I hate to put an end to this party, but we should clean up since I need to go. We both have to work tomorrow."

"Are you sure I can't convince you to stay? I promised you kisses and more when you first walked in." His eyes flashed with mischievousness.

"I would love that, but I need sleep and I will not get that here."

"You're right." His roguish grin confirmed his words. "Let me walk you out to get a cab. I'll clean up later. If you stay and help me, I know I won't be able to keep my hands off you."

A slow fire burned inside, and Ava knew it wouldn't take much more than a stroke to ignite it into a full-fledged flame of desire and need.

As they stood out on the sidewalk hailing a cab, Brian spoke. "I'm out of town Thursday and Friday, but don't make plans for the weekend."

A cab arrived, and she kissed him goodbye. "I'm all yours."

****

Peter poked his head into Ava's office first thing Tuesday morning. "Hi. I'd like to meet with you and Max in my office for a few minutes. Is now a good time?"

Ava looked up from her computer and nodded. "Sure. I'll round up Max."

She found him in the kitchen getting coffee, and the two of them headed down the hall to Peter's corner office. It was the best one at their firm with views of the skyline heading south.

"Come on in and have a seat. I want to run something by the two of you." They sat in Peter's clients' chairs across the desk.

"What's up?" asked Max, sipping his morning

brew.

"We were recently hired by Brian Stanhope on behalf of his company, Stanhope Natural Gas, to review and revise their standard contract to drill on private land."

Ava's heart fluttered at Brian's name. He was her secret. At least where her employers were concerned.

"He called this morning and asked if we'd be interested in getting involved in his litigation cases. There are lawsuits pending by two groups of plaintiffs alleging harm due to their drilling on nearby lands."

The neurons in Ava's brain collided.

Max spoke first. "You know we don't represent the defense in these types of cases. We're a plaintiff's firm."

"I know, but there's no conflict and there's no reason why we can't get involved. He and his company could be a good business generator. Ava, what do you think?"

Ava paused to hopefully put a coherent sentence together. "I thought this firm was built on representing plaintiffs in environmental contamination cases. I understand business is business, but if we take on this one client in a defense capacity, more may follow. Surely we'll find ourselves in conflict situations down the line."

Peter nodded as he considered her statement. "Maybe. Maybe not. I hate to turn away good work. Max, would you have a problem representing the defense?"

Max also took his time answering. This was clearly a thorny issue. "No, not intellectually. And I certainly know both sides of the argument. It just doesn't sit well with me."

Ava sat forward in her chair. "I don't know if this will affect your decision, but there's something you need to know." Embarrassment over having to reveal anything about her personal life singed her to the core. "I'm dating Brian. I don't know what will happen between us, but I thought I should let you know in case that affects your thinking in some way."

Peter sat back and stroked his chin. "So that's why he wants us to take on all his work. Because of you."

Ava shook her head. "No. That can't be it. He never even mentioned he wanted to hire our firm to do his litigation. I'm sure it's because he's heard that Max is an expert litigator."

Max smirked. "Nice try, Ava. He probably heard that from you. And knowing you're dating the man tells me he's here to boost you up the ladder."

Heat flushed Ava's face, and she wanted to dive under the desk. Why hadn't Brian told her about this? Given her a warning so she'd be better able to deal with it? "I'm sorry if it looks that way. But I can't believe his company would change law firms because of me."

"Why not?" said Max. "The two of you are dating. You do the work he needs done. You're an excellent lawyer and a hard worker. And he already has his corporate work here. There's no downside to him. Unless, of course, the two of you split, and you decide to tank his cases."

Both Peter and Max chuckled over Max's joke. Unfortunately, Ava didn't see the humor in it. If she and Brian broke up, she'd be devastated. Again. She would have to leave the firm. She would never be able to pass him in the hall, or god forbid, work on his litigation cases, if their relationship didn't work out.

Peter broke into her somber thoughts. "So, what's the verdict?" Peter steepled his fingers and waited for a response. He looked pointedly at Ava.

"I don't think it's a good idea." She stopped there, since her opinion was rooted in her personal life.

Max nodded. "I'll go along with Ava on this. No point in changing our focus on this work for one client. Besides, it may be disconcerting to our current clients."

Peter nodded. "Fine." He turned back to Ava. "Since you know Brian so well, you should be the one to tell him our decision on this. Of course we'll continue representing him on the corporate end, we just can't do the litigation. Bring up the potential conflicts in the future, as well as the focus of our representation. No need to blame it on your dating relationship." Peter chuckled. "That way he won't break up with you just so we'll change our mind and do the work."

Very funny. And nice of Peter to make her the bearer of bad news.

Despite her stunned state, Ava found her way back to her office. What was Brian thinking? And why did he call Peter this morning without saying a word to her throughout dinner last night? Was this some tactical move on his part to conflict them out of future cases that might be against his company?

She slowly picked up the phone and dialed his work number.

"Good morning, gorgeous. I missed you after you left." Brian's opening words did nothing to melt the angst burning in her system.

"I just got out of a meeting with Peter and Max. Why didn't you talk to me about moving your litigation cases to our firm?" She wanted to reach through the phone and strangle him for putting her in such an awkward position.

"I didn't think you had the authority to make that decision. At least not yet. And I didn't want to put you in the middle of it." He was always so calm and rational. While true, she didn't have the authority, he could at least have thrown it out there for discussion.

"I am in the middle of it. Because of your request, I had to tell Peter and Max we were dating. It was very uncomfortable raising my personal life with them."

"You sound angry. Are you?" His tone morphed from calm to incredulous.

How had he turned this around? "I'm..." At a loss for words, she could only repeat his. "Yes, I'm angry."

"What's the problem? I thought you'd be happy to have garnered more business for the firm. You convinced me last night when you were talking about your upcoming trial that you and Max are an excellent team. I thought about it more after you left and made the decision to give Peter a call. Find out if your firm was interested."

"I just think you should have spoken to me about it before you called Peter. So I wasn't blindsided at a meeting this morning." She couldn't melt her frosty tone. "In any event, the partners talked it over and decided against representing your litigation cases. Not that they weren't intrigued by your request. It just presents too many problems in the long run given our usual practice of representing plaintiffs. We appreciate your corporate business. But at this time, we don't want to get involved in representing the defense. They—we thank you for your trust in our firm."

"Trust. Now there's an interesting word coming from your mouth." The sarcasm couldn't be missed. "I completely understand the business decision made today. I'm not totally surprised by it. But I won't lie by saying I'm not disappointed in your seeming distrust of me. As if I went behind your back to obtain something that would somehow be a negative for you. I've told you before, I respect you and the lawyers at your firm, and I thought I'd kill two birds with one stone, as they say. I'd be receiving great representation, and you'd get the credit for landing a client."

Of course he made it sound so sensible, so reasonable. As always. But she couldn't dismiss the initial shock she'd felt upon hearing his request.

"I'll talk to you later. I have to go." She hung up without resolving the strained atmosphere between them.

Brian was right about one thing. Trust kept flying its white flag in her face, and she still refused to surrender. A lifetime of heartache caused by abandonment could do that to a woman. But Brian was doing everything possible to win her trust back, yet she seemed bent on finding fault with him. She knew the reason. To protect her heart. But if she didn't make some changes soon, she may find her heart encased in stone, and no one would ever be able to get at it. Not exactly her game plan.

Attempting to put aside her anxiety over their situation until she could deal with it productively, Ava kept her head deep in trial preparation. By the end of the day, her initial anguish had dissipated, and she allowed Brian's reasoned explanation to take hold and battle back her original mistrust. Gathering her resolve and her pride, she headed for a face to face with Brian, where she just might have to fall on her sword.

****

Brian opened the door and let her in, with a serious set to his jaw that sometimes looked so sexy. Tonight it foreshadowed a negative emotion—frustration, anger? She wouldn't know until he said something.

Standing in the foyer, she jumped right into the purpose of her visit. "I'm sorry if I sounded brusque this morning."

Brian's jaw tightened, but he said nothing.

She bowed her head. "Of course I explained the reason earlier. But you have a right to speak to your corporate counsel about representation without my input. It's hard to separate my personal feelings from business considerations. Which is why the conflict of interest rules exist."

She studied his face to gauge his reaction. The planes and angles had softened marginally, but she couldn't detect even the slightest smile on his lips.

His blue eyes darkened with emotion. "Why does everything have to be so hard between us? You weren't angry because of some conflict of interest. You were angry because you thought my motives were suspect. I understand your reactions are rooted in the past and I haven't managed to win over your complete trust yet, but I don't know how much longer I can try." His eyes held sadness, and Ava's heart squeezed so tightly, she could barely breathe. He couldn't break up with her, not now, not after they survived her confession about their child.

Unwanted tears burned her eyes, and she bit her lip to hold them back. Men hated tears. Brian would feel manipulated, and she didn't want that. She considered escaping to the safety of the city streets, where her tears could flow unchecked among the apathetic throngs surrounding her. But she couldn't run. If she wanted Brian, she'd have to stay and fight for him—convince him they would work out.

"Please don't give up on me." Her voice rasped with agony reeling all the way to her soul. "I promise to consider your views before I speak. I promise to give you the benefit of any doubt. Please." She was precipitously close to begging, and she stopped herself from continuing.

He reached out and hugged her close. She breathed him in, replenishing the oxygen she needed to survive. He stroked her back and some of the angst that suffocated her began to dissipate. Still, he said nothing.

She didn't want to move from this place of comfort and security. Ever. But more words needed to be spoken. By him.

Regretfully, Ava stepped back, but refused to break their embrace. She questioned him with her eyes, since she'd said all she could say.

Brian traced the curve of her jawline, the whole time studying her eyes, her face. "I love you, Ava. But I don't want to walk on eggshells around you. The issue we're dealing with right now is much more than a question about whether I should have conferred with you concerning representation. The fact that you thought I was going behind your back and doing something that would negatively affect your firm's bottom line, and perhaps your future with the firm, is not only disturbing but very hurtful. I know I let you down in the past. I can't be held responsible for something I knew nothing about. I've apologized over and over. I've tried to make things right by setting up a trust. You need to let go of the past—at least between us. You have to start trusting me."

Ava swallowed, but the lump in her throat wouldn't budge. "I know. I will. I do."

A small smile, or was it a grimace, moved his lips. "What exact statement are you responding to?"

"All of them. In order." Her gut twisted and bunched as Brian apparently considered his options.

She held his gaze, willing him to choose her.

He shook his head. "Ava, Ava, Ava. What are you doing to me?"

His eyes flashed, and in them she could clearly see the hurt and pain she'd inflicted. That agony unleashed the torrent she'd been attempting to hold in, and hot tears streamed down her face. "We can do this. I know it. Let's start over. Right now."

Wrapping her arms around his neck, she embraced him with everything she had—trying to convey every emotion: sorrow, hope, love, regret. He crushed her to him accepting, at least for the moment, her total abandon.

His mouth devoured hers, as if starved for her love, and she breathed in his breath as she willed his heart to merge with hers.

"I need you," she rasped between kisses.

Her words escalated his erotic assault, and she reveled in his embrace, a more than willing participant. Dragging his mouth from her lips to her neck, and back again, icy heat coursed through fevered veins. His mouth scorched as his tongue mated with hers in a frenzied dance. Brian seduced and incited Ava's passion, and all control evaporated. Her hands roamed, caressed, and grabbed at the same time, pulling him closer, pushing him away.

"What do you want?" he gasped, roughly.

"Make love to me. Now." Her husky demand drew a chuckle from him.

"Not a problem."

He slid his hand around her upper arm and tugged her toward his bedroom. This man was on fire, and Ava craved his scorching burn.

As they entered his sanctuary, Brian tore off his T-shirt, displaying his sculpted physique. He hastily unzipped his jeans and slid them off along with his shorts. Ava's mouth watered at the athletically built body on display—wide shoulders, muscled arms, tight abs. He cocked his head and raised a brow.

"Take off your suit." His order was wildly arousing. "Do it now, before I do it for you. I don't think you want it ripped."

With trembling fingers, Ava removed her jacket and fumbled with the buttons of her blouse. His intent stare burned through her clothing, yet she couldn't seem to shed her clothes fast enough.

"Turn around," he demanded.

She followed his instructions and felt masculine hands at her waist, unhooking the clasp on her skirt before yanking down the zipper and pushing the impediment to the floor. She stepped over the material, slipped off her shoes, and discarded her blouse all at the same time. Brian turned her back around to face him, fingering the lace of her bra before moving his thumbs back and forth over her nipples.

Their tight peaks pushed at the see-through

material begging to be released. But Brian had taken charge, and Ava rejoiced in his wicked seduction. She closed her eyes and felt her breasts swell as she leaned into his caress. A moan escaped her mouth, and Brian possessed her lips with his, silencing her.

His previous fevered onslaught had gentled, and now delicate fingers whispered over her face as his velvet tongue tangled with hers. Ava's splayed hands caressed his broad chest, sliding lower and lower until she took hold of his throbbing erection. A low growl erupted from deep within, and Ava savored the power she shared with him.

Brian backed her onto the bed and tenderly removed the last items of clothing before easing beside her and pulling her into his embrace. "I need you, too. I can't survive without you." His words pierced her heart and the powerful emotions that cascaded over her hurt at the same time they eased the torment bombarding her mind.

He moved over her, locking his intense gaze with hers. Ava was powerless to let go, staring into beautiful, soulful blue eyes that chained them together. He grabbed a condom from the nightstand before rocking against her, his hard length stroking and stimulating the delicate folds between her legs. She opened herself to him and he glided into her, moving leisurely at first until the exquisite arousal built and he quickened the pace.

Moving as one, Ava's mind blurred with passion and lust, but most of all love.

Chapter Nineteen

Awakening to the insistent buzz of her cell phone, Ava felt drugged from the exquisitely erotic night she'd shared with Brian. Not falling asleep until after three, she missed her usual rising hour of seven. She hung her arm over the bed and felt around the floor for her purse, eyelids heavy with sleep. Grabbing the strap, she yanked the bag toward her and plunged her hand in to stop the offending noise.

Brian stirred next to her. "Who is it?"

Ava squinted at the phone screen. "It's Dan, Kim's husband." Confused over his early call, she answered instead of letting it go to voicemail.

She listened for a few seconds, then screamed and jumped out of bed. "Where is she?" Ava's heart beat out of her chest, and she could hardly hear Dan over the roar in her ears. "I'll get there as soon as I can."

She threw the phone in her purse and started gathering her clothes from the floor, nausea threatening to take her down.

Brian pushed off the covers and came to her side. "Ava, what?" He held her shoulders to force her to stop and face him.

Her tongue felt thick in her mouth, suffocating. "Briana and Kim. Hospital. There was a car accident. Going to school." She knew her words weren't forming sentences, but she got out the gist before pulling away from Brian and trying to straighten her clothes.

"I'll get a car to drive us." He moved quickly around the bed, picked up his phone, and called someone. "It will be here in a few minutes."

He grabbed his jeans and T-shirt from the night before and dressed in record time.

"What exactly did Dan say? Are they in the ER? Have they been treated yet?" Brian kept his voice calm, undoubtedly for her benefit.

Hot tears streaked down Ava's face even though she tried to keep it together. "Briana's in surgery. They had to take them both by ambulance. Kim is banged up, may have some broken bones, but she's conscious."

Ava couldn't see through her tears, but she heard an unmistakable gasp from Brian. He hugged her, then stroked her back. "Don't jump to conclusions. She'll be fine. She'll be fine."

He couldn't be saying that just for her benefit. Brian had been biding his time, waiting for the right moment to meet Briana, to take the next step in the process of dealing with his parentage. He'd been patient, not pushing, yet anxious for the day to come.

A sob escaped Ava's mouth, but she nodded. "Of course she'll be okay... She's young...resilient." Ava rushed to the door. "Let's go."

Brian followed in her wake, calling after her. "I can have our driver stop off at your apartment to get something more comfortable to wear."

"No. We have to get there as quickly as possible. There's no time to go across town. This is fine." She smoothed her skirt, which hardly pressed out the wrinkles from lying in a heap on the floor all night. But she didn't care. "Hopefully the car is here."

It wasn't. Ava paced the sidewalk in front of Brian's building, cursing and stretching her neck to zero in on their transportation. "Where is it?" Ava's initial panic escalated with the wait, and her stomach cramped.

When the car finally arrived, Ava threw open the door and climbed in, not waiting for the driver to do his job. She consulted her phone, barked out the address of Nassau General Hospital in Princeton, and then stared out the window.

The ride took an hour and a half in the heavy morning traffic. Brian held her hand throughout, but little was said between them. Ava prayed and begged God to help Briana through this. She had no idea what Brian was thinking.

Sporadically she checked her phone to be sure she didn't miss a call or text from Dan, who had promised to notify her as soon as he knew anything more. Nothing.

Finally they pulled up to the hospital ER. Ava flew out of the car and dashed through the sliding glass doors. She searched for Dan in the sea of people seated in the waiting room, but didn't see him. She strode to a receptionist.

"I'm looking for Briana and Kim Reynolds. They were brought in by ambulance after a car accident."

The receptionist checked her computer. "And you are?" she asked without looking at Ava.

"Briana's moth—" She stopped cold as Brian, who'd caught up to her, slipped his hand around her waist, tugging her back. A clear sign to reconsider her words. "Her aunt. I'm Kim Reynolds' sister." Ava raced through her explanation, and her voice rose with panic as she considered that this woman might not give her the information she needed.

"Briana. Reynolds is on the third floor in surgery. Kim Reynolds is registered in the ER but out for x-rays. You can take the elevator halfway down this hall"—she pointed to the left—"up to three. Then follow the signs for the family waiting room."

Ava started sprinting away before the woman finished her sentence. Brian ran to catch up, then grabbed her arm. "Ava, wait. Just for a second. She spun toward him barely able to contain her impatience over his delay.

"What?"

"Are you going to let the staff know we're Briana's natural parents so we can see her? Does Dan know about me? What if your father's here?"

Damn. In the interminable time it took to drive here, these particular thorny issues hadn't crossed her mind. "You couldn't have asked these questions while we were caged in the car?"

Ava knew her ire shouldn't be directed at Brian, who had done nothing but try to help her this morning, but she couldn't stop herself.

His jaw clenched at her verbal assault, but he didn't address it. "I didn't think about it until just now. You clearly didn't think about it either."

"For the moment, I'm Briana's aunt and you're my…my boyfriend. Let's get up there and find out what's going on. Once I know Briana is okay, we can discuss this further."

Disappointment etched his face. She should apologize to him. But fear had replaced all other emotions from the moment she received Dan's call.

She'd apologize later. After she got word of Briana's condition.

He kept whatever response he had to himself, being a much better person than she at this moment.

They travelled by elevator to the appointed floor and found their destination quickly.

"Dan! How's Briana?" Ava couldn't even bring herself to ask about Kim in the same sentence.

His eyes were rimmed in red, and he shook his head. "She was unconscious when they brought her in. They rushed her to surgery to stem the internal bleeding. I don't know." His voice broke, and although she'd never hugged Dan in her life, she tried her best to comfort him.

Out of the corner of her eye, she saw her father. He stood but didn't approach as she patted Dan on the back. "She'll be fine. I know she will." That's the only thing she could say to Dan, to herself, to anyone who would listen.

When she disengaged from Dan, she turned to Brian and introduced the two of them just as she said she would. Then she went over to her father.

"Hi, Dad." No kisses or hugs for him.

"Ava. I haven't seen you in a while."

Instead of answering, she introduced Brian to him, taking up the awkward moment. Brian followed her script and tried for some small talk to ease the tension in the room.

Finally, Ava asked Dan about Kim.

"She has a broken femur and a fractured wrist. She's in a lot of pain or was until they gave her something for it. I've been running down there, checking on her, too. They were taking her for more tests."

Brian broke into their conversation, looking directly at Dan. "Who is Briana's surgeon?"

"I don't know," he shrugged.

"Then you didn't check on his credentials?"

"No."

"Maybe she should be flown to CHOP? Did you discuss that with anyone?"

"What's CHOP?" Dan's dazed look took on a wary edge.

"Children's Hospital of Philadelphia. It's the best in the area."

"This was the closest hospital. Are you a doctor? What's with all the questions?" Annoyance punctuated his comeback.

Brian matched his tone. "You should be asking these questions."

Ava slipped her arm through Brian's and steered him out of the room.

"What are you doing?" she hissed.

"I'm in a situation where I have no control. I'm not used to it, and I don't like it. Worse than that, I'm angry about it." He paced near her in the hall, hand thrust in his pockets, his eyes trained on the floor, working his jaw as his teeth gritted.

"What are you talking about?"

"Briana should be getting the best care possible. Her adoptive father is just sitting back waiting to see what happens."

"Maybe she is getting the best care. She's in emergency surgery. There was no time to check credentials, consider CHOP, ask questions. You need to calm down and remember that Dan may not know who you are. We need to be supportive, helpful. Not attacking." A lesson she needed to learn as well.

Ava inhaled, recognizing that she had also jumped into mother mode the second she heard about the accident. Brian was only acting like a father.

Guilt lashed at her over the harsh treatment of the man she loved. "I'm sorry about the way I spoke to you before. I seem to always be apologizing to you for something. I'm just so scared." Her eyes sought his, trying to convey the fear that streamed to her every pore. "What if…" She couldn't finish the question.

"I'm scared, too. What if I never get to meet my daughter?"

Ava could barely breathe. This was all too much. Briana's situation. Brian's presence. All the secrets. Where would it take them? She dared not ask.

Brian sighed, avoiding eye contact with her as he obviously pulled himself together. "I know now is not the time to battle over this."

He took Ava's elbow and led her back to the family sitting area where they waited in uncomfortable silence in their own form of hell.

****

Before long a woman in scrubs stood in the doorway. "Mr. Reynolds?"

Dan, Brian, Ava, and her dad all rushed forward.

"I'm Dr. Strauss. The surgeon in charge of Briana's procedure." Neither her tone nor manner suggested a dire outcome, and Brian's angst waned ever so slightly. "Briana is in the recovery room. Her surgery went well. She had a lacerated spleen. We were able to stop the internal bleeding. This was a major operation, although I feel confident she'll pull through.

233

We'll be moving her to intensive care when she comes to. After she's settled in, you can go in and see her, Mr. Reynolds."

"What about us?" Ava asked, dismay prevalent in her voice.

"Only her parents for now." Ava received a small sympathetic smile. "We'll keep you informed of her condition as the day progresses."

As soon as Dr. Strauss left, Dan said to no one in particular that he was going to see Kim to let her know.

Brian pulled Ava out into the hall, away from her father's ears. "We should tell Dr. Strauss we're her birth parents. I'm sure we'll be able to see her then."

Ava seemed to consider this before a steely determination took over. "No. That's not a good idea." She paused, then softened her tone. "I don't know if Kim told Dan you're Briana's father. I have to talk to Kim when Dan's not around and find out."

Brian steered her out of the way of an oncoming cart filled with towels and linens. "Why don't you talk to him and tell him who I am? How could he object?"

Ava stared at the floor, clearly contemplating something in that mind of hers, however, Brian couldn't even guess at what those wheels were spinning.

"Ava? What are you thinking?"

She looked at him warily and waited for a nurse to pass, her shoes squeaking loudly against the floor. "My father doesn't know Kim and Dan adopted my baby. He never knew I was pregnant." She twisted her hands and bit her lip, refusing to look at him.

"You're kidding? How did you pull that off?" He couldn't keep the incredulity from his tone.

"I told my father I was going to Paris for six

months to study abroad. I stayed at school. Every once in a while Kim and I got together when no one else was around, either at her house in Lawrenceville or my apartment in New York."

"You had Briana in March. What about the holidays? Thanksgiving, Christmas?" This new information had him reeling.

"I spent them alone."

The kick to his gut made him nauseous. He stared at her face looking for a sign she was joking, but the grief and sadness etched there confirmed her words.

"Oh, Ava." He pulled her into his arms and held her tight. Their night of passion together changed her life in so, so many ways. It was agonizing to think about her alone in the City, pregnant, without family, without the comfort and traditions of the holidays. Going through the ups and downs of pregnancy with no supportive partner. While he got to enjoy the holidays with his family, blissfully ignorant of the upheaval he had caused in Ava's life. "I'm so sorry."

He'd apologized dozens of times, but what could it mean in the scheme of things? It wouldn't change the life she'd led from the moment she learned of her pregnancy to this moment, standing in the hospital, waiting for more news about Briana's condition.

Yet, he couldn't fathom why she would keep something like that from her father. Sure they weren't very close, but how could anyone keep such a secret?

"Do you ever plan to tell him?"

Ava shrugged. "I suppose. Kim has been seeing a counselor to help her decide when and what to tell Briana about the adoption. I'm willing to do whatever is right for her. Up until now, she was so little and wouldn't understand, so there seemed no reason to raise the issue. Now that she's six and in school, Kim has been trying to deal with it."

"Why didn't you want your father to know?"

Ava bowed her head. "It seems so childish now, but I was angry with him. I still am. I didn't want to share any of my personal life with him. I didn't think he deserved to know." She sighed. "I was also afraid he would try to influence Kim and me, maybe interfere with our plan. Once I got Kim and Dan to agree to the adoption, I didn't want any outside intervention to affect our decision."

Brian shook his head. "The secrets your family holds are incomprehensible to me. Things have to change, Ava. I want to see Briana and I know you do. I don't care who has to learn the truth today to accomplish this. But either you start talking, or I will." Given everything Ava had suffered in the past, Brian winced at his no-nonsense tone and ultimatum, but it had to be done.

Ava's sapphire eyes held so much misery that Brian's chest ached. If he could shoulder some of her grief, he would gladly do so, but he also had to acknowledge he was causing some of it. Yet, he would not back down on this. He had a right to see Briana, to talk to her, to stroke her forehead. He'd been patient up until now, waiting for Ava to dictate the right circumstances for him to be introduced. Unfortunately, a life-threatening event changed everything and he was no longer willing to sit back.

Ava cleared her throat. "I'll go see Kim and Dan. Tell them we want to see Briana. I'll be back."

"I'll come with you," he offered.

"No. Stay here. Wait for word on Briana. I need to ease into this given Kim's reaction a few weeks ago, when I told her you knew about Briana. Besides, I don't know what condition she's in."

Brian accepted her request. It was the least he could do given the circumstances. His gaze never left her retreating back. She still moved with the grace and poise of a ballet dancer. While it must be difficult for her, she held her head up high as she strode into potentially hostile territory—and as her history dictated—she did it alone.

****

Several hours later, the coast was clear for Ava and Brian to visit for a few minutes with Briana in intensive care. Ava didn't share with Brian much of her conversation with Kim and Dan, but he was satisfied with the bottom line.

They entered Briana's cubicle, with curtains drawn around the sides, but the front visible to the central desk where lifesaving machines were monitored. She looked so tiny and helpless lying in an adult sized hospital bed hooked up to a heart monitor, pulse oxometer, and an IV with some clear liquid dripping into her veins through a stent.

Brian stared at the child—his child—waiting to feel the connection, the innate paternal bond that would reach his soul. Her face and arms were bruised and her long blonde hair matted in places. She looked nothing like the photo of the vibrant, adorable child from Ava's office.

He walked closer to her bed, intending to touch her arm. But something kept him from reaching out. He didn't have the right. He didn't know this little girl.

They'd been advised she slept most of the time and might not be responsive. That was fine with Brian. He just wanted to see her. To confirm she was breathing and being well cared for.

He looked at Ava who stood on the other side of the bed. Ava had no trouble stroking her, talking to her, smiling at the child she knew so well.

"Hi, honey. It's Aunt Ava. I came to see you." She talked softly, soothingly, and even though Briana wasn't awake, she continued. "You gave us a scare today, but you're going to be fine. We're all here for you. Your mommy and daddy, Pop-pop. And I brought another special person who's been wanting to meet you so badly. His name is Brian."

Ava glanced up at Brian, possibly seeking his approval over her words. He nodded for her to go on, for he knew he couldn't speak over the lump choking his throat at Ava's love for their child.

"Brian and I go way back. You'll like him when you meet him. He has blond hair and blue eyes, just like you. And your names are similar." She gave a little laugh. "I told him all about our dance routines. The next time we make up a new dance, he wants to see it. So you have to get better real soon." Ava's voice caught and she was unable to say more, but she didn't stop rubbing Briana's arm.

A nurse came in to check one of the machines. "Your time is up. You can come back in a few hours."

Ava nodded, then bent and kissed Briana on the forehead. "We'll see you soon, sweetheart."

Tears flooded Brian's eyes. He tried to control them, but seeing how tender and loving Ava was with Briana undid him. A few escaped, and he swiped them away.

Although he couldn't speak, he patted Briana's hand. A touch. The first time he touched his daughter. Ava came around the bed and gently took his arm as they exited the Intensive Care area.

Ava stopped him before they got back to the waiting room, her eyes filled with misery.

"What is it?" he asked.

"This brings back all the emotions I felt after your accident. Those same feelings are swarming through me and the agony of those memories is gut-wrenching. I put those days behind me, but seeing Briana in that hospital bed…" She choked back a sob. "I can't believe it's happening again. It's not just a horrible feeling. I feel physically ill. The same as I felt with you."

Brian's heart ached. "I never knew, Ava." He swallowed. "I don't even know what you're feeling now. I can only guess at the intense level of pain. I don't know Briana like you do. I didn't give birth to her and hold her and love her like you did. Like you do. But please know I'm here for you. And if I can share your burden in any way, please let me."

Ava nodded and they slowly walked to their destination. As soon as they arrived back at the visitors' room, Ava's father pounced.

"How did you and your boyfriend get to see Briana? He's nothing to her. I'm her grandfather and I've been told I can't go in." Anger flashed in his gray eyes as he glared at Brian.

Brian clenched his jaw, but he remained silent.

Ava's father continued his verbal assault. "You're a stranger. I want you out of here. This is the family visiting area. We don't need any interlopers."

"That's enough, Dad." Ava stood toe-to-toe with her father. "Brian is Briana's biological father." The words seemed to come out so easily, yet her hands fisted and her face paled.

The horror displayed on Mr. Harrington's face competed with the guttural noise that escaped his mouth.

Brian exhaled to rid himself of a fraction of the tension ricocheting around the room. He was sure it hadn't been Ava's intention to play this card, but her father's personal attack and look of disgust at her "insignificant" boyfriend must have pushed her to it.

"I'm sorry to have shocked you, Dad, but it's time to share my secret." She turned to Brian who nodded his approval at her sudden revelation.

"What are you talking about?" Ava's father sputtered as he glared at Brian. "Do Kim and Dan know you're the father? Where did you come from? If you're here, why isn't the mother?"

His questions made sense in an odd sort of way. Should he start talking and explaining, or should he leave it to Ava? Since she was protecting him with the truth, maybe he should put himself in harm's way and try to share her burden. He glanced at her, looking for an answer to his unspoken question.

Ava's exhale could be heard down the hall "Dad, let's go find somewhere to talk. I have a confession to make."

Chapter Twenty

Ava steered her father into an empty sitting area. Thankfully it had a door to close, since she couldn't gauge the type of reaction she'd get. His initial anger had turned to what looked like shock, his mouth open, his face gray, and his eyes unfocused.

She tugged him to sit in the chair beside her. "I realize this may all seem very odd to you. That Briana's biological father is here. With me." Ava's mouth was drier than a dead leaf and talking was almost painful. "We've been dating for a few months. But I met him seven years ago at my roommate's Newport house one weekend."

Her dad frowned, trying to put the pieces together that were not interlocking. Ava searched for the words to fill in the blanks. "I was really taken with him that weekend. You know, head over heels. A Harvard grad. Charismatic. And really, really nice." She swallowed, biding her time before delivering the blow. "We were together that weekend." Ava searched her father's face to see if he understood where this was going without her having to get graphic. Unfortunately, his brow furrowed even more.

"Dad, I got pregnant."

"What?" he yelled. "Pregnant?"

Ava looked past him at the door to assure no one would come to her rescue at his outburst. Although, that might be nice.

"You weren't pregnant." His unreasonable statement almost made her laugh.

"I hid it from you. I told you I went to Paris for a semester. Remember?"

He blinked rapidly as if a bright light shone in his eyes. "You lied to me?" His tone had gone from loud to a whisper in mere seconds.

Guilt washed through her in a torrent, a guilt she had never felt before when it came to hiding this huge secret from him. She stared at the squiggly lines in the tile floor while she pulled words together, telling him the rest of the story. A very brief version of that long, dreadful year.

She inhaled, hoping the oxygen would give her strength to bring him to the here and now. "When we reconnected a few months ago, I was curious about Brian—who he had become, what my baby's father was like now. I never thought I'd fall in love with him, again. But I did." A smile threatened to take over her lips, but she held it at bay given the seriousness of the conversation. "I just told him recently he's Briana's father. He didn't take it so well, either."

Her father shook his head. "I don't understand why you didn't tell me. I'm your dad, your family." Shock morphed to defeat, and a deep sadness penetrated his eyes as he looked directly into hers.

"You and I weren't close. Nor are we now. I didn't think you deserved to know my personal business. You pushed me away when I was fourteen, sending me to boarding school." Ava heard the anger creep into her voice.

"Is that what you think? That I didn't want you

around?" Her father's eyes widened as he questioned her.

"It was pretty clear. Mom left us. You were upset and angry and whatever else. Maybe I was a reminder of her. Or maybe you were too wrapped up in your own grief to care about what I was feeling—what I needed. But whatever the reason, you shipped me off to go live at school. I was only fourteen, and I was literally on my own." Ava's face burned with the all too familiar anger over her father's selfish decision.

"I thought I was doing you a favor, Ava. I was always working. I had to be at the gas stations, or I'd be robbed blind. I didn't want you to be alone at home. I thought that would be worse for you. Make you even sadder than you were that your mother left. You went to a great school. One of the finest in the state. I knew you'd be well taken care of, have friends around. Especially since Kim was off at college."

"Did it ever occur to you that you could have hired a manager or even sold the gas stations and gotten a regular job so you could have been home at a normal hour? You had a daughter, Dad. A daughter who needed you." Her voice caught in her throat, and she was dangerously close to crying for that little girl who desperately wanted her father to show her he cared.

He stroked his chin, almost perplexed at her bold suggestion. "It never crossed my mind to sell the stations. I've owned that business for over thirty-five years. That's what I do. I don't have a college education. What would I have done?"

Ava threw up her hands. "How do I know? The point is, you never tried for something else because you never thought you had a responsibility to me. And as a result, I felt no obligation to you. That's why you didn't know I had a baby and gave her up for adoption to Kim and Dan."

She stood and began pacing. "You know what else I've noticed? You spend a lot of time with Briana. You cut back on your work hours now and give her much more than you ever gave me." It sounded so petty, yet she decided to put it all out there—all her father's sins.

He pushed his hand through his thinning gray hair. "When your mother left, I couldn't function. The only thing I could do was what I had been doing for years, what I could do in my sleep. And that was work at the service stations. Being in the house was too awful. So I spent as many hours as I could away from it. I thought you'd feel the same way. So I freed you from coming home to an empty house, from the memories of your mom. I thought I was doing you a favor."

Ava stopped pacing and stood in front of him. "Did you ever think to ask me? To find out what I wanted? What I needed?"

Her father's mouth drooped along with his shoulders. "No," he rasped. "You were too young. At least that's what I believed. I didn't think you were capable of voicing your feelings on the whole subject. By not talking about it, I shielded you from reliving the pain."

"Psychologists would wholeheartedly disagree with you on that one. Talking things out is a good thing. Communicating, making joint decisions that affect two people is a good thing. Because of the decisions you made without talking to me about them, because you banished me from your life without any explanation, I've been angry with you for thirteen years. And I have a very hard time trusting people. Because of you. Dad."

The blame dripped from her words, but Ava didn't care. She didn't care if she traumatized her father or wounded him to his very core. He deserved it and more.

She glanced at him. Her words had left their mark. He looked battered and bruised. He held his head in his hands as if covering his face would shield his ears from hearing further blame.

But she didn't back down. She didn't leave. She stood her ground, waiting for a response.

Finally he looked up at her, tears in his eyes. "I am so sorry, Ava. I didn't know. I didn't know how to deal with a fourteen-year-old daughter who was the spitting image of her mother. Who had the same goals and dreams as her mother—to dance professionally. Your mother grabbed her dream at our expense." The bitterness was still there after all these years.

Ava felt that same bitterness. "I'm not just blaming you. I blame her as well. She started us on the collision course we ended up on. And I will never forgive her for what she did. She called me several times over the years, thinking time would heal the rift between us."

Her father's head shot up. "She contacted you?"

"Yes. But I never spoke to her. Why are you so surprised?"

"No reason," he mumbled.

"Dad? Tell me." Her demand was harsh, authoritative.

"She asked where you were. I wouldn't tell her. I didn't want you to suffer because of her ever again."

Ava squinted her eyes at him. "So, again you made a decision that affected me greatly, without ever speaking to me about it."

"You just said yourself you will never forgive her, even though she tried to reach out to you."

Ava chewed the inside of her lip to keep from lashing out. Her head throbbed, and she desperately wanted to lie down, put a cool washcloth over her forehead, and sleep for hours. Maybe this whole nightmare would go away.

She made a snap decision. "I need to be alone. I'm going for a walk."

She marched out of the room, slamming the door on her father. With purposeful strides she headed in the opposite direction from Brian. If he or Dan had heard anything about Briana, they would have interrupted their talk. She cruised the common areas of the third floor, then the second, then the first. Until she finally found what she was looking for. The chapel.

The atmosphere was dim and quiet. No one else had made her discovery. It smelled of incense, that smoky, pungent aroma that was so distinct, bringing back memories of her childhood when she, her parents, and her sister would go to church. She hadn't been in years.

She slid into a pew and sat on the hard bench. A small marble altar graced the front of the chapel and a gold cross hung above it. A statue of the Blessed Virgin Mary stood on a pedestal on the left and a statue of St. Anthony—how did she remember what he looked like?—stood on the right. Her gaze moved along the walls where small paintings of different saints decorated the gray walls.

Ava allowed the peaceful atmosphere to envelop her and clear her mind. Just for a little while she wanted to think about nothing. Inhaling and exhaling slowly, she practiced long-ago learned meditation techniques and pulled out her mantra. Closing her eyes, she escaped.

After a time, she allowed herself to think about the conversation she had with her father. And although his actions were devastating, she realized for the first time he actually thought he was helping her. He had no clue he should have discussed things with her or changed his life to accommodate his child. His mind didn't work like that. He was a blue-collar worker who did what he did to support his family, never recognizing the support she needed was emotional and not financial.

The click of the door told her she was no longer alone. Ava turned her head to see what stranger would be joining her. But it wasn't a stranger.

Her father's eyes were rimmed red, and he looked like he'd aged ten years in the past hour. He sank into the pew next to her and placed his hand on her leg. He stared straight ahead, but began talking.

"I know saying I'm sorry can't bring back all the years we've been apart, nor can it erase the mistakes I made. Maybe I didn't talk to you about things like I should have, but you didn't talk to me about things either. Of course, you were the child and maybe you didn't know what to say, or even know you could voice an opinion. We can't go back and change anything. But we can go forward. I want to be here for you. For whatever you need from a dad. I can't believe I didn't know you had a baby. That Briana's your child." He shook his head. "How can a father be so in the dark about what's going on right under his nose? And to think I not only didn't have your trust, but I didn't have Kim's either."

247

His words twisted and tore at her heart. She had to throw him a lifeline. "Kim wanted to tell you. I wouldn't let her."

He nodded slowly. "Thanks for that."

She turned her head to look at his profile. Lines creased his cheeks and around his eyes. He'd had a hard life working outside in the heat of summer and the cold of winter, early mornings, late nights, and weekends. He'd saved every penny to put his daughters through school, even though Ava barely acknowledged his financial help. She'd wanted more from him, much more.

Tears leaked out of her eyes, and she let them stream down her face as similar tears slipped down her father's cheeks. Covering his hand with hers, she tried to smile, but everything hurt.

Her father draped his arm around her shoulder and pulled her toward him so their heads touched, side by side. "I love you, Ava. I always have. I may have never said it. Those words don't come easy from a hardened guy like me, but they need to be said."

Ava sniffed and wiped some tears from her face, but it was useless because they kept falling. "You're right. I needed to hear that." She struggled to come up with an acceptable way to say what she had to say. "You probably need to hear the same thing, but right now, Dad, I can't. I need some time to process all this. I'm sorry."

He squeezed her shoulder. "I understand. We need to build on this. Talk more. Spend more time together. Get to know each other again."

She nodded. "We should go check on Briana."

"You go. I'll be there in a little while. I want to say

a few prayers while I'm here. I think we can all use them."

A truer statement couldn't have been made.

****

Brian jumped up from his seat as soon as Ava approached the waiting area. She knew she looked as if she'd been through a hurricane, tornado, and maybe locusts. But he looked worse. His handsome face had taken on a greenish hue, perhaps from the fluorescent lights, and his eyes, those beautiful blue eyes, had lost their spark.

Are you okay?" She glanced at Dan who slouched in an uncomfortable chair and stared at the wall. Then panic set in. "Has something happened to Briana?"

"No. No." Brian took hold of her elbow and guided her out of the room.

"Then what's wrong?" Electrons buzzed around her body as Brian steered her down the hall and into the same room she had used to deliver the unsettling news to her father. "You're scaring me."

Brian folded his arms over his chest and looked directly into Ava's eyes. "You knew Kim was taking pain medication, didn't you?" His tone was accusatory.

"Y-yes. I knew she was seeing a pain management doctor. She had pulled something in her back a month or so ago while working at the hospital. I don't know how those nurses do it, lifting people all the time—"

"Stop." It was almost a yell. "Stop with your excuses. Your secrets." Anger tightened his jaw and the planes of his face looked like carved stone. "Kim's doctor came to talk to Dan while you were with your father. It was impossible not to hear the conversation. He wanted to know how long Kim had been taking pain medication and how much she was taking. Dan said she started last winter and was taking at least four pills a day, maybe more on the days she worked. By the time evening rolled around, she'd be knocked out by 7:30, if not sooner."

A chill coursed down Ava's spine. Yes, she knew Kim had been taking pain pills, but she didn't think much about it. Kim was a nurse. She knew what she could take and how it affected her. "I didn't know she had been taking them that long," was all she could say.

"Apparently, the prescription she's taking is addictive. And it affects her reflexes. How could you and Dan sit by while she's clearly impaired and allow her to drive Briana around?"

Tingles ran from Ava's head to her spine. "I-I honestly didn't know. When I saw her take a pill, it was in the afternoon and Briana rode the school bus home. She would never have gotten in a car and driven Briana if she didn't think she was capable."

"You can't be that naïve, Ava. People who take drugs always think they're clear headed and unimpaired. Usually they try to hide their addictions from their families, but it appears you knew. And didn't do anything to stop it."

"Wait a minute." Ire forged to the surface. "I knew Kim was seeing a doctor and I saw her take one pill. How am I supposed to jump to the conclusion she's addicted to pain medication and she shouldn't be driving?"

"You go and visit Briana almost every Sunday. Dan said Kim has been on medication since last winter. You can't be that blind."

Ava thought back to her Sundays at Kim's. As

soon as Ava showed up, she and Briana would either go to her room to choreograph a new dance or Ava would take her shopping or to the movies. Kim and Dan did whatever they did on Sundays. Sure Kim was always tired and often took naps in the afternoon if Ava had Briana. She worked hard all week and had a six year old that kept her running. What mother wasn't tired?

But the reality of Brian's words smacked her in the face. "Oh, my God." She shook her head. "It never occurred to me." Ava covered her face with her hands and massaged her forehead.

"I told you I wouldn't do anything to disturb the adoption as long as I knew Briana was safe. But now, after what your sister has done, I can't just let things stay as they are. I have no other choice."

Ava's knees buckled. Brian's strong grasp caught her before she hit the cold, hard linoleum.

"Ava, are you okay?"

She heard his voice as if in a tunnel and felt herself being guided to a chair. "Breathe," he commanded. His hand tapped lightly at her face, but she hardly felt it.

This nightmare was overwhelming and she needed an escape; the enveloping blackness a welcome respite.

****

Brian's anger dissipated as Ava collapsed. He grabbed her arms before she hit the floor, calling her name, instructing her to breathe. But it must have been all too much for her, and she slipped into a faint. He kept calling her name as he gently shook her.

Her eyes fluttered open and confusion momentarily marred her face until she obviously remembered the hell she was in. She looked at Brian and reached out to him as she struggled toward consciousness.

He helped her to a chair and sat beside her, stroking her face, her arm, trying to bring her back to reality—a reality she wanted to escape.

"Please don't do anything before I can figure this all out." Her eyes pleaded with him to reconsider his prior statement. "Accidents happen. We don't know if it was definitely Kim's fault. Maybe the sun was in her eyes. Maybe Briana distracted her. There could be a dozen reasons." She closed her eyes and inhaled. "Kim loves her. She would never do anything to harm her. You have to believe that."

"I wish I could, Ava. But drugs are involved here. I don't understand how you can give your sister a pass on this." His anger returned at the dilemma they now faced and it interfered with his clarity.

"I'm not. I just need some time to deal with it." Her voice was thin, fragile.

Ava's anguish trumped his ire. She loved Briana more than anyone. She'd sacrificed her life for her. His tie was only that of a sperm donor thus far. He didn't know the little girl.

Could fathering a child produce a bond so great he was willing to ignore Ava's near impossible decision to have her sister adopt Briana and fight her in court to overturn it?

She cut into his thoughts. "So your plan is to vacate the adoption? What if you're successful? Are you prepared to raise Briana?" Her reasonable questions deflated his resolve.

"We can do it together. We'll be a family."

She shook her head. "No. We can't. I gave up my rights to be Briana's mother. I realize you didn't sign the consent forms. I know you can legally wage a battle, and maybe you'll even win. But I will not help you. I will not rip Briana away from the only parents she knows." Ava's voice was hoarse and strained. Her watery eyes pleaded and demanded that he let this go.

"You're emotional now. Not thinking straight. This is the perfect solution. I love you, Ava. We'll get married. We'll finally do what we couldn't have done seven years ago."

Ava looked away, avoiding eye contact. "We should never have started down this road. I should never have gotten together with you."

"What are you talking about? We finally found each other. We're clearly meant to be together."

"We're too different. You think you can pull a few strings, throw money at a problem, do whatever it takes to get what you want. Maybe that works in your world. But it doesn't in mine." Her voice caught in her throat. "This was all a mistake."

"That's not true. How could you say such a thing?" Confusion laced with fear tore through him.

"We need to end this. I can't do this—us—anymore."

He took her hands in his. They were so cold. "Yes, we can. We can make this work. It's the perfect solution. We love each other." Why couldn't she see this?

She shook her head, staring at the floor.

"Are you saying you don't love me?" She couldn't be. He knew better.

"I'm saying…" She faltered, then started again. "We're not meant to be. It's over." This time her voice was strong, determined. There was no hesitation, no room for discussion.

He considered her words, ready to deny their veracity. Just yesterday, a lifetime ago, she'd indicated otherwise. "I don't believe you," he rasped.

"If that's what you need to hear to understand what I mean, then I'll say it." She paused. "I don't love you." Ice penetrated her eyes as she spoke those awful words.

The sword hit its mark.

She didn't waver as she stood, ramrod straight, her face a mask. "You should go."

When he didn't move, she turned and opened the door. And without a backward glance, walked out of the room and out of his life.

****

Ava's gut twisted at the finality of her statement. She had no choice. She had to wash her hands of him. A clean break.

The pain stabbed at her heart. She loved him so much, she couldn't breathe without his presence. From that first day in Newport when he flirted with her in the gazebo until this very moment at the hospital, she loved him with her entire being. But she could never go back on her promise to Kim and Dan. She wasn't that type of person. She had to shut Brian down, no matter how hard or torturous. And it was.

When she told him she didn't love him, she drove the stake in deep. Even though she loved him to Antares and back. But if she admitted it, he'd push for her to go along with him in vacating the adoption, and she just couldn't do that.

Ava slowly wandered back to the family waiting room, numbness taking over her body. In her own hell, she nearly ran into a group of interns discussing some medical procedure in the hall before entering the room she could no longer bear.

"Have you heard anything new on Briana?" She zeroed in on her father, begging to hear some good news to combat the war she'd just been through.

"She's still in critical condition, but stable. That's supposedly good news." Her dad grimaced at his statement.

"When can I see her again?"

"They just wheeled Kim up to see her. Dan's in there too."

"How is Kim?" Anger and guilt collided and crashed over Ava. Anger at her sister's stupidity and gross negligence. Guilt over her own blindness.

"She's okay. Casted up, bruised up, in a lot of pain despite the medication. But her worries are all about Briana."

Ava swallowed the bile seeping up her throat. "Brian overheard the doctor talking to Dan. Apparently, Kim has been over-medicating for her back spasms. Brian thinks Kim was incapable of driving because of the medication she's on. He blames Kim. Me. Dan. For not seeing what's been going on." She looked at her father. "Did you know Kim's been taking prescription drugs since last winter?"

Her father hung his head. "I knew she was taking something. I didn't think it affected her that much."

Ava sighed. "We're all to blame. How could we all have missed it? Especially Dan who lives with her." Ava inhaled in an effort to bring some life back into her. "We have to deal with this now. Talk to Kim, her doctors, figure out what she needs to do to deal with her back issues. Figure out whether she needs to go to rehab."

Ava's father gasped. "Rehab!"

"Did you hear what I said?" Ava's voice escalated. "Kim is addicted to drugs. She almost killed Briana."

"That's going a little too far, don't you think?" Her father's anger rang out loud and clear.

"Do you think, Dad? Do you think she should have been driving after taking heavy-duty pain pills? Do you think taking pain killers for eight months—highly addictive pain killers—is a good thing?" The disgust in her voice was palpable, but she didn't care. Her father was still burying his head in the sand. "If you need to hear it straight from her doctor, be my guest."

Dan's voice came from behind. "She's right, Frank."

Ava turned as Dan entered the room, his shirttail hanging from his pants, his hair disheveled.

"Kim has been taking too many pills, too often. I've been nagging her about it, but she claimed she was fine. She's a nurse. She knows." His shoulders stooped. "But she didn't know. Dr. Faulkner came to see me before. He's very concerned. We're going to have to deal with this as soon as she's released from the hospital."

"What does Kim say?" Ava's voice gentled.

"She'll do anything. She's devastated that she caused Briana's injuries. She can't stop crying."

Ava nodded. "That's good. She's hit rock bottom."

Chapter Twenty-One

As evening approached, Ava's father asked the inevitable. "Where's Brian?"

Just the sound of his name sent daggers to her heart. She could barely breathe. "He went back to New York." She considered lying about the reason, but enough lies and secrets had peppered the past. "We broke up."

Her father's eyes questioned her statement, but she didn't have the strength or courage to discuss what went down.

"I can't talk about it now, Dad. Someday. But not here, not now. We have other more important problems."

Hours morphed into evening, then night when they finally got word that Briana was being upgraded from critical to guarded. Although Kim had been assigned a hospital room, the nurses wheeled her to Intensive Care twice so she could visit Briana, who'd been in and out of consciousness all day.

Ava's father whispered to her as the clock approached ten p.m. "Do you want to go to the house to get some sleep? We can come back first thing in the morning."

"No." That was one question she had the answer to. "I wish I had brought clothes with me." She looked down at her rumpled suit, which she had now worn for two days. "I don't want to leave Briana. What if she wakes up tonight and calls out for her mom. Kim can't comfort her, but I can."

Her dad considered her statement. "But you should get some rest. You're exhausted and won't be worth anything to Briana if you can't think straight."

Ava glanced over at Dan who had fallen asleep in a chair, his head slumped to the left. "Maybe I should send him home for the night. You go, too. We can do this in shifts. When Dan gets back tomorrow morning, I'll buy some clothes, then go to your house so I can shower and change."

There was no way Ava was leaving Briana tonight and the more she talked about her suggested plan, the more she thought it made sense. Of course, her brain might not be functioning at a hundred percent given the emotional warfare of the day, but as Briana's birth mother, she would relish time alone with her daughter under these difficult circumstances.

After some further discussion with specific timelines, both her dad and Dan left. Dan promised to be back by six a.m. and her dad by nine.

Finally Ava had visiting hours to herself. Every two hours, she was given five minutes alone with Briana.

Bleary-eyed but happy to have the opportunity to comfort her, whether Briana was awake or sleeping, she slipped into her room and thanked God she was alive.

"Hi, sweetheart," she whispered, taking her small hand in hers and squeezing it. Briana's eyes fluttered open. "How are you feeling?"

"Not good," she croaked, her voice rusty from non-use. "I want my mommy." Tears shone in her eyes and

Ava's heart broke for the little girl—and for herself. "She's resting. You remember she has a broken leg. But she's doing great. She just needs to sleep. Like you." Ava smoothed Briana's hair back, desperately needing to touch her, to comfort her. "She'll be up to see you first thing in the morning. Are you in pain? Do you want me to call the nurse to get you more medicine?"

"No. I'm so tired." Her eyes drifted closed and within seconds, she was breathing softly in sleep.

Ava stayed for her allotted time, just looking at her child, taking in every feature along with every bruise. She willed her to have a miraculously fast recovery so she wouldn't suffer much longer.

As she left for the waiting area, she made the nurse on duty promise to come out and wake her when she could spend the next five minutes allowable with Briana.

Taking time off from work, the hours blurred into indistinguishable days until Briana was moved from intensive care to a regular hospital room. The relief among her family was palpable, and the once-tense and stressed-out group became more jovial, more friendly.

After discussing Kim's course of treatment going forward, with everyone on board including Kim, Ava left for home on Sunday night in a rented car, promising to return the next weekend, maybe sooner.

Ava called daily, sometimes more often, for status reports and to talk to Briana. In between, she worked to block out the pain of losing Brian. But everything she did, everywhere she turned reminded her of him. Just being in the office and talking to Peter had her swallowing her questions about whether he'd talked to Brian, whether Brian had been in to confer on some matter. When she walked through the lobby, which became a crazy hourly habit, she studied every client, hoping Brian would appear one of those hours, one of those days. But he didn't. Even if he did, what would she say to him?

The streets and sights of New York bombarded her with memories. Passing the theater district in a cab called up the play tickets he had given her when they first reconnected. Passing Lincoln Center sent ballet dancers spiraling through her head, including Carrie. Even if they hadn't gone to a specific venue, the generic Italian restaurant, furniture store, or the deli on every corner wreaked havoc on her bruised and battered heart.

Once Briana got out of the hospital, she healed quickly and was soon attending school. Kim agreed to go to a drug rehab facility in Pennsylvania and while she was gone, Dan and her father took up the weekday responsibilities of Briana's life, while Ava chimed in on the weekends. She took Briana to her ballet classes and worked with her to catch up on the lessons she'd missed in school as well as dance class. Her winter recital was coming up and Briana stubbornly refused to sit in the audience while her class performed a number from *The Nutcracker*. So she practiced, nonstop.

As the weeks passed, Ava hoped the grief over losing Brian would dull. But it got sharper, clearer. More damaging. And oh so familiar. Those weeks and months after his accident seemed to be on a continual repeat cycle, and those old feelings of despair returned with a vengeance. Back then, she'd been pregnant, living each day with the knowledge that the course of her life had veered off track, and she'd never be able to maneuver it back. So too, now.

As she sat at her desk at work, a few errant tears slid down her face. They appeared frequently, and she brushed them away quickly. Her productivity was at an all-time low, and if she didn't pull herself together soon, she'd be out of a job. Peter and Max had tiptoed around her gloomy state, attributing it to Briana and Kim's accident and the aftermath. Thankfully they gave her the time she needed to travel back and forth to Lawrenceville, but she couldn't expect their patience and sympathy to last much longer, especially since Kim had come home a few days ago. If all went as expected, and there was no reason to believe it wouldn't, their lives would take a turn for the better. Even if Ava's didn't.

Ava had to let Brian know that everything in the Reynolds household was under control. He deserved to know. For his peace of mind. She'd contemplated calling him, but feared she'd start crying. An email seemed like a better idea, but she wanted it to be more personal than that. And not so easy to delete. So she decided on an old-fashioned hand-written letter. One that would get to him by snail mail. Something he could hold in his hand and reread, if necessary, before throwing it in the trash.

She took a piece of paper from her printer and started:

Dear Brian:

I know it's too late for confessions, and it would be better for both of us if I kept one more secret. But I can't do it. It's selfish of me, I know, and it's not fair to you, but I can't stop myself. I can't sleep, can't work, can't turn off the memory of our last conversation at the hospital.

I lied to you. At the time, I felt I had to. To protect Briana, to honor the promise I made to Kim and Dan before Briana was born. I promised them I would let them adopt Briana, legally. That I would never interfere with their parenting of Briana. I would never come to them pleading for them to give her back because I made a mistake, and I would never question their judgment. I made these promises when I begged them to adopt Briana. I didn't want strangers to raise her. If I couldn't do it, which I couldn't, I wanted her close.

When you said you loved me and wanted to marry me, that we could be a family with Briana, I wanted nothing more. What a wonderful, happy ending to our sad saga. But that was a fantasy. I couldn't go back on my promises to Kim and Dan. I knew you could probably vacate the adoption. You never consented to it. But I could not condone that action and participate in the outcome, no matter how perfect the result might be. Because we would not only be shattering Kim and Dan's life, but Briana's.

So I lied to you. I told you I didn't love you. The truth is, I will always love you.

I am so sorry things ended as they did. I want you to know that Briana healed quickly, and she is home and back to school. Kim recently got out of rehab and is on the path to recovery. She's actually doing great. It wasn't hard to get her to go. She was devastated that she caused the accident—that she harmed Briana. She loves her so much. So does Dan. I know you believe that.

I want to apologize to you for ignoring Kim's problem. I've beat myself up over it since that day, but we can't redo the past. Maybe that's what I should take away from all this. You and I—the past. I was trying to recapture the magic. But your guilt and my mistrust of your intentions made for a lethal combination. The agony we caused each other in the short time we were together still haunts me. But the happiness and love we shared far outshines our difficulties. Yet, I know a relationship shouldn't have so many ups and downs. The highs were so high, but the lows were unbearable. I guess we just have to let it be.

But I do want you to know you were everything I had remembered—kind, caring, thoughtful, insightful—which is why I'm having such a hard time moving on. You understand me. The good and the bad. Maybe it's because you're so connected to Carrie, so you know how a passion for something can overtake your life.

Briana has been my passion since she was born. At the time, I didn't think I'd be a good mom to her. I was young and trying to find my way. But I've always been in her life. Yes, I made the choice to have Kim and Dan adopt her. I acknowledge the decision was mine alone. Without input from you. And I know I've asked you to believe in and trust that decision even after Kim's accident. But Briana is their child. They are her parents. She loves them despite their faults. She is happy. I know Kim will not slip up. She has her child to think about, and Briana is the most important person in the world to her.

Kim also knows it's time to tell Briana that she's adopted. But we have to do this right. She's talking to a counselor, finding out the best way to approach it. I want Briana to know we're her birth parents, but since I've kept you out of every decision so far, I didn't think it was right to continue making decisions as it relates to you and Briana without your input. Too little too late. I know. So the question is, do you want Briana to know you're her birth father or do you wish to remain anonymous?

Whatever you decide I will make sure that Briana knows the decision I made seven years ago was to protect her. I keep hearing my father's words echoing in my head. I despised him for so long, thinking he didn't want me when, from his point of view, he did what was best for me. Now, here I am in the same situation with Briana. But I would never allow Briana to think she wasn't wanted. She wasn't loved. I will do everything in my power to convince her she was loved so much that she has more than a mother and father in her life.

Things are going much better with my father and me. Since I've been going to Kim's so often, helping with Briana while Kim was away, we've had time to talk more. It's been good.

While this accident was a horrendous event in all of our lives, some good has come out of it. Kim has gotten the help she needs, Dan is more involved in both Kim's and Briana's lives, we're all working together to tell Briana about her adoption in the best of all possible ways, and my father and I are building a good relationship.

The one casualty in all this was us. Maybe it was inevitable, and it would have happened whether or not Briana was injured. I would like to think we would have found our way.

I hope this letter gives you some comfort in knowing that Briana is safe and happy and that her family is pulling together and doing well.

All my best,
Ava

The words *I love you* fought for space on the page, but Ava tamped them down, then squashed them. Her letter was sentimental enough, and she didn't want Brian to rip it to shreds because of one final emotion.

She quickly sealed the letter in an envelope, addressed it, and put it in the mailroom. If she thought about it more or reread it, she might trash it. Putting herself out there, exposing herself, had never been a strong suit of hers. But rationalization was her friend. She needed to know the answer to the one burning question she posed?

Would Brian want to be a part of Briana's life going forward, or would he want to stay as far away from Ava and her family as he possibly could?

Chapter Twenty-Two

Ava's hands hurt from clapping as she stood and gave the cast of *The Nutcracker* a standing ovation. "Briana was wonderful," she gushed as Kim and Dan joined her with their enthusiastic applause. "I've never seen a better snowflake. And her pirouettes were amazing."

"Thanks to all the time you put in with her." Kim beamed as her daughter bowed with the rest of the performers. "I have to meet Briana backstage. I'll see you and Dan in the lobby in a few minutes."

Ava gathered up the bouquet of flowers she had bought for her star ballerina, and she and Dan inched toward the front of the auditorium with the rest of the parents and family members. She had her phone ready to take pictures of Briana in her snowflake costume next to one of the giant nutcrackers that decorated the entrance.

"Ava." The warm rumble of her name came from behind. A hand touched her arm.

She turned and there was Brian, just inches from her.

Her phone slipped from her hand, and she took a breath so she wouldn't end up down for the count. No words formed on her lips. She just stared at his face with its strong, chiseled planes, expressive blue eyes, beautiful mouth. And his perfect smile. And he was smiling. At her.

He stooped to pick up her phone and handed it over. "Briana was fantastic."

"How did you know?" was all she could manage.

"Kim told me."

"You've been talking to Kim?" Why didn't she know that?

"After I got your letter, I thought about it. A lot. Whether it was best if I just stayed out of the picture. I didn't have the answer. So, I called Kim. I figured she'd have the most insight into the issue. You said she was talking to a counselor."

Ava nodded, unable to speak.

"We spoke for a long time. She brought me up to date on Briana and the steps they were taking to tell Briana she was adopted. She said she would be grateful if I would agree to be a part of the process, part of Briana's life, but she would understand if I chose to stay out of it."

"And?" Ava's heart was beating out of her chest, and she could barely breathe.

"I'm in." Brian's smile lit up the lobby

Oxygen failed to reach her brain, and Ava felt dizzy. "I need some air." She spun on her heel and headed out the door into the cold December chill. Snow flurries bombarded her face as she walked briskly down the sidewalk, heading nowhere in particular.

Her mind had paused, and she found it impossible to think, to feel.

"Ava, wait." Brian was on her trail and spun her around. "What's wrong? I thought you'd be happy."

She bit her lip, searching for the emotions she felt. "I don't know what I am right now. When you didn't respond to my letter, I assumed you had no interest in being known to Briana. I accepted it and even convinced myself it was the right decision. We wouldn't have to run into each other at...recitals, or other important events in Briana's life."

Tears clouded her eyes and clogged her throat. "At least that's how I rationalized it. And it was all for the best. Of course, that's the selfish me talking because I knew it would hurt too much to see you." The tears spilled down her cheeks. "I don't think I..." She exhaled and swiped at her face with her glove. It didn't really matter what she thought. She needed to consider what was good for Briana. She tried to smile. "Please ignore me. I'll get through this." Ava nodded, trying to convince herself.

Brian put his hands on her shoulders. That one small gesture sent electricity raging through her veins. She focused on his lips instead of his eyes. She didn't want to see the pity in them. But his lips held other memories. Like the times they devoured hers in a passion so great that her heart burst. But now they were set in a straight, grim line. She raised her hand and caressed his jaw line, trying to soften the edges.

"What is it, Ava?" His eyes held hers, and she fell into their depths.

"I love you," she whispered. "I miss you so much."

His eyes glistened, and she knew she was inflicting more harm than either of them could handle. They both knew they weren't meant to be. Two strikes were enough to end this game. She swallowed, hoping to find some words that would allow them to part without having to engage the paramedics. Up until now, she had not done a stellar job.

"It was really good of you to come." She sounded ridiculous, like she was talking to some acquaintance. "I'm sure Kim and Dan will let you know when it would be good for you to be introduced to Briana as her birth father. You probably shouldn't have wasted your time driving all the way here today."

She started to turn away, at a loss for appropriate words, yet, feeling like a fool for the words that did spill forth. But Brian grabbed her elbow before she could flee. "I didn't come here to rush anything with Briana. As I told you, I've spoken to Kim and when the time is right, I'll be on board. I came to see you."

"Me! But why?" Confusion ricocheted around her brain. He could have spoken to her on the phone or sent an email. If he wanted to see her, they both lived and worked in New York City. Why come to Lawrenceville?

"It was important for me to see you in the role of Briana's aunt. Cheering her on. Being so proud. Suspending your role as her mom, but loving her unconditionally. Because that's what's right for Briana. I need to learn from you, Ava."

He caressed her cheek, then wrapped his arms around her and drew her in, molding her into his body, holding her close as if to assimilate her strength into him. Yet, she didn't feel strong. She felt fragile where he was concerned. But his embrace felt so good. So right. She never wanted to move from this place.

He nuzzled her head and whispered, "I love you, too."

Had she heard him right? She pulled back to search his eyes, the windows to the truth. And she saw in their beautiful depths, his heart and soul.

"I'm here to tell you I want to make this work. With us. With Briana. Maybe she'll learn to call me Uncle Brian."

Ava's heart soared and she gave him a fierce hug. "This is the best day of my life."

Why had it taken so long to get here?

****

As they drove back to New York together after a dinner celebration with Briana and family, Brian cut into Ava's private thoughts. "I've been thinking about starting a new business."

"What? You have a business that takes up all of your time. Why would you add more work to your schedule?"

"Stanhope Natural Gas is going in a direction I'm no longer comfortable with. And I know you aren't. It's been your delicate but true remarks about what we're doing to the environment that have been replaying in my head—especially during the last few months. How can I be so cavalier about how we extract natural gas from the ground and not consider the effects it has on the water systems of those who live in the area? Looking at Briana and thinking about all the other children who have their lives ahead of them, I can't rationalize the negative effects on their environment, on their health."

Ava couldn't contain the surprise that was surely written all over her face. "You would leave your father's company, your company, to start a new business?"

"That's what I've been tossing around. Of course, it's not that easy. My father will most likely have a heart attack, and I'll be throwing away my lifestyle for an unknown venture."

"I have every confidence in your success once you put your mind to it. What is this new business you're thinking about?"

"An environmental cleanup company dealing exclusively with water remediation. A friend of mine from Harvard recently started the business, and he's been looking for investors. I met with him a few times in the past months to learn about it. But now I'm more interested in becoming involved, not just as an investor, but as a participant. He'd love to have a partner, and since the family business has been instrumental in polluting groundwater in certain areas, I think it's only fitting that I work to clean it up."

"What do you think your parents will say?" She had some idea, given their vision that Brian would work for the family business since he was in kindergarten.

"After they get over the initial shock, my father will want to know all about it, and my mother will give her blessing."

"Really." Would it truly be that easy? "You've always done what your family wanted you to do. This is off track."

"I know. I have faith in them."

She smiled. "You do have an incredibly supportive family. You're very lucky."

"It sounds like your family dynamic has changed for the better."

Ava nodded, acknowledging that truth. "It's taken some time for Dad and I to get to a good place, but I'm glad we've accomplished it. It's unfortunate it took Briana's accident to make it happen."

"Sometimes you need a traumatic event to set you

on a better course."

Ava grunted her acceptance of his statement before turning the conversation back to Brian's news. "Has your friend gotten the business off the ground yet? Does he have clients? Employees? Does your expertise translate to this business?"

"All great questions. Zack started the business last year and has a few clients as well as employees. His goal is to grow it, which is why he was originally looking for money. I have money to invest, but I also know how to market and sell."

"Zack. Carrie really liked one of your friends by the name of Zack. Is it the same guy?" She recalled Carrie's infatuation that weekend in Newport.

"Yes. They dated for a while. But Carrie's career takes her away from home, and Zack was looking to settle down."

"Did he?"

"Not yet. He's seeing someone. But I think he still has it for Carrie."

"Hmmm. Very interesting. How does Carrie feel about him?"

"She still cares. Didn't want to break up. But I give her credit. She understood his reasons and let him go."

"That's sad." Ava knew the heartache too well. "Is Carrie seeing anyone now?" She recalled her date at the Ballet Gala.

"No one special that I know of. But I can't say we talk about that when we get together. She's all about dance, new choreography, where she's going next, what role she's playing."

Ava's soul ached for what could have been. She stared out the window at the Sunday night traffic lost in thought. She loved Briana with her whole heart and could never fathom a life without her, even if that life excluded dance. Her decision was right, and she just had to keep telling herself so when thoughts of a dancing life interfered with her true reality.

"Where'd you go?" Brian's voice held concern, as if he knew what she was thinking.

"Where I shouldn't be." Ava shrugged, showing her helplessness.

"I see the sadness in you every time we talk about Carrie's career. Is it too late for you to get back into it?"

He was really so kind to even think it, ask it. "Yes. That dream has sailed."

"You're only twenty-seven. That's not ancient. I'm sure there are plenty of dancers in their thirties. And although I can't remember much about your dancing, both Carrie and my mother have said you were fabulous. You'd be fabulous again once you got back into it."

She reached over to touch his leg. "I appreciate your suggestion as well as your enthusiasm. I have been taking a dance class on Saturdays. But not with the hope of getting back to my former goal. I've invested too much time and money in my legal education. I can't just toss that to the side while I chase an old dream. Even when I was in college, I knew the odds of getting picked up by a company were against me." She exhaled trying to rid herself of the melancholy attitude. "I made my choice a long time ago."

"At the time you were pregnant and alone. Things are different now. Briana has a loving family, and you don't have to worry so much about her financial future."

"I agree, things are different." A smile hijacked her mouth. "You know what would make me happy? Teaching children to dance. I love doing it with Briana. Maybe I'll check with some of the dance studios to see if they could use a very part-time dance instructor."

Brian nodded. "Great idea. Who knows where it will lead."

Ava glanced over at him and gave his shoulder a nudge. "It won't lead anywhere. I'm just talking about teaching one or two classes."

"Fine. You should do what you want. Teach dance. Practice law. Marry me."

"What?" Had she heard him right? Her heart stammered, then beat uncontrollably.

"I realize this isn't the most romantic of proposals. Driving up the New Jersey Turnpike after not seeing you for a while. And I will do it right. I just thought it should be one of your considerations—while you're considering."

Ava threw her arms around his neck, hugging him tightly while trying to let him drive without crashing. "You're serious, right?" Her smile took over her entire face.

Brian laughed, but his words were solemn. "Yes, Ava. I love you. These past few months have been hell. I want to spend the rest of my life with you. And I can't believe I'm having this conversation at the most inopportune time."

"It's the perfect time." She couldn't keep the blazing smile from her mouth or her hands from touching him.

"As soon as we get back to my place, I'm going to ask you again. Properly. And then I'm going to show you how much you mean to me."

His eyes locked on hers. "And it's going to take all night."